The CROW FOLK

The Witches of Woodville

Mark Stay

SIMON &
SCHUSTER

London · New York · Sydney · Toronto · New Delhi

First published in Great Britain by Simon & Schuster UK Ltd, 2021

1 3 5 7 9 10 8 6 4 2

Simon & Schuster UK Ltd
1st Floor
222 Gray's Inn Road
London WC1X 8HB

Simon & Schuster Australia, Sydney
Simon & Schuster India, New Delhi

www.simonandschuster.co.uk
www.simonandschuster.com.au
www.simonandschuster.co.in

A CIP catalogue record for this book is available from the British Library

Paperback ISBN: 978-1-4711-9797-0
eBook ISBN: 978-1-4711-9798-7
Audio ISBN: 978-1-3985-0169-0

Typeset in the UK by M Rules
Printed and bound in Great Britain by CPI Group (UK) Ltd, Croydon, CR0 4YY

For Claire and the magic she makes.

June, 1940

War rages in Europe. The defeated British Expeditionary Forces and their allies have retreated from Dunkirk, and France has fallen to Hitler's Blitzkrieg. In Britain, food is rationed, and children are evacuated from cities to the countryside to escape the coming bombardment. With so many men away fighting, it falls to the women on the home front to keep the country running. The Women's Land Army helps on the farms, the Air Raid Precaution wardens watch the skies and the Women's Voluntary Service supports them all. Men too old to be conscripted sign up for the Local Defence Volunteers (soon to be known as the Home Guard) and prepare for invasion.

Meanwhile, in a quiet village in rural Kent, strange things are afoot …

PROLOGUE

A field in England

Under a sunset sky streaked with pinks and yellows, a scarecrow stands alone in a field. A sorry sight in a tatty red gingham frock that was once someone's Sunday best, she has a sack for a head, buttons for eyes and stitches for a smile. Draped in a musty old shawl, she hangs on her cross like forgotten laundry. She has a name, Suky, but her mind is as empty as her pockets.

Across the tilled soil comes the metronomic clonk of a cowbell.

A figure stalks over the field, swinging the cowbell like a priest with incense, but he moves unnaturally, limbs all herky-jerky. His dusty dinner jacket billows behind him, his scuffed top hat at a jaunty angle. Jackdaws warn him off with salvos of kar-kars, *but he keeps coming. His head: a pumpkin of prize-winning orange. His smile: a jagged sawtooth. His eyes: triangles of black.*

The jackdaws know enough to fly away as he approaches, leaving Suky alone with him. He rattles the cowbell some more to ensure they don't come back. The echo dies and there is only the gentle rumble of the breeze. The air is summer-sweet, the soil flaky, the sky turned blood-red. Pumpkinhead slips the cowbell into his dinner jacket as he moves closer. He circles Suky, his feet skipping like a dancer's, then he cradles her sackcloth head and whispers words in a language not heard since his kind were banished.

The words sink inside her, filling her to the brim. It takes time. Pumpkinhead is patient.

Suky shudders, her straw stuffing rustles and she looks up, a light in her button eyes.

'That's it,' Pumpkinhead tells her. 'Here, let me help you.' He takes a folding knife from the band in his top hat and cuts her bonds.

Suky's head darts around. A frightened newborn.

'You are free, sister,' he tells her. 'We all are.'

A jangling and clanging comes across the field. Suky looks to the horizon where a dozen or more scarecrows dance in a parade towards her.

Suky's sackcloth head creaks as her stitches form a smile.

1

Wynter's Book of Rituals and Magic

Faye Bright's dad once told her the old hollow oak marked the centre of the wood. She was six at the time and they had been walking Mr Barnett's dogs when they came across the tree. Dad said it was the oldest in the wood. Young Faye half expected to find a fairy-tale wolf peering out from behind it.

Faye was seventeen now. There weren't any wolves in Kent. And the hollow oak was as far as she could get from prying eyes. That was where she would open the book for the first time.

Faye had found the book in a trunk of old knick-knacks when she and her dad had been clearing out a corner of the pub's cellar. They were looking for bits of old scrap metal for the 'Saucepans for Spitfires' collection run by Mrs Baxter when Faye unlocked the trunk tucked in the shadows behind the ale barrels. Inside was a box of letters, a hairbrush with an ivory handle, a few cheap necklaces and earrings, a cracked gramophone record of 'Graveyard Dream Blues' by Bessie Smith and this leather-bound book.

Faye's dad Terrence was busy sorting through a box of dull cutlery when she took the book from the trunk. It was ordinary enough to look at. Red leather, much like a ledger or a diary from a stationer's, and the cover and spine were plain with no title or author. All the same, a voice at the back of Faye's head told her she should keep its discovery to herself. She opened it to the first page. The words scrawled there in Indian ink nearly stopped her heart.

Wynter's Book of Rituals and Magic by Kathryn Wynter.

Wynter. Mum's maiden name.

And then, beneath that, and written in darker ink:

To my darling Faye, for when the time is right.

Faye closed the trunk, hid the book under her dungarees, told Dad she had ringing practice and legged it.

Faye didn't want to open the book in the pub, she didn't want to open it in the village, she didn't even dare open it in the privacy of her room. She had to get as far away as possible from other people, which was why she made a beeline for the hollow oak in the middle of the wood.

All the road signs had been removed to befuddle invading Nazi spies, but Faye could have cycled this route blindfolded. She pedalled from the village along the bridleway by the Butterworth farm, over the Roman bridge and into the wood until the path surrendered to tangles of ferns and bracken. She left her bike leaning against a silver birch and continued on foot, all the while thinking ahead to how she would explain the book in her satchel if anyone were to see her reading it.

The ancient wood had shrivelled over time, eaten away by farming, roads and housing. Now it was little more than a few square miles of ancient oaks, yews, pines, birches, beeches and alders packed together.

Explore it long enough and you would reach chalk cliffs and the coast, but the wood's roots clung onto Woodville. The village sat snug on its border, and the two existed in a sort of truce. The villagers took only what they needed, and the wood tolerated their odd little rituals, like when they pootled about in groups with maps and compasses and got lost, or when they brought their dogs to chase squirrels and piddle on the trees. It was perfectly happy to let the girl in the dungarees with the nut-brown hair and big round spectacles wander along its hidden trails in the fading light. Had the wood known what was to follow, it might have put a stop to her there and then, but it was getting complacent in its old age.

Faye crossed the stepping stones of the glistening Wode River and hurried up the muddy bank where she had once found a flint axehead. The local vicar, Reverend Jacobs, reckoned it dated back to the Stone Age when folk first settled Woodville. He had put it on display in the church next to the few bits of Saxon clay pots he had found when hiking with the Scouts. Faye briefly considered pursuing a career as an archaeologist, but two summers ago one of the Scouts, Henry Mogg, had told her girls weren't hardy enough for outdoor pursuits, so to prove him wrong she kicked him in the shins and got thrown out of the Girl Guides for unruly behaviour.

She was too old for them anyway. Seventeen and ready for anything. Even a war.

The summer sun was dipping below the treeline when Faye arrived at the hollow oak's clearing. She shuffled around to make sure there was no one about, catching a flash of red, green and yellow as a woodpecker swooped between the trees. Confident she was alone, she sat at the foot of the tree. Centuries old, the oak leaned over Faye like a curious onlooker. Its gnarled roots reached through the soil, twisting around her like a nest as she got comfy.

Faye leafed through the pages of the leather-bound book.

'Blinkin' flip, Mother,' Faye said to herself in an awed voice.

On every page were pencil and charcoal sketches of symbols, runes and magical objects, alongside watercolours of strange creatures that couldn't be found in any zoo. Around them were notes scrawled in ink. A few times, the notes were made in steady cursive handwriting, but it was mostly in smudges and smears scrawled in flashes of terrified inspiration.

This wasn't like any book that Faye had ever read before. She enjoyed detective novels where some clever clogs solved a murder. There was none of that here.

Here were rituals, magic, monsters, demons and, for some reason, a recipe for jam roly-poly.

She flicked through the pages until the sketches and words became a blur. A scrap of notepaper slipped out. Faye snatched it up before it hit the ground and turned it over.

'Bloody Nora,' Faye said, not quite believing what she was seeing.

Eight handwritten columns of numbers filled the page, with lines of blue and red ink zigzagging between the numbers. Few folk would know what they were looking at; some might suspect a code, but Faye recognised it immediately.

This was a ringing method for church bell-ringers.

Eight columns meant eight bells and the red and blue zigzags were the working bells. Faye rang at Saint Irene's every Friday and Sunday, as she had done since she was twelve. Her mother had been a ringer, too.

Mum had gone and created her own ringing method.

And it had a name. At the top of the page, Faye's mum had written the word *Kefapepo*. It didn't sound like a ringing method. They had odd names, to be sure, but they were usually called things like Bob Doubles, Cambridge Surprise or Oxford Treble Bob, but not this Kefa-wossname nonsense. And it was a peculiar method, too. Faye tried to play it in her head, but something wasn't quite right.

Magic, rituals and bell-ringing.

And jam roly-poly.

Beneath the method, Faye's mother had written

more words: *I break the thunder, I torment evil, I banish darkness.*

'You what?' Faye muttered to herself. 'Oh Mum, what are you babbling on about?'

Faye had been four when her mother died. Old enough to have memories, even if they were ghostly. Details would come to Faye in little flashes at unexpected moments. The scent of rosemary sparked a recollection of helping Mum in the garden when she was a toddler. The blanket on Faye's bed reminded her of kisses goodnight. Mother was comfort and happiness.

Which was why Faye was so angry with her.

Faye knew it was wrong. It wasn't Mum's fault she died so young – diphtheria wasn't picky – but any mention of Mum made Faye's blood boil. All those years growing up without her, all those birthdays and Christmases and summers, and all the things they would never do.

And so Faye shut her away. Mum was in the past, a stranger, a fuzzy memory. Faye was all right with that and got on with her life.

Turned out that Faye had been fibbing to herself. When this book fell into her lap, Faye stupidly allowed a little flicker of hope to flame. Finally, there might be some clue to who her mother really was. Finally, that big gap in her heart would be filled.

Sadly, if this book was anything to go by, then her mother was either a witch or off her rocker.

Faye read through the pages from back to front, then

front to back, mesmerised by the words and pictures, wondering why her mother had made it, and why her father had never mentioned it, not that he spoke about her much these days. Not without getting all evasive or soppy.

Rain pattered on the yellowing paper and Faye looked up to see the sky was a shade of indigo. It was Friday night. She was late.

'Oh, buggeration!' Faye jumped to her feet, clutched the book to her chest and dashed back into the tall ferns, heading for her bicycle, a Pashley Model A. She stuffed the book in her satchel and wedged the satchel in her bicycle's wicker basket, then pushed away, gripping the handlebars. The Pashley was a boys' bicycle – one she had bought second-hand from Alfie Paine after he gave up his paper round – and she had to swing her leg over the crossbar as she gathered speed.

As she was beetling over the old Roman bridge, she almost ran down a lad coming the other way with a trug full of elderflowers in the crook of his arm. Faye dodged around him as he jumped back with a cry of surprise. Faye brought her bicycle to a skidding stop in the undergrowth, sending the satchel flying. The book spun out of the satchel and onto the path.

'Bertie Butterworth, what the blimmin' 'eck are you doing skulking about in the woods at this time of night?' Faye hopped off the bike and scooped up the book and her satchel, shoving them back in the wicker basket.

'I'm, er, well, y'see, here's the thing, I'm, oh, uh …'

Bertie was a little younger than Faye and had been soft on her when they were at school. Though Faye was sure he had a thing for Milly Baxter now, as he never stopped staring wistfully at her in church. He worked on his dad's farm, which had given his cheeks a ruddy stripe of freckles and made his hair go as wild as a hedgerow. 'I'm making elderflower cordial,' he said once he got his words in order, proffering the trug full of berries. 'Funnily enough, your dad wanted some for the pub.'

'Dad?' Faye squinted one eye as she wheeled her bicycle back onto the path. 'Did he send you? Are you spying on me, Bertie Butterworth?'

'Er, n-no,' Bertie stammered. 'I mean, yes, he sent me. To get the berries, that is, but I ain't spying on you. I mean, I did see something moving about and I wondered if you were a, uh, a . . . well, no, it's daft.'

'No, go on. What did you think I was?'

Bertie leaned forwards, eyes darting from left to right, before whispering, 'A Nazi spy parachuted in by the Luftwaffe to infiltrate the village.'

Faye looked up at his open mouth and sincere eyes and couldn't help but snort a laugh. 'You great loon. What would the Nazis want here?'

'We have to be vigilant,' he said as they walked together. Bertie did so with a limp, having been born with one leg shorter than the other. 'They said it on the wireless the other night. If the Nazis invade, it'll be right here.'

'Well, there ain't no Nazis here. Just me and a few squirrels.'

'And a book.' Bertie tilted his head to get a better look at the contents of the bicycle's wicker basket. 'What're you reading?'

'Nothing.' Faye tucked the book behind her satchel. 'An old recipe book. I'm thinking of making a jam roly-poly, if you must know.'

'Oh.' Bertie looked satisfied with the explanation, but Faye could sense the cogs turning within and any moment now he would ask why she had come to the middle of the woods to read a book. She had to change the subject.

'You ringing tonight?'

'Oh blimey,' Bertie said, his face dropping. 'What's the time?'

'Late,' she told him. 'Hop on. I'll give you a backie.'

Still gripping the trug, Bertie clambered onto the saddle behind Faye, and she leaned forward on the pedals as the rain fell heavier. Faye was cross at herself for letting so much time pass unnoticed, but she had found a book of magic spells written by her own mother. The first chance Faye got, she was going to have to try one.

2

The Sound of Angels

The first written mention of Woodville Village is in the chronicles of Wilfred of Cirencester, a travelling scribe sent by Offa, King of Mercia, to assess his new lands. Wilfred passed through the village in AD 762 and described it as 'well past its prime, and in need of a good scrub,' and the inhabitants as 'dim to the point of savagery'. These were Wilfred of Cirencester's final writings, found in a ditch with a few of his blood-stained belongings not two miles from Woodville.

Around the village, travellers might encounter dense woodland, several farms, a handful of mansions, a few ancient forts, an aerodrome, rolling downs, crumbling chalk cliffs and shingle beaches. The Wode Road is the only way in or out, and few come here by accident.

Faye pedalled hard up the Wode Road with Bertie perched on the saddle behind her, clinging to her back and his trug of elderflowers. The rain was pelting down and Faye hoped it would clear up before closing time tonight. She had promised to join Mr Paine on ARP patrol after the pub closed and she didn't much fancy getting too cold and wet in the dark. They passed the grocer, butcher, baker, post office, sweet shop, tea room, general store, three pubs, a school, a library and two churches.

Saint Irene's Church was by far the oldest of the village's two churches, the other being Our Lady of the Sacred Heart, a relative newcomer built in 1889. The nave of Saint Irene's dated back to the sixth century and was built with Roman bricks and tiles salvaged from a church that once stood on the same spot. Other nooks and crannies were added over the centuries, the final addition being the bell tower in 1310. The church was named after Saint Irene of Thessalonica, who was martyred along with her sisters for, among other things, reading banned books. Irene's sisters were executed, but she was sent to a brothel to suffer molestation by the patrons. No one touched her in the end, and the story goes she converted many of the brothel's patrons to Christianity with her passionate readings from the Gospels. Another story says the very same readings drove them to frequent another brothel up the road, but either way, Saint Irene's stubbornness inspired the villagers to this day. No one ever brought up that she was burned alive as punishment for her refusal to compromise, but the villagers of Woodville weren't the sort to let a grim ending dampen a good story.

'Off you hop,' Faye told Bertie as she brought the bike to a stop.

'You go ahead,' he said, stretching his uneven legs. 'I'll catch you up.'

Faye leaned her bicycle against the foot of Saint Irene's bell tower, ducked in out of the rain and scuffled up the uneven stone steps of the spiral staircase. She could hear the voice of the tower captain, Mr Hodgson, preparing the other ringers for their final course of Bob Doubles. 'Look to!' he cried. Faye peered through the narrow stone arch into the ringing chamber as Mr Hodgson took hold of his sally. 'Treble's going . . .' He pulled on the sally, bringing his bell to the balance point. Then, as it tipped over to ring, he added, 'And she's gone.' The treble bell rang, followed in quick succession by the others.

It was nearly nine and Faye and Bertie had missed the whole practice. The tower gently rocked from side to side as the bells rang and Faye wavered with it, wondering about turning around and heading back to the pub to help her dad, but the ringers would all congregate there in a minute anyway, so she might as well show her face and make her excuses.

She squeezed through the arch into the ringing chamber, staying close to the wall and giving a meek wave to Mr Hodgson as he led the rounds. Bertie appeared behind her, still carrying his trug of elderflowers and slightly out of breath.

Even by the strange standards of Woodville Village, the bell-ringers were an odd lot. There was Faye, who no one could quite figure out, not least herself. Miss Burgess had more affinity for the chickens on her allotment than people, and her nails were never clean. Miss Gordon was kindness incarnate and a dead-shot archery champion. Mrs Pritchett had become quite tiny in her dotage and had to ring while standing on a box, though her concentration was as sharp as ever. The ringers were rounded off by the Roberts twins, two elderly gents, rotund and gentle in nature, who communicated with little nods and murmurs. They were known in the ringing world as the Bob Doubles, an in-joke that always got a chuckle at the County Society Annual General Meeting and polite bafflement everywhere else. They were all led by their tower captain Mr Hodgson, the Scout leader who wore knee-length khaki shorts whatever the weather. Indeed, it was said one could predict the weather by the colour of Mr Hodgson's knees. This evening they were the shade of Cox's Orange Pippin apples. Rain overnight with a slight chance of drizzle in the morning.

The rounds were ending and they began to ring down. This was Faye's favourite part of any practice. After rounds, the bells needed to be left safely mouth down and they were gently coaxed into position by the ringers. They began to ring closer and closer together, clattering into one another in what was often described by Faye's dad as 'a bloody racket that wouldn't be allowed nowhere else if it weren't for the bloody church'. But then something wonderful happened. From the chaos came a harmonic humming. It swirled around them, resonating off the ancient stone of the tower, vibrating the wooden floorboards and rattling the windows. Faye's mum used to say it was like angels singing, and when the ringers got it right, there was no other sound like it.

The ringers continued to gently hold and release the sallies with their right hands while coiling the ends of the ropes in their left. Faye closed her eyes in bliss, the hum of the bells all around them now.

The harmony was broken by a call from Mr Hodgson. 'Miss and catch in rounds after three. One … two … three. Miss and catch!' With a final round of chimes, the bells fell silent.

Faye opened her eyes to find Mr Hodgson scowling at her.

'And what time do you call this, you two?' he huffed at Faye and Bertie.

'Sorry, Mr Aitch,' she said. 'The day just got away from me.'

'Did it indeed? Did you give any of us a second thought as we stood around waiting for you to arrive? Wasting precious time twiddling our thumbs when we could have been ringing, hmm?' Mr Hodgson always found it unfathomable that one's day did not entirely revolve around ringing practice. Though even by his standards, he was unusually snippy this evening.

'Sorry, Mr Aitch, I cycled as fast as I—'

'Oh, I'm sure you did. Where have you been?'

'I was … doing stuff. Saucepans for Spitfires and all that. I won't be late for Sunday. I promise.'

There were murmurs and intakes of breath from the other ringers and their eyes darted furtively.

'There won't *be* any ringing on Sunday,' Mr Hodgson said, his upper lip trembling. The other ringers all looked as glum, pouting as they tied up their ropes.

'What . . . what's wrong?' Faye asked. 'Who died?'

'It was on the wireless,' Bertie said. 'Paris is occupied by the Nazis. Terrible news.'

'Worse, Bertie, worse,' Mr Hodgson wailed. 'No more bell-ringing. Banned till after the war!'

'Banned?' Faye's voice went up an octave. 'Who banned it? They can't ban it? Can they?'

'Word has come from the diocese and the War Office. All church bells to be suspended until further notice,' Mr Hodgson said, and then added with a roll of his eyes, 'with the exception of air raids.'

'But what about the quarter peal on Sunday? For Mum?' A quarter peal of bells was a long session, almost an hour, which required experienced ringers and were rung to celebrate special occasions. Faye had never done one before, but she was ready, and Mr Hodgson had suggested a quarter peal to honour the anniversary of her mother's passing. Faye hadn't been sure – she didn't like it when other people made her think of her mum – but Mr Hodgson insisted and she caved in.

'Off, I'm sorry to say,' he said.

'No, no, it can't be. It-it's my first. That's not fair. They must be able to make an exception for one little quarter peal, Mr Hodgson, please.'

'An exception? Why is it the young believe the rules do not apply to them, hmm?'

'I don't want to break any rules, Mr Aitch, but look, I've …' Fay lowered her voice and looked around as the other ringers filed out of the room and began the perilous descent of the spiral steps. 'I've found a new method.'

Mr Hodgson's face twitched with anticipation. New methods weren't unusual – he had concocted a few himself – but he was always keen to try something fresh. 'You have? Where?'

Faye noticed Bertie loitering by the narrow stone entrance to the ringing chamber. 'Bertie, can you tell Dad I'll be along in two shakes?'

'Oh, uh, yes, yes, of course,' Bertie said with a blush before turning sideways to squeeze through to the spiral stairs.

Faye felt a pang of shame in sending Bertie on his way, but if he saw any of what followed then he would know there was more to Faye's book than jam roly-poly. 'One moment, Mr Aitch,' she said as she unbuckled her satchel, took out the book and flicked through the pages until she found the slip of paper. 'Here.' She handed it to him and he narrowed his eyes as he played the method in his head.

'The Kefo … Kefa …'

'Kefapepo,' Faye said. 'Don't ask why it's called that, cos I don't know.'

'Most peculiar,' Mr Hodgson said, his voice baffled and intrigued. 'In all my years of ringing I've never come across anything quite like it, I must say.'

'Well, no, you wouldn't have.'

'Where did you find it?'

'It was my mum's.'

'Ah.' Mr Hodgson flexed his lips. 'Certainly explains a few things.'

'Like what?'

'Forgive me, Faye, but it's simply bizarre. It's just the bells dodging over and over again. Nothing more than noise, I'm afraid. Fine if you were trying to hypnotise someone, but quite un-ringable. And what's this at the bottom? *I break the thunder, I torment evil, I banish darkness*. Oh, I say, this is most peculiar. If we were to go ahead, I would have suggested a simple quarter peal of twelve-sixty of Plain Bob Triples, but alas, we are forbidden until further notice. Perhaps the best thing is to wait until all this war nonsense is over and then stick with tradition, hmm?'

'But, Mr Hodgson—'

'I'm sorry, Faye, I truly am.' Mr Hodgson's face crumpled sympathetically. 'Your mother was a marvellous ringer, but we shall have to find some other way to honour her memory, I'm afraid. No more ringing until this blasted war is over.'

3

The Green Man

The rain had escalated beyond mere cats and dogs and was lashing ferociously against the walls of the pub by the time Faye and the ringers arrived at the Green Man. The pub was built in 1360 and had been in a state of constant disrepair ever since. It was almost as old as the bell tower, and this was no coincidence. Bell-ringers varied in their levels of devotion to the church – there were a surprising number of agnostics and atheists to be found among their numbers – but for centuries the great majority of them had shared a true passion for local ales and ciders.

The hand-painted sign with the Green Man's foliage face creaked in the gale as they barged through the door in their hurry to escape the rain and reach the bar. Few would get in their way. Two old fellas were playing dominoes in the corner and a bloodhound was asleep by the fire. By Woodville Village standards this was quiet for a Friday night, but the hammering rain and the blackout kept most regulars at home by the hearth and the wireless.

Faye's spectacles misted up as the warmth of the fire washed over her, and she was grateful as they hid the few tears she had shed between the bell tower and here. She sniffed, blinked them away and squinted through the fog to make out her father Terrence cleaning pint glasses behind the bar.

The tobacco-smoke air of publican life had given Terrence's face the texture of a saddlebag. Receding white curls sat atop his head like clouds on the horizon, but he was as sharp as ever. This was his pub, and he knew every villager by first, second and middle names. His eyes darted to Faye as she came in and he looked at her through the bottom of a pint glass like Nelson peering through a telescope.

'Ahoy there! Here come the village's finest campanologists,' he said, gleefully using a word only ever used by non-bell-ringers who had found the noun for bell-ringers in a dictionary and wanted their bell-ringer friends to know that they knew it.

'And the thirstiest,' Faye said, the leather strap of the satchel pinching her shoulder, weighed down by her mother's book. 'One tick and I'll give you a hand,' she told him, gripping the satchel's buckle and scurrying into the narrow hall behind the bar. She checked her dad wasn't looking as she slipped the satchel into a little nook by the penny jar where it wouldn't be seen, but she couldn't resist one last peek at the wonders inside. Faye took out the book and opened it at a page full of runes and magical symbols and a sketch of a witch riding a broomstick.

'What you got there, girl?' a new voice asked, startling Faye. She snapped the book shut and found Archibald Craddock had silently emerged from the lavatory, without flushing or washing his hands. Craddock had a body sculpted from a lifetime of ale, pie and mash and the great outdoors. Bald under his cap, he was cloaked in a poacher's long coat which crumpled as he squeezed past her in the hall. His grin was three pints crooked.

'It's a book,' she said, sliding it behind the penny jar. 'It's called *None of Your Beeswax, Archibald Craddock* and it's by me. I reckon it'll be very popular.'

For a heartbeat it looked like Craddock might shove her aside and grab the book, but he had little interest in childish things, let alone reading. Instead, he wheezed a boozy cough, scruffed Faye's hair and returned to his regular haunt at the end of the bar.

Faye got her breath back, wiped her specs clean on her blouse, adjusted the clip in her hair, hid the book away in the satchel and took her place behind the pumps with her father.

'Terrence, have you heard the awful news?' Mr Hodgson asked Faye's dad, raising his arms as if proclaiming from on high.

'The Nazis have got Paris, Mr Aitch,' Terrence replied. 'Bad business.'

'No, no, no, that's not it at all,' Mr Hodgson wailed, thumping a fist on the bar.

'Er ... They're talking about putting another penny on a pint to pay for the war effort?'

'No! All church bells to be suspended until further notice, with the exception of air raids. It was on the wireless. Did you not hear?'

'Oh.' Terrence had worked in this pub since he could walk. Long ago, he taught Faye it was easier to allow the customers to vent their spleens, then sell them a pint or two. Disagreeing with them or pointing out that the bells were a bloody public nuisance would only lose custom. 'Oh, that's . . . terrible. In't it, Faye?'

'Come on, Dad, don't pretend this isn't the happiest day of your life.'

'Don't be like that, girl. I know how much the old ding-donging meant to you and your mother. Weren't you going to do one of them extra-long ding-dongs for her this Sunday?'

'Quarter peal.' Faye's voice cracked. 'Not any more.'

'Oh, I am sorry, Faye,' Terrence said, resting his hand on Faye's shoulder. 'No, really. You was looking forward to it, weren't you, girl?' Faye, caught off guard by her father's sudden and genuine sympathy, thought she might become a mess of tears there and then. Of course, he had to go and ruin it: 'Does that mean I get a lie-in?'

'Dad.' Faye snapped as she poured Mr Hodgson a pint of his usual.

'I can't say I'm happy about it, of course,' Mr Hodgson said. 'But we have a duty and we must do by it.'

The other ringers grumbled in assent, and Bertie piped up, 'As Mr Churchill said, we must never surrender.'

'Cobblers.' Craddock's gravelly voice came from the other end of the bar and all heads turned.

Faye watched as Bertie's face went white as milk. The lad looked down at his pint and waited for a hole to open in the Earth and swallow him up. Mr Hodgson, on the other hand, spoke up with the bravery of a man who had fought valiantly at the Battle of Mons in 1914.

'I beg your pardon?' the tower captain asked.

'I said, cobblers, bollocks, balls and what a load of old toot,' Craddock replied, not looking up from the bar. '*Never surrender*, my arse. We got stuffed at Dunkirk, the Frogs got stuffed today. The Poles, the Dutch, Belgium, all done for, and we'll be next. Hitler's Blitzkrieg can't be stopped, and Mussolini and the Eyeties just declared war on us, too.' Craddock took a long drag on his roll-up. 'We should never've got involved.'

'This is treason, Mr Craddock,' Mr Hodgson said. 'I should report you.'

'It's common sense, you old fool,' Craddock said, wreathed in smoke. 'We should stop now and make a deal before they send more of our boys to die. In the meantime, they expect us to farm the land with naught but women, cripples and pansies.'

'And which one are you?' Faye asked, flashing him a smile.

Bertie snorted and blushed, though the other ringers looked at her in horror.

The big man snarled and got to his feet, the chair

scraping the floorboards with a noise like a wounded animal. 'What did you say . . . ?' He moved towards Faye, the pub floor creaking beneath his weight.

'Easy now, Archie,' Terrence said. 'She didn't mean nothing.'

'Oh, I did.' Faye stood her ground, all the time wondering if having the bar between her and Craddock's hulk would be enough to keep her safe.

'Faye, pop a cork in it.' Terrence had known Craddock with his short temper and quick fists his entire life. Faye had heard all the stories, of course, but lacked the experience of witnessing Craddock in his full-blooded rage, smashing a bar to splinters over little more than a spilled pint.

Faye steadied her voice and folded her arms. 'All I'm saying is, if you don't like it, then maybe you should go off and fight the Nazis, too?'

'He's too old,' Bertie blurted.

Terrence gave him a glare. *And you can belt up, too!*

Craddock turned on Bertie. 'I went to war last time round,' he said, and the boy shrank. 'I've done my bit and I ain't going again. I'll stay here with the women, cripples, pansies . . . and witches.'

Faye tingled with guilt and just about stopped herself from sneaking a glance at the book hidden behind the penny jar. But Craddock wasn't looking at her or the book. He'd turned his head to the woman sat next to the two old fellas playing dominoes. Faye's hair stood on end. She could have sworn the woman hadn't been there just a moment ago, but now there she was, ensconced in the armchair under an old sepia photograph of some hop-pickers.

Charlotte Southill's hair was cotton-white, her face pale, lipstick blood-red. She was smoking a clay pipe and reading an unmarked black book; her big eyes reflected the light of the fire as she returned Craddock's glare with an enigmatic smile.

Faye watched as Craddock tried to stare Charlotte down. His face began to tremble and beads of sweat appeared on his top lip. The woman gently closed her book, stood and glided to the bar, slender as a rose stem in her fur-lined coat. Faye's specs started misting up again.

Charlotte Southill slapped some coins on the bar. Charlotte didn't come to the Green Man often, but when she did, she always had a bit of Mother's Ruin. Faye nodded and poured her a gin.

'Evenin', Miss Charlotte,' Terrence said cheerily. 'Didn't see you there.'

Charlotte offered no reply, keeping her eyes on Craddock.

The poacher leaned so close to Charlotte that Faye wondered if he was going to kiss her. 'I ain't afraid of you,' he said, curling his lip then adding, 'witch.'

No kissing, then. Faye placed the gin by Charlotte's elbow.

Charlotte's hand was a blur as she reached for it.

Craddock flinched.

It wasn't much. A twitch in his eye and a spasm in his arm, but they all saw it. The ringers nudged each other. Charlotte's smile widened as she downed the gin in one.

Craddock pulled his coat tight and, with a wordless mumble, strode out into the rain, slamming the door behind him.

For a moment, the only noise was the crackle of the fire, then Miss Burgess ordered a half of pale ale and the friendly hubbub of chatter returned.

Faye's mind whirled as she tried to recall every bit of gossip she had ever heard about Charlotte Southill. The witch thing was a common rumour; others said she was descended from Romany gypsies, and the most ridiculous one came from Mr Loaf, the funeral director, who reckoned Charlotte was over three hundred years old, a direct descendent of Mother Shipton, who had survived the plague and made an immortal pact with the Devil. Mr Loaf would have been less than delighted to learn he was closer to the mark than most.

'Get you another?' Faye asked.

Charlotte didn't look directly at Faye, but rather at the air around her, her head twitching like a hound with a scent. Her eyes rolled down to meet Faye's as the tobacco in her pipe glowed red. Charlotte gently exhaled smoke from her mouth and nostrils and Faye felt it waft over her. It wasn't the usual acrid pipe smoke that made Faye's eyes water. This was warmer, sweeter, with a hint of honey. 'And what have you been up to today?' Charlotte asked, her voice husky.

'Oh, y'know, bits and bobs, Saucepans for Spitfires, doing my bit.' Faye couldn't help but inhale some of the smoke and it made her cough a little. She glanced over to her dad. He was chatting with the ringers and serving pints, unaware of Faye and Charlotte's conversation.

'Anything else?' Charlotte asked.

Faye stood wide-eyed, feet rooted to the floor, befuddled by Charlotte's sudden interest in her. 'Er . . . no,' she said, all the time thinking, *She knows! She knows about the book. But how?*

'Anything special?' Charlotte took another puff of her pipe, exhaling more of the honey-scented smoke. Charlotte raised an eyebrow and Faye felt an uncontrollable urge to tell her everything about the book, how she had found it and what was inside, along with all of her conflicted thoughts about her mother. Faye's mind was foggy and soft as a duck-down pillow. She shook her head but her lips tingled, the world swam around her and the only point of clarity was Charlotte's face. Faye had to think very hard to ensure the only words she uttered were, 'I went for a walk.'

Charlotte's eyes narrowed. Her smile returned. 'How delightful,' she said, then added, as if coming to a disappointing conclusion, 'It's not you. Have a lovely evening.'

Charlotte took a final puff on her pipe, pulled up her hood and sashayed to the door.

The fog in Faye's mind cleared, her ears popped and the hound by the fire began barking. Reality washed back over her, as if waking from a daydream. Voices became more distinct and she could hear Mr Hodgson talking to her.

'Say what you want about that Charlotte,' Mr Hodgson said, tapping his fingers on the bar then pointing at Faye, 'but she was kindness itself to your mother. They were thick as thieves, y'know?'

'No,' Faye said, turning to her dad, who was scowling at Mr Hodgson. 'I didn't know. And I'm wondering, Dad, when you was gonna tell me?'

'Eh? What?' Terrence blustered, looking like he could murder Mr Hodgson.

'And you're going to start right now,' Faye said.

4

Mrs Teach's Midnight Rendezvous

'Ill met by moonlight, Mrs Teach?'

Philomena Teach strode into the circle of standing stones as if she owned the place. Indeed, whenever Mrs Teach arrived at any destination she drew the eye. She was a large woman. Shaped liked a ripe pear and taller than most men, she moved with a regal grace, chin tipped up, and just the hint of a saucy smile tucked between round cheeks. Most days she wore a striking frock and slingbacks. Tonight, the rain and slight chill in the air found Mrs Teach in her Women's Voluntary Service woollen coat, hat and sensible shoes.

'If you want to have a chat, just knock on the door,' she said to the woman waiting for her. 'Slipping notes through my letter box and inviting me to occult places in the middle of the night is liable to give a lonely widow pause. What the bleedin' 'eck do you want, woman?' This last was delivered with a snap. Mrs Teach maintained a speaking voice worthy of the finest elocution school, but every now and then her natural common-as-muck Thames Estuary inflection would make itself known with a curse.

Charlotte Southill stood at the foot of the slaughter stone that lay flat in the centre of the circle. Mrs Teach took her place at the opposite end of the stone. Both women had agreed long ago that it was a good idea to have some small distance between them. The standing stones weren't as mighty as those at Stonehenge, but they were much older. Tucked in a corner of the wood that few wanderers found, they were a perfect meeting place for those who liked to keep secrets.

'How do I put this?' Charlotte scratched a match into life and lit the tobacco in her clay pipe. 'Have you been . . . ?' She took a few puffs. 'Doing what you shouldn't be doing?'

'I don't think I like your tone, madam.'

'Like it or not, the question remains. Have you?'

'No, I most certainly have not.'

Charlotte exhaled and smoke billowed around her. 'Someone is,' she said.

'Well, it was not I. How dare you accuse me.'

'Forgive me, Mrs Teach, but you have form.'

'Once, that's all.' Mrs Teach's eyes glistened with tears and her voice began to crack. 'One little mistake, and a long time ago at that.'

'You can turn off the theatrics, Philomena. I'm immune.'

'Yes, you are, aren't you. And do you know why? Because you're a heartless—'

'Something has broken through.'

Mrs Teach sniffed the tears away. 'From where?'

'Below.'

'Oh. Bugger.'

'Quite.'

'You're sure?'

'It's like someone left a door open and I can feel the draught,' Charlotte said. 'It is powerful and moves among us, and it could not have done this on its own.'

'If it's not you and it's not me, then who?' Mrs Teach asked, then gasped. 'Ooh, do you think it's Kathryn's girl?'

'Faye? No.' Charlotte shook her head. 'I spoke with her tonight. She's still a child. Naive. No power. I don't think she has anything to do with this.'

'What did you say to her? She's not supposed to know . . .' Mrs Teach trailed off as she caught a whiff of Charlotte's tobacco. 'Oh, you are incorrigible. Did you try and read the poor girl's mind?'

'I might have had a little peek.'

'Charlotte, you should know better than to poke around in a young lady's thoughts. Goodness knows what you might find.'

'There was nothing to find. The girl is empty-headed.'

'She always seemed quite clever to me.'

'Perhaps, but she has none of her mother's talents.'

'Who else can it be, then?'

'That's what I intend to find out. I will meditate on it in the morning. Reach out and see what I can discover. There's a ritual I've been wanting to try.'

Charlotte nodded, half lost in thought before adding, 'I need a toad.'

'I can try a reading, see if there's—'

'You're on probation,' Charlotte snapped.

Mrs Teach made little fists, digging her nails into the palms of her hands. 'Then why drag me out to the stones at this ungodly hour if you don't want my help?'

'I had to ask the question.' Charlotte shrugged. 'And look you in the eye when I did so.'

Mrs Teach stepped onto the slaughter stone, fixing Charlotte with a glare. 'And just who put you in charge?'

'Vera Fivetrees.'

'Did she, really?'

'Yes, and you did, in a way. When you disobeyed our laws.'

'One day,' Mrs Teach said, her voice all aflutter, 'I hope your heart is broken the way mine was. Only then will you have any clue what I went through. But what am I saying? For you to suffer heartache, you would have to actually *possess* a heart in the first place.'

Charlotte's red lips broke into a smile. 'I have a heart, Mrs Teach. I'm wise enough to keep it to myself.'

'Thank you for wasting my time,' Mrs Teach said, turning and heading back towards the village. Charlotte watched her go, idly wondering where she might find a toad at this time of night.

5

Put that Light Out

'Put that light out!'

'Get stuffed!'

Rain pattered on Faye's steel ARP helmet as she strolled the dark streets of Woodville with Mr Paine, the newsagent. Both were on Air Raid Precaution patrol. Their job was to ensure that no house lights were visible at night. The government had advised that Luftwaffe pilots not only used the lights from towns and villages to navigate but would also target them with bombs. The policy was designed to save lives, but not everyone enjoyed hiding in their homes at night behind blackout curtains, leading to some heated exchanges.

'I said put that light out!' Mr Paine repeated.

'And I said get stuffed!' replied a voice from inside the house on the corner of Bogshole Road.

'Don't make me come up there,' Mr Paine hollered. 'I can issue you with a fine, y'know.' The blackout curtains of the offending house were tugged shut and the darkness returned. The village used to be quite lively at night, even after closing time, but the blackout applied to cars, torches and even bicycle lamps, so folks stayed at home, curtains drawn. It got so dark that Mrs Brown at the stables painted her horses white after one of them had been hit by a car. Faye even painted the mudguards on her bicycle white for what good it did.

'That was Mr and Mrs Mogg's place,' Faye said, her night vision returning. 'He'll have a moan when he next sees you.'

'That'll make a change.' Mr Paine was a big man who lumbered from side to side as he walked. He spoke with a deep voice, a frown and pursed lips, leading those who didn't know Freddie Paine to mistake him for a simpleton. He was anything but, and Faye liked his dogged sense of duty. 'Remind me to put it in the logbook later. Sherbet lemon?' Mr Paine offered a little brown paper bag to Faye, but she didn't reply. Her mind was still all of a jumble after what she had learned earlier in the Green Man.

Mum, Faye's mum, Kathryn Bright, née Wynter, had been friendly with a witch.

And not just any witch – not that Faye knew any others – but Charlotte Southill who, rumour had it, would curdle your milk if you gave her so much as a funny look.

Faye had interrogated her father until closing time, but he clammed up and refused to say any more. She turned on Mr Hodgson who, taking his cue from Terrence, got all evasive and claimed he needed an early night, leaving half a pint of his pale ale undrunk.

This never happened, and Bertie was so confused by Mr Hodgson's behaviour he began to wonder if he had been replaced by a German spy, and that became the topic of conversation for the evening instead.

At last orders, Mr Paine turned up in his ARP helmet to collect Faye for lookout patrol. She popped her own helmet on, pinned her silver ARP badge to her lapel, strung her gas-mask box over her shoulder and stepped out into the night with the plodding newsagent.

They started at the Green Man and made their way down to the Warden's Post at the bottom of the Wode Road. By the time their shift was done they would have covered the whole village.

'Wake up, sleepyhead,' Mr Paine said, shaking the bag of sherbet lemons under Faye's nose.

The noise brought Faye out of her daze. 'Oh, sorry, ta very much,' she said, pinching one of the little yellow candies and salivating as she popped it in her mouth. Another reason to go on patrol with the owner of the village newsagent and sweetshop.

'Thanks for covering tonight, Faye,' Mr Paine said. 'Poor Kenneth's lumbago is playing up something chronic. You're a credit to the ARP.'

'It gets me out and about and . . . PUT THAT LIGHT OUT!' she called across the street to where Reverend Jacobs could be seen through the vicarage cottage window scribbling a sermon by candlelight. He hurried to the window, waved in apology and pulled his curtains shut. 'And I get to yell at people, which is just what a girl needs after a long day.'

'You did the right thing,' Mr Paine said, making sucking noises on his sherbet lemon. 'I heard what happened with the LDV.'

'Nothing happened with the LDV,' Faye protested.

'I heard they laughed at you.'

'They didn't laugh.' Faye bunched her lips, blushing at the memory. A call for Local Defence Volunteers had been announced on the wireless, just after Dunkirk. Volunteers were needed to defend the country in the event of invasion by the Germans in occupied France. Faye was one of the first to try to sign up. 'It was more of a sneer. Said they didn't take girls.'

'Why would you want to join that lot, anyway?' Mr Paine said, crunching down on the remains of his sherbet lemon. 'Bunch of old men playing soldiers with broomsticks.'

'They let Bertie sign up. He's too young, but they took him cos he's a boy and he's keen and he makes a good cuppa tea. He says you get a gun.'

'They've got Morris Marshall's shotgun and Harry Newton's old blunderbuss. The rest of 'em have broomsticks and an armband that makes 'em think they're Bulldog bleedin' Drummond. Hardly a match for the Nazi Blitzkrieg. Y'know what everyone's calling 'em? The Old Contemptibles, the Look, Duck and Vanish brigade, the Last-Ditch Volunteers, Dad's Army – PUT THAT LIGHT OUT! – at least in the ARP you get two quid a week, a steel hat and a silver badge.'

'And sherbet lemons.'

'Only if you're good.'

'Bertie said he'll let me have a go with his gun when he gets one.'

'Don't hold your breath.'

'I just want to be useful,' Faye said. 'But none of them want me.'

Faye left school when she was fifteen and had helped her dad in the pub ever since. She got on with most folk, she had her head screwed on, was good with numbers and loved nothing more than a juicy murder mystery from the library with a good twist or two.

She didn't much fancy getting married and having kids, though that's what was expected of girls her age. She didn't look good in a frock, and she didn't turn the boys' heads. She much preferred her dungarees with proper pockets and a pair of good boots. Now and then she thought she could be a teacher, but none of the teachers she'd met were anything like her, so she didn't reckon she'd fit in.

Dad told her not to worry too much, which was good of him, though she suspected he was hoping she would work behind the bar her entire life and take the pub over when he retired.

Faye just wanted to help people, even though some thought she was just poking her nose in. It didn't matter what it was – a leaky roof, a flat tyre or picking up your ration – Faye would volunteer to help you fix it. Unfortunately, 'Fix-It Girl' wasn't a recognised vocation at the employment exchange, and so Faye drifted from task to task, doing the best she could.

They came to the Warden Post, a tiny concrete

shelter surrounded by sandbags at the bottom of the Wode Road. Faye and Mr Paine sheltered inside and he poured tea from his Thermos flask into a pair of tin cups.

The village slumbered in silence. The houses and shops were lined with sandbags and their windows criss-crossed with tape to reduce flying glass in the event of a bomb dropping. All the curtains were closed tight and the clouds above were breaking apart, revealing clusters of stars as the rain abated. Faye loved night patrol. The stars glistened without the glow of street lamps to dull them. As she picked out the constellation of the Plough, her mind drifted back to what Mr Hodgson had said about Charlotte and her mother. *Thick as thieves*.

'Mr Paine.' Faye bit her lip before asking, 'Did you know my mum much?'

'I know everyone in this village, Faye. That's the privilege of being a newsagent. Sooner or later they all come through your door. Every Monday, your dear mother would pop in for a copy of *Woman's Weekly* and a bar of Cadbury's. Lovely woman. Always said her pleases and thank yous and very good with her exact change. You don't forget stuff like that.'

'Did she ever do anything . . . peculiar?'

'In what way peculiar?'

'In an . . . odd way. Strange. I dunno . . . er . . . witchy.'

Mr Paine slurped on his tea as he cogitated. 'No,' he said.

Faye puffed out her cheeks. That was that. Her

mother was an ordinary woman who bought magazines and chocolate and never so much as—

'Except that one time,' Mr Paine added. 'Gave me the right willies.'

'What time? What do you mean, *Gave you the willies*?' Faye asked. 'What did she do to give you the willies?'

'Nothing horrible, you understand, just . . . it was peculiar.'

'Peculiar how?'

Mr Paine stood as he screwed the lid back on his Thermos flask. 'Tea break's over,' he said, marching off at a clip towards Gibbet Lane.

'Like what, Mr Paine?' Faye hurried after him. 'Mr Paine, tell me, please.'

Mr Paine slowed his pace and scratched at his ear. 'I was just a lad,' he said, 'helping the hop-pickers who came out for the harvest. A sparrow got trapped in a sack of hops and the poor thing panicked, its ticker stopped and it dropped dead right in front of us. Stiff as a board, legs like that.' Mr Paine raised his hands like frozen claws, crossed his eyes and stuck his tongue out of the side of his mouth. 'Your mum – she weren't much older then than you are now – she was nearby, hears the kerfuffle, comes over, fishes out the sparrow, cups it in her hand and whispers in its ear. And blow me if the bloody thing didn't come back to life and fly off. She wouldn't take no praise for it, no thanks nor even the offer of a beer. She scarpered off like she'd done something . . . like she'd done something she'd been told she shouldn't have. Half the hop-pickers thought she was Saint Francis of Assisi, the other half thought she was a . . .' Mr Paine stopped walking as he trailed off. Faye had the feeling that he'd told this story to countless others in the past with the same punchline, but never to the daughter of the protagonist.

'Go on, say it,' Faye said, folding her arms.

'I don't rightly think I should.'

'A witch?'

'You said that, not me. Personally, I think the dickie bird had a funny turn and the warmth of your mother's hand woke it up again. She was a lovely woman, your mother. All pleases and thank yous and exact change, like I said.'

'Did she know Miss Charlotte well?'

'Miss Charlotte? What do you want to know about her for? She's a proper fly-by-night, if you know what I mean.'

Faye didn't, but persisted, 'Did she? Did she know my mum?'

'Not especially,' he said. 'I heard they had some sort of falling out. But don't go asking me for any more details, cos there aren't any. Why don't you ask your father?'

'I did. He kept changing the subject.'

'The thing about this village, Faye,' he said, 'is it's *all* peculiar, odd, strange and witchy. Did you know the River Wode turned red in the summer of 1911? There's a path near the convent where if you were to leave a cart unattended it would roll uphill, and they reckon if you hold a magnetic compass in the middle of the standing stones in the wood it would go all doolally. Peculiar, odd, strange and witchy is standard operating procedure for this place, Faye. Just this week on Larry Dell's farm, he said someone pinched all his scarecrows.' Mr Paine took another sip of tea.

'Larry Dell . . . Is he the one with the brassica farm? He's got that dent in his head.'

'That's him. I saw him in the Heart and Hand last Friday—'

'What was you doing in the Heart and Hand?' Faye didn't like it when villagers went to pubs other than her dad's.

'Darts night. Now, where was I?'

'Someone else's pub, apparently.'

'Where was I in *my story*?'

'Someone pinched Larry Dell's scarecrows.'

'That's it. And here's the peculiar, odd, strange and witchy bit. He said whoever pinched the scarecrows left the crosses. It's like the scarecrows just hopped off their poles and walked away. And then yesterday I heard about Doris's boy, Herbert.'

'He's at sea, isn't he?'

'Just got back on shore leave the other day. He was on the train home from Portsmouth, and as he's coming into Therfield Station, you'll never guess what he saw.'

Faye shrugged. 'Larry Dell's scarecrows?'

Mr Paine smiled, opened his mouth to speak, then angled his head, listening.

'What's up?' Faye asked.

Mr Paine raised a silencing finger. His voice dropped to a whisper. 'Someone's out there.'

Faye mouthed, 'Out where?' and Mr Paine pointed to where Gibbet Lane veered off to a bridle path into the wood. From the darkness came a rhythmic *t-tap* of heel-toe, heel-toe. Boots on cobbles, and they were coming this way.

Only today, a leaflet had arrived in the second post called *When the Invaders Come*, and Bertie had been filling Faye's head with stories of German paratroopers dropping from the sky for sneak attacks with machine guns and grenades. Faye's heart began to thump in her ears and she wished she had Morris Marshall's shotgun or Harry Newton's old blunderbuss. Even a broomstick would be something.

'Who goes there?' Mr Paine bellowed. No answer. Faye saw him clench his fists as he called again. 'Who goes there?'

The footsteps drew closer and closer.

6

Brief Encounter

Philomena Teach marched through the midnight gloom of the wood. Most people would fear the oppressive darkness, but there was nothing for Mrs Teach to be afraid of here. The wood was an old friend. There were paths that only she knew of, and she followed one now to the village.

Mrs Teach's encounter with Charlotte had made her blood boil. Accusing her of breaking the rules like she was some naughty schoolgirl. How dare she, indeed. Mrs Teach had considered telling Charlotte the truth, but the snooty cow had made it clear she wouldn't be requiring Mrs Teach's help, so she could go and take a running jump.

That said, if Charlotte was right about an incursion from below … it didn't bear thinking about. No one in their right mind was daft enough to open the door to anyone – any*thing* – from down there. Mrs Teach's own little mishap had been a complete accident and she had taken immediate steps to rectify her error.

The path led to the edge of the wood where the trees were further apart, cliffs dropped away to the sea and the sky and the water came together as a silent curtain of darkness. Waves hissed across the shingle beaches far below. The chalk path was bumpy here and she had to watch her step as she wound her way to Gibbet Lane. Chalk became a bridle path and then cobbles. Her heels clacked on the stone.

This incursion wasn't her fault. Nothing to do with her. Yes, she had done wrong before, but that had come from a place of mourning and love. There was no malice in her actions. She knew she had broken the rules, but those rules were unjust and she had still been grieving and all she wanted was to—

'Who goes there?' a voice bellowed from the darkness.

'Bloody Nora.' Mrs Teach clutched her chest. She snapped out of her angry daze to find she had left the wood and was at the bottom of Gibbet Lane. Two shadows in ARP helmets huddled together in the dark. One was much bigger than the other. The familiar bulk of a friendly purveyor of cigarettes and sweeties. 'Freddie? Freddie Paine, is that you? You nearly gave me a heart attack, you great lummox.'

'Oh, sorry, Mrs Teach,' Mr Paine said, tipping back his helmet. 'Can't be too careful these days. Hope I didn't give you a fright.'

'A fright, Freddie? A fright? I think you took ten bloody years off me. I'll say goodnight to you both.' She started to head home when another voice chirped up.

'Might I ask what you was doing out and about so late at night, Mrs Teach?'

It took her a moment to recognise the voice. 'Faye? Faye Bright?' Mrs Teach bit her lip to stop herself from blurting, *I was just talking about you.* Instead, she took a step closer to the young girl, her face blue in the pallid moonlight. 'Oh, look at you, doing your bit. How wonderful. You're an inspiration to young women everywhere. Well, it's getting chilly, so I'm off to make some cocoa and—'

'Begging your pardon, Mrs Teach,' Faye persisted, 'but you haven't answered my question.'

Just like her mother, Mrs Teach thought. Kathryn Wynter never knew when to keep her mouth shut. Always asking impertinent questions. Constantly prodding and poking her nose in where it wasn't wanted. One of the many reasons Mrs Teach quite liked the woman.

'Only, we have to report any suspicious behaviour,' Faye said. 'And someone wandering about in the woods in the middle of the night might be construed as somewhat suspect, if you get my drift, no offence.'

'None taken, young lady. Now, if you don't mind, it's a bit nippy and—'

Mr Paine blocked her path. 'Kindly answer the question, Mrs Teach,' he said.

In her youth, Mrs Teach had taken many lead roles in the Woodville Amateur Dramatics Society and received good notices in the parish gazette, but it had been nearly three decades since she last trod the boards, so she was pleasantly surprised at how easily she was able to summon her thespian powers of old. Mrs Teach burst into a flood of tears that would have won her a standing ovation in the West End. 'Everywhere I look I see him,' she said between sobs. 'I just had to get out of the house, even for a short while. Too many memories.'

'Oh, oh, I'm so sorry, Mrs Teach.' Faye hurried over and took her hand. 'What's it been? Three months?'

'Three months, three weeks, two days, my love,' Mrs Teach said with a sniff. 'But we must soldier on, mustn't we? Bigger worries in the world than me and my Ernie.'

Up close, Mrs Teach took a moment to look the girl over. There was a sharp mind behind those big specs. Charlotte was wrong to dismiss the girl. Mrs Teach wanted to ask her all sorts of questions, but Mr Paine was taking her by the elbow and steering her in the direction of home.

'Come along, Mrs Teach,' he said in his low, slow voice. 'We'll see you to your door.'

'Oh, you're too kind,' she replied. 'What would we do without brave folk like you watching over us?' Mrs Teach allowed herself to be guided home like an invalid, but once inside she clapped her hands together and with a new determination marched to the kitchen to make her cocoa. She flicked the light switch on and immediately a voice cried from the street, 'Put that light out!'

7

The Crow Folk Rally

Clouds boiled from inside, pulses of lightning throwing long shadows that swooped across the forest floor.

Craddock slipped between the trees at the edge of the wood, a silent silhouette as he checked his snares. A hare for the pot. Or maybe for one of the mugs in the village? Since rationing started he had been raking it in with a bit of black market game. When the butcher was only permitted to give you a few ounces of meat every week, and when you were sick of corned-beef fritters, a rabbit or hare could be a very welcome change and there were plenty in the village who were willing to pay over the odds for it.

He stuffed the hare in his sack and slung it over his shoulder, still simmering at the way he had been spoken to in the pub earlier. Pompous old farts like that bell-ringer Hodgson, or a mouthy little bint like that Faye, or witches like that Charlotte. Sod 'em. They could get their own game. This one was for him.

Craddock passed a badger drinking from the pond.

Another lightning flash revealed the cluster of barns at Newton's farm. Lamplight flickered within and Craddock wondered what the bloody hell Harry Newton was playing at this late at night. More than one barn had burned down around here thanks to a forgotten oil lamp, so Craddock took it upon himself to investigate. He moved quietly, peeling away from the cover of the wood and scurrying down the footpath, dashing over bloody feathers on the ground where a fox had pounced on a pigeon.

This was a friend's barn, but a hunter's instinct told him to be cautious. Craddock froze when he heard a rousing cheer from inside, followed by a smattering of applause. He ducked down to sidle up to the barn and the voices became more distinct.

'For too long have we suffered under their yoke. No longer will we endure their mockery.' It was a man's voice, and he was more than a bit full of himself, giving it all like a soapbox preacher. 'For now, we have our freedom.' Another cheer.

Communists? Craddock wondered. *Bolsheviks? Nazis?* He recalled last winter when a chap went from door to door handing out pamphlets urging villagers to join some fascist organisation. Constable Muldoon had chased the loon from the village on his bicycle while waving his truncheon. Woodville didn't have any truck with such nonsense, so how had someone filled a barn with village revolutionaries? He peered through a crack in the barn's timber frame.

He could only see the legs of the talker, who was

standing on a podium of hay bales with his back to Craddock. Flanked by flickering oil lamps, the speaker addressed the crowd of twenty or so that filled the barn, but he couldn't make out any faces beyond the glare of the lamps.

'But for how long?' the speaker asked. 'They will want to take it from us, brothers and sisters, yes they will. How long can we remain free?'

Craddock backed away and hurried around to the front of the barn to get a better look.

'We must leave this place,' a woman's voice cried from inside, 'and find a new home to call our own.'

'No. This is our land,' said another.

'Yes, brothers and sisters,' said the speaker. 'We have watched over this land and it is ours by right. We must take it and keep it.'

Craddock decided that was quite enough and barged in, swinging the barn door open. 'What the bloody hell is—'

Craddock lost his voice as every head turned towards him.

Some were featureless bundles of straw under floppy hats, others had crude cloth blackbird faces with yellow beaks, most were sackcloth with buttons and stitches for eyes and mouths. Each one was the stuff of nightmares.

Scarecrows.

Living, walking, talking scarecrows.

Craddock was a simple man at heart. A hunter who knew the cycle of life and death, and he was well acquainted with the laws of Mother Nature and how harsh and unforgiving she could be. But he wasn't equipped with anywhere near enough of an imagination to make sense of what he was seeing. So he ignored the fact that he was talking to a barn full of scarecrows and went about his business of telling them to bugger off private property. 'This . . . this is Harry Newton's barn. What are you—'

'I know this man.' One of the scarecrows stepped out of the crowd, pointing an accusing finger at Craddock. She had a sack for a head and a red gingham frock. She pulled her shawl tighter around her as she stared with her button eyes at the speaker on the hay bales.

The speaker's head looked just like a pumpkin, but that couldn't possibly be the case because people don't have heads shaped like pumpkins, but this one really, really looked like a pumpkin.

'Speak up, sister Suky,' Pumpkinhead said.

'I have seen him at night, I have,' Suky said, her cross-stitch mouth moving in time with her words. 'A poacher. He traps hares and rabbits and more. Craddock, his name is. Wilfred Craddock.'

'Wilf?' Craddock hadn't thought he could be any more baffled, but now this lass was mistaking him for his grandfather. A poacher like him, to be sure, but long dead and buried.

'He cannot be trusted. He must not leave, he will betray us, I'm telling you,' Suky said, gripping Craddock's arm.

He shook her off, but she grabbed him again

and Craddock would be buggered before he let any woman touch him like that, so he backhanded her across the face.

Her head spun around so far it was facing the wrong way. Had he broken her neck? Craddock's blood began to rush as he readied to fight his way out.

There came a creaking noise. At first, Craddock thought it was the barn door, but this sounded more like wood being twisted to the point of breaking, and he watched with cold dread as Suky the scarecrow's head slowly turned back to face him.

Craddock might not have had much of an imagination, but he was playing catch-up and not liking what he saw. 'I . . . I don't know you,' he said, backing away, 'and this ain't none of my business.'

The scarecrows had formed a circle around him and were closing in.

'I won't be telling no one,' he said, angry at himself for letting his voice tremble. 'You can trust me. I won't say a word. You ask people around here about me. I'm known in the village.'

The circle of scarecrows tightened around him. A few reached out, stroking his long coat.

'Are you indeed?' said the man with the pumpkin for a head. 'Known for poaching? Stealing? Do you consort with thieves? Do you dabble in the dark arts? Do you keep company with witches?'

'Witches?' Craddock slapped the stroking hands away. 'I won't have nothing to do with no witches.'

'But you know of them?' Pumpkinhead's triangle

eyes narrowed somehow. 'Tell me. Tell me their names. Tell me where I might find them and you shall be free to go about your business.'

'Oh, will I now?' Craddock bristled. 'Most people you meet round here couldn't be trusted to tie their own bootlaces, and I have no truck with anyone who calls themselves a witch or any such nonsense, but I won't be betraying any of them to you, sir. If you think I'm going to be told when I can or cannot go about my business by some berk with a pumpkin on his head, then you've got another think coming.' Craddock dropped his sack with the dead hare and clenched his fists. 'Now, if you're done, you can all sod off before I—' He glimpsed a tiny nod from Pumpkinhead just before the scarecrows threw themselves on top of him. Craddock stumbled to his knees as their gloved hands gripped his arms with a strength that took him by surprise. One grabbed his collar and forced his head down. With a roar from the depths of his gut, Craddock thrust his arms up, knocked them back and broke free. Two more tried to block his path, but Craddock punched one and shoved the other out of the way, then hurried to the barn door and out into the storm.

He had taken about three steps when he heard cries behind him and scarecrows poured out of the barn, rushing after him. The hunt was on.

❧

Craddock dashed into the thick of the wood, flitting between the trees. The rain had stopped, though lightning still flashed and thunder shook the air. He dared to glance back at his pursuers.

The scarecrows moved fast, their arms and legs whirling madly, boneless and inhuman as they closed in.

Craddock tripped and tumbled into a ditch. For a moment, he saw white as the back of his head hit a rock. He could only flounder, grasping for any kind of handhold to haul himself out of the ditch when a jolly scarecrow with a beaming smile leapt on Craddock, beating him about the head with a flurry of punches.

Craddock kicked him away and got to his feet, but two more scarecrows joined the fray, raining clumsy blows on him, wild and savage with flailing arms.

Craddock knew how to fight in a bar, in the streets, and according to the Queensberry Rules, but he had never known anything like the relentless insanity of the scarecrows. They were fearless and brutal and knocked him to the ground again. The jolly scarecrow's sackcloth face filled Craddock's vision, giggling like a loon.

Craddock had landed awkwardly and something poked into his buttocks. He knew what it was and how it would save him, and he tried to ignore the incessant punches as he reached for the box in his back pocket.

The jolly scarecrow's head twitched at the scratch of a match on phosphorous, but it was too late to move as flames licked across his face. The jolly scarecrow howled, trying to pat the fire out. The others wanted to help, but they scurried back, afraid of the flame.

Craddock limped away into the darkness. Behind him, the jolly scarecrow ran blindly, a glowing ball dashing between the trees, wailing like a banshee.

8

Goliath Spooked by Low-Flying Spitfires

Faye couldn't be sure what time she had finally made it home last night, but it was well after midnight as Dad was already in bed. It took her even longer to get to sleep, her mind buzzing with all the strange revelations of the previous day. When she got up for breakfast, her father was already gone. He'd left her a note on the kitchen table:

Goliath spooked by low-flying Spitfires. Gone to fetch him out of a ditch.

Goliath was the brewery's dray horse, a friendly giant who delivered the cart laden with a pyramid of beer barrels to the pub twice a week. He was a docile fellow, fond of apples and carrots, and frightened by all the aircraft buzzing back and forth from the aerodrome. It wasn't uncommon for him to do a runner across a field, spilling barrels of ale as he went. Faye knew that her dad didn't *have* to help coax Goliath out of a ditch. He was avoiding her. At least until he thought Faye had forgotten all mention of her mother being in cahoots with a witch.

But if he reckoned Faye was going to let this one drop, he was dead wrong.

Faye wolfed down her porridge, rushed through a few of her chores, then lost patience and jumped on her Pashley Model A bicycle. She had a witch to interrogate.

ꝑ

The bike's wheels cut through the puddles from the previous night's storm as she cycled through the village. Woodville shone glorious in the morning sun. Tudor buildings leaned over thatched cottages and cobbled streets. Red, pink, white and lilac petunias clustered in hanging baskets by every front door. Even the blemishes of wartime – sandbags on every corner, buckets of sand and water ready for fires, and windows criss-crossed with tape – felt oddly normal and comforting after last night.

The butcher and baker were open for business and villagers queued outside their doors in an orderly fashion, ration books in hand. Faye smiled and waved at the faces she knew, which was everyone. Any other day and she would have stopped to chat, but she was on a mission this morning and Charlotte's cottage was hidden deep in the woods, which meant a long cycle till the path petered to nothing, followed by a longer walk.

As Faye came to the bottom of the Wode Road, she dodged a line of schoolchildren wearing gas masks, following their teacher in an air-raid drill. That's when Faye caught sight of the white horse and cart of Doris Finch's milk float turning off the road and heading out of the village.

Doris lived in a cottage on the corner of Allhallows Lane. After her husband Kenny passed away, Doris had taken over his milk round. Doris was much liked in the village. She was always on time with her deliveries and had a cheerful smile, whatever the weather. The same could not have been said for Kenny, who had been snippy with his customers and his family. It would be uncharitable to suggest that Kenny's sudden death from pneumonia two winters ago had been the best thing to happen to Doris, but it couldn't be denied that she walked with more of a spring in her step since they buried him in Saint Irene's.

Her son Herbert, looking fine in his Navy uniform with his cap at a jaunty angle, was hitching a ride on the back of the cart and leafing through the sports pages of the *Daily Mirror*. Faye remembered the story Mr Paine had started to tell her last night, and she pedalled harder to catch up with them.

'Morning, Herbert,' she called as she weaved behind the cart. Its empty bottles clinked as it trundled down the road.

The lad lowered his newspaper and smiled, revealing a missing tooth. 'Faye Bright, as I live and breathe.' It wasn't quite the same happy-go-lucky smile he'd worn when first marching off to war last autumn, but there was still a hint of his chipper nature. He was only two years older than Faye, but he looked so grown up in his uniform. 'How's your old man?'

'Yeah, he's all right,' Faye said, standing on her pedals as she coasted. 'You got a bit of shore leave, then?'

Herbert's smile shrank a little. 'Just a couple of days. I'm heading back now. Got a train to catch.'

'Dad said you was on the Atlantic convoys on a big old battleship. That must be exciting.'

Herbert's smile remained in place, but his eyes looked down. 'Has its moments.'

Faye had read in the papers about the terrible battles faced by the Atlantic convoys, and Herbert had probably been in the thick of it. She got the feeling she should change the subject. 'I was having a chinwag with Mr Paine last night,' she said.

'Oh, yeah. How is the big man?'

'Tickety-boo, can't complain. We was on ARP patrol last night and he mentioned you saw something peculiar on the train when you came here the other day.'

'Oh, for—' Herbert slapped his newspaper shut and turned to where his mother was steering the cart. 'Mum, did you tell everyone in the bleedin' village?'

Doris craned her neck around. 'Don't blame me. You're the one who— Oh, hello, Faye.'

'Hello, Mrs Finch.'

'How's your dad?'

'Tickety-boo, can't—'

Herbert cut through the niceties, snapping at his mother. 'Who else have you told?'

'I don't recall, Herbert, and I wasn't aware that it was privileged information.'

'That means everyone on your round.'

'Not *everyone*,' Mrs Finch said, flashing Faye a cheeky grin.

'Oh, wonderful. I know that look, Mother,' Herbert said. 'The only people who don't know are the hard-of-hearing and the dead in their graves. Everyone's going to think I'm off my chump.'

'No, they won't,' Mrs Finch said. 'You were all tuckered out after a long journey, that's all.'

Faye pedalled to keep up with the cart. 'What did you see, Herbert?' she asked.

'I didn't see nothing,' he said, hiding behind his *Daily Mirror*.

'Scarecrows,' Mrs Finch said. 'He saw folks dressed like scarecrows and one of them had a pumpkin on his head. Actually, no. How did you put it? Not *on* his head. *For* his head.'

'Give it a rest, Mum.'

Mrs Finch added, 'He said this Pumpkinhead fellow smiled and waved at him as he went by.'

'Mu-um.'

'This pumpkin, was it like a mask? Or a funny hat?' Faye asked.

'No, a pumpkin,' Mrs Finch asserted. 'A right and proper pumpkin for a head.'

'Mum!'

'I'm just telling her what you told me,' Mrs Finch insisted. 'He was white as a sheet when I brought him home. Like he'd seen a ghost or something.'

'It was nothing,' Herbert said. 'I was half asleep and probably dreamed it and I ain't never telling you nothin' ever again, Mother.'

The milk float came to the junction at the bottom of Fish Hill and Mrs Finch steered it away from the village towards the train station in Therfield, the next town along.

Faye pulled on her brakes, skidding to a stop at the junction. 'Bye, Herbert, stay safe,' she called after him. He waved back and a little of his smile returned.

Faye gripped the handlebars of her bicycle and tingled at the thought of a walking, talking scarecrow with a pumpkin for a head. The poor lad was seeing things. For a start, pumpkins were out of season and wouldn't be ripe till the autumn harvest. As the *clip-clop* of Doris's horse faded away, another horse came cantering up the road.

It was Goliath, being led by Mr Glover from the brewery and Faye's father, who puffed up his chest when he saw her.

'You found him, then.' Faye lowered her bike and greeted Goliath, stroking his face. 'Hello, big fella,' she said, and the dray horse nodded his head in greeting. 'Did those noisy Spitfires give you a fright? Eh? Oh dear. Mornin', Mr Glover. Dad.'

'Morning, Faye,' Mr Glover said cheerily. He was a man as round as he was tall, topped with a flat cap and mutton chops. He took his yellow neckerchief off and dabbed his forehead. ‘Silly bugger ended up under the railway bridge. Shaking like a leaf.’

‘Oh, bless his soul.’ Faye gave Goliath a hug around his neck. He shook her off, embarrassed by the attention.

‘All right, suit yourself,’ she said, stepping back.

‘You done your chores?’ Faye’s dad greeted her more cautiously.

‘’Course.’ This was mostly true.

‘What you up to now?’

‘Out and about,’ she said with a shrug. ‘Just saw young Herbert Finch off.’

‘Did you hear about that?’ Mr Glover’s face broke into a grin. ‘Says he saw a man with a pumpkin for an ’ead. How about that, eh?’

‘How about that indeed,’ Faye said, not taking her eyes off her dad. ‘Do you not believe in magical notions, then, Mr Glover?’

‘Nah, a lot of old rot. Fairy stories for little’ uns. For me, the only real magic is how a bit of hops, barley, yeast and water can become beer. There’s a miracle, right there.’

‘You don’t believe in witches and such?’ Faye ignored the steely glare she was getting from her father.

‘Er, no, course not.’ Mr Glover began to falter. He looked from Faye to Terrence and back again, sensing some unspoken hostility between father and daughter.

‘Did you know my mother, Mr Glover?’ Faye asked.

Terrence said nothing, but oh-so-slightly shook his head.

'Of . . . of course.' Mr Glover was cautious, wondering where this line of questioning was going.

'Was she a . . .' Faye was ready to ask, ready to say the word, but she couldn't bring herself to do it. Did she really believe her mother was a witch? That she could do magic and fly on a broomstick? It seemed so likely last night, in the woods, in the dark. But what had her mother really done? Written a book with some odd things in it. Been kind to people. Helped a bird that had been stunned. The more Faye thought about it, the more ridiculous it sounded. On the cusp of her thoughts, she could sense Mr Glover awaiting the rest of her question. She blinked herself back to the real world and adjusted her specs. 'Was she . . . nice?' Faye asked lamely.

'Oh, she was lovely, your mother,' Mr Glover said, slapping his hands on his belly. Terrence released the breath he'd been holding. 'Kindness itself, always smiling and as wise as the day is long. And she helped my mother with her *down-belows*, if you know what I mean.'

Faye didn't exactly, but let the man continue.

'Of course, there were plenty who reckoned she was some sort of witch, but I don't believe that.'

Four things happened in quick succession.

Terrence looked at Mr Glover as if he would strike him dead on the spot.

Faye's heart skipped a beat.

Three Spitfires thundered overhead in formation, their Merlin engines splitting the sky.

And poor Goliath whinnied in fright, reared up and bolted down the Therfield Road.

'Curse you,' Mr Glover cried, giving chase. 'Those things are a bleedin' menace,' he hollered as he dashed into the distance.

Terrence hesitated, torn between helping Mr Glover and warning his daughter.

'Tell Mr Glover,' Faye said, 'he should maybe stuff some cotton wool in Goliath's ears.' She leaned on the pedals of her bike and rode towards the wood.

9

A Toad, a Goat and a Witch

When the wood grew too dense, Faye left her bicycle leaning against a tree and continued on foot down the narrow woodland path. The brambles were in flower, pink and white, well on their way to becoming wild blackberries. One of Faye's few distinct recollections of her mother was coming here to collect baskets full of them to make jam. She was four years old and she could still remember licking her sticky fingers clean and her mother doing the same. They walked home together that day, hand in sticky hand. Their last summer together. Faye's belly twisted at the memory and the familiar flash of anger returned. How many other days like that had been stolen from her?

If Mum had been a witch, she wasn't like any that Faye had seen in books or at the flicks. Faye and the ringers had gone on a day trip to London to the Whitechapel Bell Foundry, and in the afternoon they went to the pictures to see *The Wizard of Oz*. The witch in the film was bright green with a pointy nose.

Faye's mum was the colour of eggshell with freckles and had a smile that could brighten the darkest day.

The air had grown muggy and squadrons of mozzies circled Faye as she ducked under them. The path became little more than a track and soon Faye was trudging through knee-high ferns and occasionally being slapped in the face by a branch before she found the clearing with Miss Charlotte's cottage.

It was a squat home, made of short logs piled cross-wise and bound by cob, all hunkered under a turf roof in the depths of the wood. It didn't want to be found.

An axe rested by a chopping block. There was an outhouse and a herb garden. White smoke gently spiralled from the chimney and the aroma of aniseed lingered from the ground elder that grew in the shade.

Faye stood some distance from it, making little fists and biting her lip. This was it. She would finally discover the truth about her mother. With a sniff, she marched to the cottage's little wooden door and raised her knuckles to knock.

'Go away.'

Faye jolted at the unmistakable sound of Charlotte's husky voice, and she looked for spyholes, wondering how the witch knew she had come.

'I'm behind you, girl.'

Faye spun to find Charlotte striding towards the cottage from the wood, a trug cradled in her arms full of mushrooms and herbs. A black and green toad sat on her shoulder like a pirate's parrot. The toad croaked and Faye felt certain it was giving her a snooty look.

'Mornin',' Faye said, trying to sound like she was just passing and decided to pop in. 'Have you got a mo'?'

'No.' Charlotte marched past Faye and stepped inside the cottage, closing the door behind her. There followed the clunk of a bolt being slid into place.

Faye stood where she was, feeling a right old lemon. She wriggled her toes in her shoes, wondering if she should just turn around and go home, but this was her morning off and she had a million other things she should be doing and she hadn't come all this way for nothing.

'Blimmin' cheek,' Faye muttered under her breath as she rat-a-tat-tatted on the cottage door.

'Bugger off,' Charlotte hollered from inside. This was followed by a dismissive *croak* from the toad.

'Dad told me you knew my mum.'

'A little.'

'That's more than I ever did,' Faye said. 'You were friends?'

'I would love to reminisce,' Charlotte said in a tone suggesting she would rather drench her body from head to toe in petrol and set herself on fire, 'but I have urgent business to attend to. Leave me in peace, child.'

'It's just ...' Faye wondered if she should tell her everything. After all, Charlotte was probably the only person in the village who might possibly understand. 'It's just, I found this book, y'see. It was hidden in the cellar in a trunk with Mum's knick-knacks. This dusty leather-bound thing, I reckoned it was maybe a ledger at first, or a Bible p'raps, but then I opened it up and right there on the first page it says *Wynter's Book of Rituals and Magic* by Kathryn Wynter, which is her maiden name of course, so she must have started it before she met Dad, and she must've kept writing it cos it's full of notes and sketches. There's pictures of plants and herbs, and she invented her own bell-ringing method. And there's all sorts of strange creatures and this stuff about magic and spells and there's even a recipe for jam roly-poly. I mean, none of it's real, of course. Except the jam roly-poly. But when you look at what she wrote in the book and the stuff she drew, I have to wonder if she believed in it or if she was a bit funny in the head. And if she knew you . . . Well, you get what I'm saying, don't you?'

Faye left the question hanging and cocked an ear, waiting for a reply. All she heard was the bucolic bustle of the surrounding wood. Birdsong, squirrels scurrying for nuts and the wind rustling through the leaves.

'Hello?' Faye called.

From inside the cottage came a *croak*.

Faye fumed. How rude could this woman be? Faye had come all this way for answers and she was blimming well going to get them. She shuffled around the cottage to find a high window. Trying not to step in the bed of brassicas, Faye stood on tiptoe, wiped the condensation from the window and peered through the warped glass.

The room was murky, with a low ceiling propped up by timber beams, and on the white plaster walls there were strange markings that looked like the runes Faye had seen in the book. Clothes had been tossed in every corner and dust twirled in the air. There was a bed with no sheets and on that bed was Charlotte. Fast asleep, quite naked, skin pale as milk, hands clasped across her breasts and with the toad resting on her belly. The toad turned its head to look straight at Faye.

Croak.

Faye jumped back, blushing, hand to her mouth.

Bleat.

Faye spun to find a white goat glaring at her.

'She's all in the nuddy!' Faye told the goat, but the creature just lowered its head and kicked the dirt with its cloven feet. 'Righto, fine, I know when I'm not welcome,' she told the goat.

The goat just stared at her with ancient intelligence.

'Good,' Faye said and marched back to her bicycle, all her determination leaving her like the air from a leaky balloon. She was a fool to have thought such things about her mother. She was an idiot for believing in magic. All she had found was a naked oddball who slept with toads and kept angry goats. Even if this magic malarkey was real, Faye was pretty sure she wanted nothing to do with it, thank you very much.

ß

A yellow-striped damselfly hovered above the reeds then flickered away, startled by the breathless man grabbing a reed and yanking it from the water.

Craddock snapped the hollow reed, blew through it to clear it, held it tight between his lips and slipped under the surface of the pond. He had seen John Wayne do this in a film once.

Craddock took a breath through the reed and choked as his throat clogged with muck from the stem. He surfaced again and tossed it away, trying to suppress his coughing and cursing John Wayne's name.

There was a movement in the wood and Craddock backed further into the reeds. He froze, holding his breath as he watched the scarecrows pass as silhouettes, their heads darting from side to side as they searched for him.

They had hunted him all night, cropping up wherever he turned, closing in and giving him nowhere to run. Craddock was strong, but even he needed to rest, and these ungodly creatures were relentless and never tired.

A scarecrow with a floppy straw hat waded into the pond and Craddock tensed. Exhaustion weighed on him, his bones ached and his wet clothes clung to his chilled skin.

The scarecrow kept moving, but more followed and Craddock tried not to shiver.

10

A Murmuration of Starlings

Faye took a longer route home, pushing her bike along a path thick with nettles that meandered by the River Wode. A pair of swans kept her company, gliding in the water, a nonchalant entourage. Faye was sure they were staring at her.

'Mornin',' Faye said with a tip of her chin.

One of the swans nodded back. The other honked at its partner, as if scolding it for replying.

Faye stopped, tilting her head at the swans. 'Do that again,' she said.

Both swans raised their wings and began kicking in the water, splashing and gaining height before veering off into the sky. Faye watched them till they were tiny dots on the horizon.

'Suit yourself.' Faye had to wonder if they really understood her. Of course they hadn't. Once again, she was allowing her imagination to run away with her. This was her curse. Too much of a flighty imagination. She had to learn to keep her feet on the ground. Faye resumed pushing her bike along the path, head down, shoulders hunched.

Of course, it didn't help that she lived in Woodville. Mr Paine was right. The village had more than its fair share of peculiar, odd, strange and witchy stuff going on. But that didn't make magic real. Sleeping in the buff with a toad on your belly and being rude to everyone you meet doesn't give you any kind of supernatural powers. To Faye it was simply evidence that you were a sandwich short of a picnic.

Faye felt a flush of sadness: her dear departed mother had probably been just as bonkers as Miss Charlotte. She would put the book away when she got home. Back in the trunk with the other relics of her mum's life, along with all the anger and sadness. Faye preferred her fuzzy memories of warmth, laughter and sticky jam.

A whiff of smoke tickled Faye's nostrils and she looked up. At a bend in the river, the ranks of the Local Defence Volunteers had gathered around a pair of braziers that glowed white hot. Black smoke swirled into the air.

The LDV were having another one of their training exercises. Knocking this Dad's Army of wheezing enthusiasts into shape was no easy task. Every other day they were marching through town with broomsticks for rifles, practising hand-to-hand combat in the church hall or tossing home-made Molotov cocktails at old barns.

Today was a fire-drill day.

Bertie was there, knee-deep in the water, manning

a pump that fed a hosepipe gripped by Mr Baxter the ironmonger. Mr Marshall, captain of the bowls team, was shouting at everyone, which meant he thought he was in charge.

'More pressure, laddie,' he hollered at Bertie. 'Put some effort into it.'

Bertie, red-cheeked and puffing like a steam engine, doubled his efforts. At the other end of the hose, little gushes of water began to spurt out.

'Aim it at the base of the fire,' Mr Marshall bellowed at Mr Baxter who, tongue sticking out of his mouth in concentration, took aim at one of the burning braziers. The water continued to huff in sporadic bursts, barely reaching the brazier. The fire crackled on, unimpressed.

Faye hopped on her bicycle and pedalled to join the men, giving Bertie a wave. 'Mornin', Bertie.'

'Oh, morning, Faye,' he said, his voice straining as he intensified his efforts to impress a girl.

'Much better, Bertie my lad, much better.' Mr Marshall raised a triumphant fist in the air as the water began to spray over the flames.

'Want any help, gents?' Faye asked.

'Fire drill, move along, young lady, move along,' Mr Marshall said, gesturing for her to keep going down the path, but Faye planted her feet on the ground and perched on her saddle, enjoying the show. 'Need any help, Bertie?' she called, but before the boy could take a breath to reply, Mr Marshall butted in.

'I must insist that you move along,' he barked. 'This is a dangerous drill and not for the uninitiated.'

'I tried to get initiated, but you lot told me I weren't wanted,' Faye said, folding her arms. 'I'll just watch. I won't get in the way.'

Mr Marshall raised a finger to object but found himself distracted by the trot of hooves coming around the bend.

Lady Aston arrived on horseback, along with three more of her Woodville Mounted Patrol. Her ladyship had organised the patrol back in March after seeing terrifying illustrations in the newspapers of German paratroopers armed to the teeth. The article described the threat of troops descending from the sky into the English countryside, dropping grenades on unsuspecting folk below before wreaking havoc with their machine guns. Lady Aston was having none of that, and immediately kitted out her staff and tenantry with matching armbands, tweed jackets, bowler hats and binoculars. Every day and night they rode out from Hayward Lodge – her ladyship's sizeable mansion house – to patrol the countryside, with occasional breaks for tea and tiffin.

'Morning, chaps,' she called to Mr Marshall's men. 'Need any assistance?'

'We're fine, thank you, Your Ladyship,' Mr Marshall said, his cheeks reddening.

'Jolly good.' Lady Aston spotted Faye. 'Ahoy there, young Faye. You enjoying the show, too?'

'Certainly am,' replied Faye, beaming.

The Local Defence Volunteers shifted uncomfortably at finding themselves with an audience.

'I thought you said this was going to be a quiet spot,' Mr Baxter said.

'Stick a sock in it, Gerald,' Mr Marshall snapped.

'All this coming and going, it's like bleedin' Piccadilly Circus,' Mr Baxter continued.

'I order you to be quiet,' Mr Marshall said.

'I signed up to do my bit, not become a bloomin' street performer.'

'Right. You're off hose duty, Mr Baxter. Stand down and let someone else have a go.'

'That's not fair. I've hardly made a start.'

'That's what you get for insubordination. Now step back, or I shall I have to reprimand you.'

Mr Baxter pouted, refusing to relinquish the still-gushing hose. 'Shan't,' he said.

'Should I stop, Mr Marshall?' Bertie cried from the river where he continued to lower and raise the pump handle.

Mr Marshall ignored the boy and went to grab the hose from Mr Baxter, who jerked away, spraying Lady Aston and her horse with freshly pumped river water.

'Goodness,' Lady Aston cried as her horse reared up, kicking its hooves and startling Mr Marshall who stumbled back into one of the braziers, knocking it over. White-hot coals tumbled out and flames caught on the stalks of dry corn in the field. Before Mr Marshall could get to his feet, a fire was rapidly spreading.

'Fire!' Faye yelled, leaping off her bike to kick dust on the flames, but they danced from stalk to stalk faster than she could kick. Everyone around here knew that a farmer's field was his livelihood, especially now there was a war on, and the other LDV volunteers joined in. They piled dirt on the flames, but still the fire grew.

Mr Baxter did his best to regain control of the hose as more water spewed forth, but his aim was poor. Mr Marshall intervened and the pair of them tussled as the fire spread.

'Gentlemen, please,' Lady Aston said, drenched yet still retaining her decorum. 'This is *most* unbecoming.'

Mr Marshall shoved Mr Baxter away and aimed the hose at the base of the fire. 'Faster, Bertie, more water.'

Bertie pumped as hard as he could, arms straining with the effort, but he was tiring. Faye splashed into the river, rushing to help Bertie.

'C'mon, lads,' she cried and more LDV men joined them, all hands to the pump.

Alas, their efforts were a little too enthusiastic and after a few moments the handle broke off with a crack. Bertie raised it aloft for all to see.

'Oh, blimmin' heck,' he said. 'Mr Marshall, I—'

All looked to Mr Marshall, who was holding the dripping hose, silhouetted by intense flames. There was nothing they could do. The fire was too big and the field would be lost.

A noise came from above like a sheet flapping on a clothes line. The air shifted and blackened. Faye squinted into the morning sunshine to find a murmuration of starlings swirling over the treeline. They expanded and contracted in perfect synchrony and their dance brought a smile to Faye's face. She had been lucky enough to see starlings flock like this a few times, but only at dusk. They twisted and spun, hundreds of them breaking like waves on a rock then coming together again, wings shivering, before diving to where the fire burned. The birds swirled around the flames like the tornado Faye had seen in that *Wizard of Oz* film. In moments, the fire was out, the braziers were smoking husks and the birds spiralled upwards before bursting apart like a firework and flying away over the fields.

All stood about, looking at one another, trying to slot what they had seen into any bit of brain that might possibly comprehend it.

Lady Aston was first to break the silence. 'That was jolly lucky,' she said.

'Wasn't it just?' Mr Marshall agreed.

'That's quite a well-known phenomenon, actually,' Mr Baxter chipped in. 'I read about a similar incident in the newspapers, if I recall.'

Faye looked agog at Bertie as the LDV began to tidy up the mess. 'I can't be the only one who saw that, can I?' she asked him. 'That wasn't natural. That was . . . something else.'

Bertie pursed his lips. 'Like what?'

'Like . . .' Faye lowered her voice. 'Like magic.'

Bertie creased his brow. 'It *was* very pretty,' he half agreed.

'No, not magic like *pretty*. Magic like magic. Like strange-things-that-oughtn't-to-happen magic.'

Bertie's face folded in confusion. 'But magic isn't real, Faye.'

'No. No, course it isn't. Mr Marshall,' Faye asked, raising her hand, 'what will you put in the report about this?'

'Hmm?' Mr Marshall looked at Faye as if he had just woken from a nap. 'I'm sorry? What are you doing in the river, girl?'

Faye struggled to answer that one, but Mr Marshall was already distracted. Lady Aston and her riders bade them farewell as if nothing had happened, and the LDV men stood back to let them pass. The fire and the murmuration were already forgotten.

'Bertie.' Faye took the lad by the arm. 'Tell them. Tell them what we just saw.'

'Hmm?' Bertie blinked and smiled absently. 'Sorry, I wasn't paying attention.'

'The birds, Bertie, the birds.'

Bertie looked at Faye with an open mouth, then squinted up into the sky. 'Birds? What birds?'

'Oh, forget it.' Faye released him. Soggy to her knees and utterly confused, she trudged out of the river, got on her bike and rode back to the village.

ℬ

The crow folk had not found the man Craddock. They had searched the wood, the ponds and the river. Suky was checking a hedgerow when a boy scampered into view, kicking a ball. The child, a moppet barely five years old with a startled mess of bright ginger hair, stood rigid and stared at her.

Suky's stitches creaked as her kind smile moved into place.

The child fled, screaming for his mother, leaving the ball behind.

Pumpkinhead reassured her. 'The child will tell his parents and they will not believe him. They will smack his bottom and send him to bed with no supper for making things up.'

Suky felt sorry for the lad but did not say it aloud. 'We cannot find that Craddock,' she said instead. 'He must be a world champion at hide-and-seek.'

'He is a hunter, a poacher,' Pumpkinhead said. 'Finding him was always going to be difficult. I wonder if we should try a new strategy.'

'What's that, my Pumpkinhead?'

'Do you know the way to the village? There are no signs.'

'I do, my Pumpkinhead,' Suky said, looking beyond the hedgerow and finding it familiar, like a half-remembered dream. 'I do not rightly know how, but I do.'

[illegible]

body is [illegible] as her [illegible] into place.

The [illegible] [illegible] [illegible]

Pumpkinhead [illegible] The [illegible] parents and [illegible] [illegible]

[illegible]

[illegible] Pumpkinhead [illegible]

[illegible] [illegible] [illegible]

[illegible] should [illegible]

'What's that, [illegible] Pumpkinhead?'

'Do you know the way to the village? [illegible]

'I [illegible] Pumpkinhead, [illegible] looking beyond the [illegible] [illegible] [illegible] buried.'

11

Mrs Teach's Warning

By the time Faye had cycled back to the village she was mostly dry, save for where her dungarees bunched behind her knees. What a waste of a morning. Given the brush-off by a nudie witch and treated like a loon by the LDV for being honest about what she had seen with her own eyes. It became clear to Faye that the only way she would learn the truth about her own mother would be to tie her dad to a chair and give him the third degree. In the meantime, she still had chores to do, and top of the list was to pick up the weekly ration. Four ounces of bacon or ham, twelve ounces of sugar and four ounces of butter. There were rumours that cooking fat would be rationed next, so Faye made sure she got double what she usually bought.

Faye was just leaving the butcher's with her bacon when she saw the widow Mrs Teach at the back of the queue, ration book and wicker shopping basket clasped to the bosom of her Women's Voluntary Service uniform.

'Nice to see you in the daylight, young lady,' Mrs Teach said, with a chortle in her voice and a rosy blush on her cheeks.

'Oh, good afternoon, Mrs Teach. Yes, sorry about last night. We have to ask those questions, it's part of our training,' Faye said, knowing this was only sort-of true. Last night she was just being nosey.

'Not at all, dear, not at all. We must be vigilant and all that. Did Mr Paine put it in his little logbook?'

'Yup.'

'Hmm,' Mrs Teach said in a way that suggested she would pay him a visit later to convince him to take it out again. 'He's right to do so, of course. Any peculiar behaviour must be noted. Did you get lost in the woods today, Faye?'

Faye tensed. How did she know?

'Mud on your shoes, dear.' Mrs Teach glanced down and Faye's eyes followed. Her plimsolls were caked with dry mud. Mrs Teach's own bright green sling-backs – a daring choice to go with her dark green WVS uniform – looked brand new and Faye wondered how she could afford them. 'And I can smell woodsmoke and aniseed. You been to see our resident witch?'

Faye's heart nearly stopped. She knew. 'Er . . . Well, yes. I . . .'

'It's fine, dear, we've all given her a visit at some point. I appreciate that blossoming into womanhood can be a little bewildering, and we'll try anything for answers.' Mrs Teach leaned closer to Faye, who couldn't help but breathe in her sweet, summery scent of elderflower. The gossip in the village was she put a few drops of elderflower dew in her bath to keep herself looking young. 'Women's problems?' she asked in a whisper.

'N-not exactly,' Faye replied, glancing up and down the queue, hoping no one could hear them.

'That's all she's good for.' The jolly smile that usually propped up Mrs Teach's face dropped and her eyes lost a little of their usual glimmer. 'She tried to help with my Ernie, but he passed all the same.'

Faye had liked Ernie Teach. A small man when compared to the voluminous Mrs Teach, Ernie had always been cheerful – one of those chaps who could fix anything. Trouble with your electrics? Ernie Teach would ping the lights back on. Motor broken down? Ernie Teach would get you on the road again. Leaky pipe? Ernie Teach would sort it lickety-split. Lacking in carnal gratification? Ernie would satisfy your every desire.

This last was just a rumour, of course, but word was that Ernie Teach had been, among his many talents, a sensitive and generous lover. There was further gossip that Mrs Teach had worn the poor man out one night last spring and his heart had given up on him.

'May he rest in peace, Mrs Teach.'

'Yes.' Mrs Teach gently but firmly gripped Faye's wrist. 'Stay away from that Charlotte, young lady, for your own peace of mind. She only brings trouble. Trust me, I know. And if it's anything other than women's problems … ?' Mrs Teach trailed off, letting the question hang.

'Such as . . . ?' Faye pursed her lips in innocence.

'Anything . . .' Mrs Teach raised an eyebrow. 'Peculiar. Odd. *Witchy.*' She whispered this last, and Faye leaned forwards.

'Yes?'

'Keep it to yourself.'

Faye wanted to act like she had no idea what Mrs Teach was going on about. That's what a normal person who had never dabbled in magic would do. But Faye got the same feeling from Mrs Teach as she had from the goat outside Charlotte's cottage. Like the widow could see through her smile to all the sadness and doubt beneath.

'Why?' Faye managed.

'Ordinary folk only see what they want to see. Remember that. If you snap people out of their daily daydream too often, they'll turn against you. Your mother learned that the hard way.'

'My mother?'

'Next!' The butcher's cry broke the spell and Mrs Teach's rosy-cheeked smile returned.

'Have a lovely day, my dear. And if you ever need any proper advice, don't hesitate to drop by. I read tea leaves, you know.'

'I . . . er . . . will. Thank you, Mrs Teach.'

Mrs Teach swept into the butcher's like a Hollywood star, greeting everyone with air kisses.

Faye, still in a daze, popped her bacon ration in her bicycle basket and was about to hop back on and pedal home when a distant banging noise echoed through the village. Around Faye, the postman, the milkman, the children in their red blazers and caps walking in line from school – all stopped in their tracks, looking for the source of the approaching sound. The noise was rhythmic. Almost musical.

The clamour was accompanied by footsteps as Terrence came hurrying down the Wode Road from the pub, a hammer in his hand. One of his chores today was to fix the hanging baskets that had come loose after last night's storm, and Faye was about to get cross with him for slacking off when she saw the puzzled expression on his face. The rhythmic noise was getting closer. A folky tarantella of sticks clacking almost in time made Faye wonder if the Morris dancers were having a do. Terrence took the red and white spotted kerchief from around his neck and dabbed at the sweat on his brow.

'Scarecrows,' he said, catching his breath. 'Loads of the bloody things.'

12

March of the Crow Folk

Faye was about to ask her dad if he was gone in the head when she saw a movement behind him. Saint Irene's Church stood at the very top of the Wode Road, and figures flitted between the gravestones, dancing and spinning as they came prancing out of the shadows. Faye tried to count. They wouldn't keep still, but she reckoned there might be twenty or so of them. Some clapped, some struck sticks together, one squeezed a battered old accordion and another honked a horn as they twirled and whirled their way down the street.

All except one. A man with a pumpkin on his noggin marched at their head, striking a cowbell.

Faye's heart thumped in her ears as he came closer. Herbert's pumpkin man was real, and he was here, and he had brought all his scarecrows with him. The pumpkin was no mask, no funny hat – it was his actual, proper head. He was taller than the others, a good seven feet from top to toe, and Faye wondered if he was on stilts or if those skinny legs were all real, too.

'Bit early for the harvest festival, ain't it?' Terrence said out of the corner of his mouth as he hurried to Faye's side. 'Maybe it's the circus?'

'I don't think it's the circus, Dad,' Faye said, her mouth dry. She noticed the scarecrows were all wet up to their knees like they had just waded through a pond.

The scarecrows fanned out around the pumpkin-headed man, leaping between the villagers who stood their ground like they all knew the rules of this odd schoolyard game. A few clapped along with uncertain smiles, but most were hesitant, waiting to see what would happen next. Faye thought about what Mrs Teach had just told her. *People only see what they want to see.*

The scarecrows were mostly stuffed with straw and had sackcloth heads. Some of the heads were shaped like a blackbird's, with yellow and orange beaks. One had an old leather football for a head; another had a smiley sunflower face with yellow petals sewn on. Another looked like a tin man, with a dustbin for a body, paint pots for his legs and buckets for arms.

Pumpkinhead brought the parade to a stop by the Great War memorial cross, and he towered over all around him as he strode up its steps. He raised his arms. The racket stopped and the scarecrows flopped to the ground with a *flump*, with the exception of the tin man who sounded like a crash in a Heinz factory.

All were prostrate before him, lifeless as rag dolls.

'People of Woodville,' Pumpkinhead said, his jagged, carved mouth moving in a way Faye could not fathom.

'Let it be known the crow folk are no longer yours to do with as you will. We are free.'

The villagers looked at one another in wonderment. Faye gripped the handlebars of her bicycle. An ancient part of her brain was politely suggesting she might want to get away as fast as possible, but she was as fascinated by these strange newcomers as the rest of the village. All the folk around her had bemused smiles on their faces, apparently happy for the distraction and no doubt wondering if there might be a puppet show and some juggling.

All but one.

Faye caught sight of Mrs Teach, skulking in the butcher's doorway and glaring straight at the pumpkin fellow like he was the Devil himself.

'Those costumes are pretty natty, aren't they?' Terrence whispered in Faye's ear. 'Clever masks. Like something from the flicks.' Then he spotted what was in the basket on her bicycle. 'Oh, you remembered the bacon. Good girl.'

Faye squinted to get a better look at Pumpkinhead. If that was a mask he was wearing, then it was beyond her reckoning how it worked. His triangle eyes shifted, his brow furrowed and his smile widened as he reached out to the scarecrows lying on the floor like corpses.

'Sister Suky,' he said, slowly raising his hand. 'Speak.' Faye felt her ears pop and one of the scarecrows in a shawl and a red gingham dress slowly rose from the ground like a puppet on strings. Her knees did not bend and her arms were all floppy. When she reached her full height, she shuddered into life and hopped forwards. *How did she do that?* A few villagers clapped in appreciation of the trick.

Suky clasped her hands before her, turning to address them all. Her wooden neck creaked like a squeaky door. 'We seek one of yous lot,' Suky said. 'A poacher, if you please.'

The villagers shared furtive looks.

'He struck me across the face and turned my neck right around, he did,' Suky continued, 'and he went and maimed two of our siblings. He burned our jolly brother and worse.'

'Craddock?' Faye spoke to her dad out of the side of her mouth, but at that very moment the world fell silent and a breeze carried her whisper all around the village into everyone's ears.

The gasps of disapproval from Faye's fellow villagers made her blush with shame. No one liked a snitch, after all.

'That . . . that came out louder than I wanted.' Faye bit her lip. 'Sorry.'

'Yes.' Pumpkinhead stalked down the steps of the memorial towards Faye. He made her want to cry out and duck behind her father, but she stood her ground. 'Craddock,' he said, extending his gloved hand to her. 'That's him. Give him to us.'

'He ain't exactly mine to give,' Faye said, trying hard not to let her voice tremble. 'But if I see him, I'll let him know you was asking after him. I like your mask, by the way. Did you make it yourself? How does it work?'

'Tell me,' Pumpkinhead said, ignoring her questions and asking one of his own, 'do you suffer witches in this village?'

Faye's cheeks blushed hot and condensation began to cloud her specs. 'Who,' she managed, once she got her composure back, 'are you calling a witch?'

'Yeah, y'cheeky sauce,' Terrence said, jabbing a thumb back up the road. 'If you can't be polite, clear off.'

'I merely ask,' Pumpkinhead began, raising his head as if catching a scent, 'as there is magic in the air.'

Faye flushed giddy at all this talk of magic and witches, and she thought of her mother's book and then tried *not* to think of her mother's book, just in case this pumpkin chap could read thoughts.

'This place reeks of it.' Pumpkinhead smiled. 'Yes, in the air, in the streets, in the trees, in the homes – and in you, Faye Bright.'

'How . . . how do you know my name?' Faye asked, breathless at the thought that this creature could see into her very mind.

'It's on your ration book,' Terrence said, snapping up Faye's junior ration book tucked in with the bacon in her basket. Her name was written in block capitals in thick pen on the front. Terrence handed it to her and she stuffed it in a pocket. The pub landlord squared his shoulders as he faced Pumpkinhead. 'I suggest you be on your way, sunshine. We'll see what we can do regarding Mr Craddock.'

Suky stepped between Terrence and Pumpkinhead.

'Sunrise, tomorrowday,' she said, addressing the whole village in a loud and clear voice. 'We'll sees you at the abbey.'

'Do not disappoint us,' Pumpkinhead added in an overly cheery voice, then raised his arms. 'Brothers and Sisters.'

The scarecrows rose as Suky had, limbs slack and boneless.

They hung there for a heartbeat.

Then, as one, they all dashed wildly about the villagers, waving their arms and shaking their heads, hooting and howling like monkeys. Villagers scurried for cover, terrified, screaming.

Faye dropped her bicycle and held her father tight, watching as Pumpkinhead loped back up the street, striding confidently through all the chaos, stopping only to doff his hat to Mrs Teach who was still half in, half out the butcher's. To her credit, Mrs Teach raised her chin and folded her arms, fearless and defiant. Pumpkinhead grinned, then joined his fellow scarecrows as they disappeared down side streets, their cries echoing. And then they were gone, a chill silence all they left behind.

Faye turned to her dad. 'What the blinking flip just happened?'

13

The Mockery of Birds

The journey back to Therfield Abbey was playful for the crow folk. They danced and sang as they moved through the wood with Pumpkinhead striking his cowbell to keep time.

Suky spun and danced with the others, happy simply not to be tied to a cross in the middle of a field. Back then, she could only stare and wonder at what lay within the wood that looked so dark and distant. Now it was a revelation to her. She could sense the heartbeats of shrews as they scurried through the undergrowth, the flutter of wings above and all around. She spotted chaffinches nesting in the fork of a tree, feeding their chicks with wriggling grubs.

All the birds sang to her, swirling above the forest canopy in time with the music. Suky twirled and they twirled with her; Suky raised her arms and they spiralled upwards; Suky splayed her fingers wide and they dispersed like leaves on a breeze, then came together again, matching her every move.

'Do you see that, my Pumpkinhead?' Suky called as she skipped through the wood. 'Ain't I clever?'

'Do not consort with the birds, sister Suky,' Pumpkinhead said, stopping his rhythm on the cowbell. 'They are an enemy of the scarecrow.'

'But, my Pumpkinhead, that was when we was scaring them off the churned-up fields for men with farms,' Suky said, whirling around him. 'We ain't their slaves no more, like you said, so why not be chums with the birds? We should—'

Pumpkinhead gently took her wrist, bringing her dance to an end. 'Do not consort with the birds,' he repeated, his zigzag smile in place, though his eyes had never looked blacker. 'Do you understand me, sister?'

'I . . . I do, my Pumpkinhead,' Suky said, glancing up to see the birds flutter away into the trees. 'I'm ever so sorry, I am. Honest.'

'Nothing to be sorry for.' Pumpkinhead stroked her sackcloth face, then called to the others. 'Brothers and sisters, cease your revels.' The crow folk gathered around Pumpkinhead. 'Closer still, siblings, come closer so you can hear me. Good, good, as close as you can. Everyone join hands. That's it. Good.'

Suky took the hand of a scarecrow sporting a straw hat, and she felt Pumpkinhead's gloved hand slip around her own. The thrill sent a shiver through her. All the crow folk were joined as one.

'Listen, my siblings,' Pumpkinhead said, his voice hushed as he glanced up to where a row of sparrows peered at them from the abbey's teetering stone cloisters. 'Do you hear the taunting of the birds? Their cawing and hooting and tweeting. How often have they mocked us in the past?'

Suky was about to object when she found the others all nodding in agreement.

'What if I told you that we, together, could silence them?' As Pumpkinhead spoke, he squeezed Suky's hand tighter and she began to feel peculiar. Lighter. Floaty. Her vision wavered like water in a pond. 'Listen, brothers and sisters, listen to my words, we as one are stronger, we as one are more powerful, we as one will . . .'

Pumpkinhead's voice became muffled. Suky's world went dark and she did not know where she ended and Pumpkinhead began.

Suky was rising high above the ruins of the abbey, the world tilting below her. She was a bird! They all were, her brothers and sisters and Pumpkinhead. They were one and they flew together, carried on the wings of the birds, hitching a ride in their minds, soaring and swooping like a child's dream.

And that's when they saw him.

Craddock. Exhausted, staggering as he splashed along the riverbank. He was heading towards the abbey. He was coming to them and it would only be a matter of time before they had him. Suky felt a sting of angry satisfaction that wasn't her own. And then she sensed something else. Another presence with them.

One bigger than Pumpkinhead. Bigger than the birds. A wise mind, not as old as Pumpkinhead, but perhaps as powerful. It rang in Suky's ears like a bell. It frightened Pumpkinhead and Suky felt his fear bleed into her, cold and stiff. His anger made her giddy, and as he lashed out she could feel countless tiny hearts stopping, and her world went dark.

14

THE HEART OF THE VILLAGE

Woodville had a perfectly good village hall. Rebuilt after a fire in 1932, it served as a venue for village council business, the Woodville Amateur Dramatics Society, wedding receptions and children's parties. It had electric throughout, parking spaces for two motor cars and even one of those fancy indoor lavvies. For the big emergencies, though, the good villagers of Woodville knew there was only one place they could gather for a rational debate.

The Green Man pub was the real heart of the village and most of Woodville's residents had squeezed themselves inside to harrumph and rhubarb about the bizarre events they had just witnessed. It was the noon-till-two lunchtime session and the pub hadn't been this busy since New Year's Eve. Faye held the fort at the bar while Terrence popped down to the cellar to change a couple of barrels.

'Travelling folk, I reckon. Passing through,' Bertie Butterworth said and got a flutter of *uhms* and *aahs* in vague agreement from the gathered throng. He had dried out since this morning's little adventure in the river.

'*Do not disappoint us*, they said.' Faye folded her arms. 'That sounds like a threat to me, and we don't take kindly to threats, do we, folks?' This got a rousing chorus of *Yuuuurrrsss* from the Local Defence Volunteers, who had also dried out. They could only recall a slight altercation between Mr Marshall and Mr Baxter when asked how this morning's training had gone. Bertie was the same. Faye brought it up when he ordered his pint and he scrunched his nose and frowned, half remembering that something odd happened, though he wasn't quite sure what. Why was she the only one who remembered the way the starlings put out the fire? Faye could understand the older men forgetting. At the forefront of their minds were Dunkirk and the war. They had been champing at the bit for a scrap since the retreat, and if they couldn't fight Nazis, then a bunch of strangers dressed like scarecrows making threats would do for the time being, thank you very much. But Bertie should have remembered.

'Ignore 'em,' Bertie said, a voice of reason. He got a few *boos* from his LDV comrades. 'Why pick a fight? They'll be gone soon enough.'

'I don't think they're going anywhere, Bertie.' Faye fixed him with a slightly miffed stare and the boy wavered, slurping his cider, unsure why she was suddenly so cross with him. 'And I don't think they're travellers,' Faye continued, wanting to scream that they were clearly scarecrows, but also remembering what Mrs Teach had told her about folk only seeing and hearing what they wanted to. She caught Mrs Teach's eye. The older woman was watching her from the end of the bar where she nursed a sherry. 'And that name. Suky. I'm sure I've heard it before. Anyone here know a Suky?' The villagers all looked to one another and in moments the pub was hosting a shrugging contest. 'They called themselves crow folk. What does that mean?' More shrugs.

'A circus, I reckon,' Terrence said as he emerged from the cellar. 'I almost ran off with the circus when I was a lad, y'know?'

'The circus?' Faye squinted at her dad through her specs. 'Since when?'

'They came here when I was a little older than you. Had a bit of a fling with a woman who could put her ankles right behind her ears—'

'Dad!'

There was a splutter as Bertie choked on his cider, followed by a raucous jeer from the men in the bar. Mrs Teach, who had been uncharacteristically silent since the departure of the crow folk, raised an appreciative eyebrow and sipped at her sherry.

Faye raised her voice. 'Can we get back to the subject: a marauding band of scarecrows just demanded we hand over poor Mr Craddock.'

'Gypsy folk, Faye,' Terrence said with a stern voice. 'It ain't nice to call 'em scarecrows.'

'*Poor Mr Craddock?*' Mrs Teach spluttered, breaking

her silence. 'Let me tell you, young lady, he's not poor, and he doesn't deserve our sympathy. He is a brute. A cruel brute. He's a proper scoundrel, and there isn't a person here who's not had an unpleasant altercation with the man.'

'That's right,' Miss Burgess said. 'When my Matilda was sick, he said I should wring her neck and be done with her.'

'Bloody hell,' Terrence said as the rest of the pub gasped along in disgust. 'Hang on, who's Matilda?'

'One of my chickens.'

'He kicked my Mr Tinkles,' Miss Gordon cried. 'Called him a flea-bitten moggy.' This got some murmurs of sympathy, though there were few in attendance who hadn't been gifted something short, brown and smelly by Miss Gordon's cat.

'He started a salacious rumour,' Mr Hodgson began, and the pub's patrons held their breath in anticipation of the punchline, 'about my knees.'

'He let the tyres down on my brand-new Austin hearse,' Mr Loaf, the usually jolly funeral director, declared. 'Said it was in his way, so quite what he hoped to achieve by making sure it couldn't move, I don't know. Delayed old Mr Gregg's funeral by an hour. Most distressing.'

'I once saw him tip over Kenny Finch's milk cart in an argument about clotted cream,' Mr Paine said, idly sucking on a humbug. 'Two miserable sods at each other. Hate to say it, but that was quite enjoyable to observe, actually.'

'He was always mocking my Ernie's height,' Mrs Teach said, a faraway look in her eyes. 'Shorty, titch, half-pint. Every time he saw my Ernie there was a new insult, but my Ernie took it all in his stride and with a smile. I can assure you that while my Ernie may have been lacking stature, he was a big, big man.'

No one knew quite where to look. They had heard the rumours about Ernie, too.

'Another sherry, Mrs Teach?' Terrence offered.

Mrs Teach slid her glass to him.

'I like to think the best of folks,' Bertie said from behind the dregs of his cider, 'but if being a miserable bugger was an Olympic sport, then Mr Craddock would get gold, silver and bronze.'

'And he was going to thump me one last night, but that's no reason we should hand over one of our neighbours to these . . .' Faye looked over to her dad, '*Gypsies*.'

'It's simply none of our business,' Mrs Teach said. 'If they've had a contretemps with Mr Craddock then let them have it out. We should, like the Swiss, remain neutral.'

'Like that Mr Hitler had a contretemps with Poland? And France? Like that?' Faye could sense her father's disapproving glare – *never disagree with a customer* – but she couldn't let this stand. 'And what if they decide to have a little disagreement with you, Mrs Teach, hmm? Should I turn a blind eye then, too? We've never taken kindly to threats round here and I don't see why we should start now. Especially with these scarecrows.'

'Gypsies,' Terrence corrected.

'Scarecrows, Dad. One of them had a bloomin' great pumpkin for an 'ead. I saw it, like you all did. I don't care if it's real or what, but if they dress up like scarecrows and act like scarecrows, I'm callin' 'em scarecrows. So what are we going to do about it?'

'I don't see what we can do,' Terrence said with a forced chuckle. Faye couldn't fathom why he was laughing at first, then she recalled seeing him do this with unhappy customers in the past. He had always told her that if anyone got a bit tasty then first try distracting them by changing the subject and having a laugh. Just pretend you hadn't heard the insult or threat and no one would feel they had to deliver on any angry promises of fisticuffs. It was an old trick, but he had never tried it on his own daughter. He was attempting to shut her up like she was some common saloon bar brawler. 'But I *can* see young Bertie needs another half o' cider.' Terrence slid Bertie's empty glass towards Faye.

'Ooh, thank you very much.' Bertie grinned.

'Good health.'

'Cheers.'

Faye scowled at her father, but he gave her a jolly wink and raised his head to address the whole pub.

'Mrs Teach is right. There ain't a person in this room who's not had a run-in with Archibald Craddock,' Terrence said. 'And who's to say they don't have him already? Anyone here seen him today? No, me neither. And if he's got some sort of beef with these gypsy folk . . .'

Faye sighed, surrendered and poured Bertie's half.

'... then knowing Craddock, he's prob'ly having a scrap with 'em now in a barn somewhere. That's how he settles things. Queensberry Rules. Let them have it out fair and square and not stick our noses in.'

'Hear, hear,' Mrs Teach said. 'One shouldn't go poking one's nose into other people's business, Faye. It's not ladylike.'

Faye spluttered at the hypocrisy of the nosiest woman in the village. 'Well, I wonder why you of all people, Mrs Teach, wouldn't want anyone digging deeper?'

'I don't know what you mean.'

'I saw that fella with the pumpkin for a head tip his hat at you as he wandered off,' Faye said. 'Looked like he knows you well enough.'

'I cannot account for the behaviour of others.'

'There must be some reason why he singled you out.'

'Perhaps he knows a lady when he sees one.'

'P'raps he—'

'All right, that's enough, Faye.' Terrence's voice boomed as he took his daughter by the shoulders and steered her away from Mrs Teach. 'Collect the empties and wash them up, please. I think we all need to—'

A heavy *thud* came from the roof of the pub.

Everyone froze and glanced at each other to make sure they had all heard it, too.

Thud!

Everyone looked up.

Thud-thud-thud!

It became an avalanche of impacts, all piling on

top of one another, each one making Faye's heart jolt. People murmured and clustered together, and then from outside came a scream. Faye hurried around the bar, wriggled through the crowd, pulled the doors open and dashed outside.

She found the elderly Mrs Pritchett out walking her two Yorkshire Terriers. The dogs whined and the old lady was trembling, her eyes wide in terror.

All around her, and littering the whole cobbled street, were starlings. Dozens of them, lying still with their little legs stiff. Some twitched in their death throes, their wings broken.

Mrs Pritchett found her voice. 'They just . . . fell out of the sky.'

ᴓ

Chilled to the bone and encrusted with dried mud, the fugitive Craddock crawled along the edge of the marsh stream. He hadn't seen hide nor hair of those scarecrows for hours and he would be home soon. His shack stood at the edge of the wood on the other side of Therfield Abbey. When he got there, the first thing he would do was feed the stove, change into dry clothes and finish off the bottle of rum he had stashed away in a box under the bed. He would try and forget whatever the blazes he had witnessed this last night and if that meant more rum, then so be it. He would forget and never speak of it again.

As Craddock clambered up the slippy bank, there came a heavy splash from the stream. Craddock looked back, only to see rings of water spreading out from the impact. A kingfisher, perhaps, or a carp coming up for air. He resumed his climbing when he heard another splash. Then something bounced off his head and he cursed.

It fell to the ground before him. A crow. Its blue-black feathers spread out in flight, frozen in death.

Birds began to fall all around him, tumbling from the sky, bouncing off branches and rolling dead to the ground. There was only so much strangeness a man like Craddock could cope with and so he ran, fuelled by fear. Scrabbling from the stream, he dodged through the wood, dead birds still falling all round him, thumping down on his head, crunching under his boots. He came to the winding path, then up uneven stone steps to the arches of Therfield Abbey, a Norman ruin with broken stone walls that rose around him.

The birds no longer fell, though the ground was littered with their bodies. Hands on his thighs, he leaned forwards to catch his breath, then dropped to his knees. His fingers trembled, his head pounded and his breath scratched at his throat. A moment here would do.

Through the cloisters came the scarecrows.

Charlotte was chopping wood and her bonfire was burning nicely when it happened. Birds bounced off branches before spiralling lifelessly to the woodland floor around her.

She swung the axe and buried its head in the

chopping block before striding to her cottage and digging out a book she had hoped she might never need to open again. A book of signs and warnings, handed down from one generation to another. She flicked through it, her eyes darting as she scanned the pages.

And there it was.

She stood back from the book as if it were infectious.

Charlotte found her pipe on the dining table, stuffed it with tobacco and puffed as she lit it. Her nerves were soothed, but what she saw still troubled her. She glanced sidelong at the book, as if she didn't want it to notice her curiosity.

Flames from the bonfire outside threw shapes and shadows around the room. On the pages of the book, the shifting light gave the illusion of movement to an old woodcut illustration of birds falling from the sky in droves. Below them danced a grinning scarecrow with a pumpkin for a head.

15

Sweeping up the Birds

The pub closed early. No one much fancied a lunchtime pint after that strange rain. Faye and Bertie swept the cobblestones outside the Green Man. Not leaves or dust, but dozens of dead birds. Up and down the village, their neighbours were doing the same. All kinds had fallen: starlings, sparrows, robins, pigeons, blackbirds and jackdaws. In a grim shower that had lasted just a few minutes, they had tumbled lifeless to the ground throughout Woodville. Now there was only a silence in the air that made Faye uneasy.

'Tea's up.' Terrence broke the hush with a clatter as he backed out of the pub carrying a tray of old mugs, tin cups and a steaming pot. He placed it on Bertie's cart and started to pour, whistling 'Polly Put the Kettle On'.

Bertie began to sing along, 'Suky take it off again, Suky take it off again . . .'

'That name again,' Faye said as she cradled her cuppa and blew the steam off.

'Suky?' Bertie dropped two sugar cubes into his cup and gave them a vigorous stir. 'Weren't one of those circus folk called Suky?'

Faye let the circus comment slide. 'It's such an odd name, but I'm certain I've heard it before. You ever known a Suky?'

'I once met a Suzy,' Terrence said. 'Lovely girl. Dancer at a revue bar in Soho. She did a trick with ping-pong balls—'

'Dad!'

'Can't say I've ever known a Suky,' Bertie said, with the sophisticated air of someone who had travelled the world and 'known' many women. Faye knew full well he never left the village without a name and address tag tied to his coat. After his one trip to London with the bell-ringers, he had vowed never to return. He spent the whole day in a state of agitation, asking his companions if they, too, thought the sky was smaller there. He insisted the moving stairs on the Underground had tried to steal his shoes, and he swore he'd seen a rat as big as a Labrador down an alley off Fleet Street. 'It's not one of them names you hear at a christening, is it? *I name thee Suky*. What's it short for?'

'Suky, Suky, Sooky.' Terrence stretched the word out. 'Sookee . . . Maybe she's a – yes! – a zookeeper?'

'Oh, good grief, forget I asked,' Faye muttered.

'Jolly quiet without their singing, isn't it?' came a voice from across the street. 'Quite eerie.' The Reverend Jacobs ambled over, drawn by the lure of hot tea. This was his first summer in the village. Many said he looked far too fresh-faced and cherubic to have his own parish, but most of the villagers appreciated his chirpy enthusiasm, even if some of the older folk thought he was a little modern for their liking. Mrs Nesbitt had seen him reading a Penguin paperback and drinking black coffee in the vicarage one morning, and the scandal had rocked the local Women's Institute to the core. Faye had her own doubts about any man who told her what to do any day of the week, let alone twice on Sundays, but she liked the vicar because he was a part-time bell-ringer and, more importantly for today, he had brought his own broom.

'Morning, Vicar,' Faye said, pouring him a tea, knowing full well the answer to her next question. 'Cuppa?'

'Oh, how splendid,' he said, taking a tin cup from the tray with a grateful smile. 'So sorry to hear that we couldn't honour your mother's memory with a quarter peal this Sunday, Faye.'

'Not as sorry as me, Vicar,' she said as she slurped her brew, then added, 'I was hoping to ring a method she invented, an' all.'

'Really? How clever of her. What did she call it? I do love their wonderfully odd names. The Kathryn Bob Doubles? The Wynter Surprise? The Woodville Treble Bob?'

'The Kefapepo method,' Faye said, then felt obliged to add when she saw the vicar's face twist in befuddlement, 'Don't ask. That's how it was written in her book.'

'Book? What book?' Terrence asked, his voice terse.

Faye choked on her tea as she gulped it down the wrong hole. 'Her book, y'know, the book, that book she, uhm . . .' Faye's mind raced as she coughed and thumped her chest.

'Oh, she had a book of diagrams?' the vicar ventured.

'Yes, that's it.'

'All the ringers have them,' Reverend Jacobs explained to Terrence. 'Pages and pages of funny little zigzags and numbers showing them which bells to ring and when. I can just about get my poor addled brain around them, but anything more complex than a course of Plain Bob and I'm flummoxed.'

'Yeah, yeah, she wrote it on a spare page in her book of diagrams, that's what she did,' Faye confirmed, getting her breath back. 'Fancy a biscuit with your tea, Vicar?'

'Oh, that's very kind, but I merely came over to let Bertie know that we've cleared the church grounds and piled our poor birds by the lychgate. Bertie, could you kindly do the honours?'

'Can do, Vicar,' Bertie said, knocking back the dregs of his own tea. 'I'll stick 'em with this lot, take 'em round the back of my barn and burn 'em. I'll go and fetch Delilah,' he added, rushing off to get his horse for the cart while reprising his rendition of 'Polly Put the Kettle On'.

'Jolly good. Thank you, Bertie, you're a brick.'

'Does the name Suky mean anything to you, Vicar?' Faye asked.

'I'm afraid not. Should it?'

'No, never mind. It's one strange thing after another here. Walking, talking scarecrows and now all the birds drop dead out of the sky.'

'These strange phenomena are not unknown, Faye. I have a cousin Dickie who lives in Bude. He claims it rained fish there once.'

'Fish?' Faye scrunched up her nose in disbelief.

'Little red ones,' the vicar said, leaning on his broom. 'All over his roof. He's a potato farmer, too. I suggested that he open a fish and chip shop and retire on the proceeds. Peculiar things happen, Faye. I find it's best not to ask too many questions.'

'Ain't that your job?'

'Beg pardon?'

'To ask questions about strange mysteries and such?'

The vicar pursed his lips in thought. 'Mysteries of the divine, certainly. Peculiar meteorological phenomena do not really come under my jurisdiction.'

'Fish and birds fall from the sky and you're not interested in why that happens?'

'There's a war on, Faye,' Terrence said, tidying away the tea things. 'More important stuff to worry about.'

'Neither one of you is curious?' Faye turned on her heels, gesturing down the Wode Road at all the folk sweeping up dead birds as if this was part of their normal daily routine. 'Does none of you lot think this is strange?'

'Faye,' Terrence started, then cleared his throat and put down his mug of tea. Faye knew this meant she was in for one of his father-knows-best speeches. 'The world is full of strange and curious things, and it's full of terrors and awful people like that Herr Hitler. If you was to rush around trying to solve all the world's problems at once, you'd go half barmy before teatime. Pick your fights, girl, and keep your noggin in what's happening here and now. Don't worry about things that you can't control.'

'Take therefore no thought for the morrow,' the Reverend Jacobs quoted, 'for the morrow shall take thought for the things of itself. Sufficient unto the day is the evil thereof. Matthew, chapter six, verse thirty-four.'

'Wot?' said Faye.

'Don't go poking your nose in where it ain't wanted,' Terrence translated.

'Actually, it's from the Sermon on the Mount,' the vicar began. 'It means—'

'Yeah, well, mine is the sermon from the pub,' Terrence said. 'Here endeth the lesson.'

'Does it now?' Faye placed her mug on the cart and leaned into her dad's face.

'Yes, it does,' he replied.

They were nose-to-nose and Faye lowered her voice. 'You still owe me a conversation.'

'About what?' Terrence's voice was a low rumble.

'My mother and why so many folk think she was a w—'

'Not now, girl.' Terrence shook his head, eyes glancing over at the vicar. 'Not now.'

'Then when?' Faye's voice tightened and she started

using words she had read in books but never said out loud. 'You have this uncanny knack, dear Father, of putting it off in perpetuity.'

'You want to talk now? This minute?'

'Yes, I do,' Faye said, hands on hips.

'Right,' Terrence said, raising his voice, standing upright, puffing out his cheeks and addressing the vicar. 'Tea break in philosophy corner is over.' He rested one hand on the vicar's shoulder and gestured with his other to where two elderly ladies were struggling to clear their doorstep of dead birds with a dustpan and brush. 'Vicar, would you mind helping Miss Moon and Miss Leach with their birds, please?'

'Oh, I, uhm, yes, I should be delighted.' The vicar, who hadn't quite finished his tea, was too polite to object as Terrence took the tin cup away from him.

Faye handed him his broom and pointed him towards the two elderly ladies. 'You push the stick bit and the brush end does the rest,' she told him, patting him on the back.

'Hmm? Oh, yes, yes. Of course,' he said and crossed the street, greeting Miss Moon and Miss Leach and offering to sweep up more of the deceased birds.

Faye turned to find her dad in her face once more.

'Give it up,' Terrence said. 'Stop going on about scarecrows and men with pumpkins on their noggins before people think you're off your rocker.'

'I don't care what people think.'

'I do. Your mother did. She was smart enough to figure that out eventually.'

'Why eventually? Tell me, Dad, tell me straight. Was she a witch?'

'Your mother ...' The words caught in Terrence's throat. He took a breath. 'Was the most wonderful woman I ever met. Like you, she saw the goodness in people. She took notice of stuff others missed in the world around her. And she would tell folk what she had seen, and they would sometimes think less of her for it because it weren't how they saw the world. They said she was away with the birds. Loopy-Lou. Half-barmy and worse. After a while, she learned to keep that stuff to herself and people liked her again. Learn from that, Faye. Don't go making the same mistakes again, before you become a pariah.'

'Mum was a pariah? What's a pariah?'

'An outcast. Someone no one wants anything to do with.'

'You told me everyone loved Mum.'

'In the end. People loved her in the end, but she had to work hard ... so hard to ...' Terrence clenched his jaw and fists. People assumed he did this when he was angry, but Faye knew it stopped him getting weepy when he thought of Mum. She thought of her own anger whenever she remembered Mum, and seeing her dad like this made her a little weepy. 'I know you're curious about your mother, Faye. I understand that, I really do. But I'm asking you to leave off with the magic and witchery stuff. It was a hobby, a silly fancy that got out of hand, and it was only when your mum put it behind her that she was happy again. Let it go, girl. I'm asking you to do this for your own good. Will you?'

Faye thought about Mrs Teach's warning to keep things to herself, and young Herbert Finch's humiliation after telling folk what he'd seen.

'I found her book, Dad,' Faye said. 'The one with all the magic and the spells and sketches of runes and creatures and demons and such. You know the one I mean.'

Terrence said nothing, but Faye could see a new fear in his eyes. He started to shake his head.

'She done that book for me, Dad. It says so in the front. Why did she go to all that trouble for nothing but a silly fancy?'

Terrence gripped Faye by her shoulders. 'Put it back,' he said. 'Put it back in the trunk, lock it away and never, ever look at it again.'

'She said it was for me, Dad. When the time is right.'

'Promise me.' Terrence's voice cracked. 'Please, Faye, this is very important.'

Faye had never known her father to be scared of anything. If there was ever any trouble he would brush it off with a joke or a groan, but holding her now he looked proper petrified.

'Everyone tells me to pipe down,' Faye said, her voice calm. 'One of our neighbours is wanted by a bunch of crow folk after he had ructions with 'em and birds fall dead from the sky, but no one wonders why.' She puffed out her cheeks. 'Yes, Dad, I'll stop going on about magic and witches. I won't embarrass you or myself any more. I'll stay inside with a bag on my head if it makes you happy, but sometimes I feel like I'm the only person in the world who *hasn't* lost their marbles.'

'Promise me.' Terrence still held her tight.

Faye shrugged him off. 'I'll put the book away, Dad. I promise. Me and magic and witchery are done.'

16

Pumpkinhead's Questions

Suky drifted between dreams and waking. When the birds started to fall, Suky's world had gone dark, but now light and life were slowly returning and she followed her Pumpkinhead like a woozy duckling.

The poacher Craddock was here at the abbey on his knees, dead birds lying around him. He had the look of a cornered fox and he raised a hand in surrender.

'Craddock, oh, Craddock, how wise you are to return.' Pumpkinhead's voice was kind with an edge like a knife blade. 'You still haven't answered my question, friend.'

Suky watched Craddock's face crumple as he tried to recall his last encounter with them.

'Question?' Craddock shook his head.

'The names of your witches,' Pumpkinhead reminded him. 'There is a book. It whispers to me, though soon it will sing loud and clear. A book of magic and it will be in the hands of these witches.'

Suky's thoughts tingled at the mention of magic

and witches. This new life, with the crow folk and Pumpkinhead, was all so floaty. Moments came and went like puffy white clouds in the summer sky, and not for the first time, she wondered if she was dreaming.

'Tell me where it is,' Pumpkinhead said, looming over Craddock, 'and we shall be merciful.'

Suky saw the flicker of recognition on Craddock's face. And if she could see it in her addled state, then so could Pumpkinhead.

'You have seen the book, haven't you?' Pumpkinhead took Craddock's head in his hands. 'Where is it? Tell me.'

The others closed in around Craddock and Suky followed. They all looked like Suky felt: half-awake and gormless.

'I remember now.' Craddock sneered at Pumpkinhead. 'I remember your question. And my answer stays the same. To hell with you and to hell with your straw men and to hell with your questions.' Craddock got to his feet and made fists. He was weak, but Suky was in no state to defend herself and neither were her siblings. A few punches from this thug and they were done for. And what if he had his matches? Would there be more burnings? Suky took a step back, and she wasn't the only one.

Pumpkinhead lunged forward, his hands a blur as he gripped the sides of Craddock's head and squeezed harder. The man's eyes bulged and he gasped for breath, falling back to his knees, his arms thrashing.

'Let me see,' Pumpkinhead said. 'That's it, let me in. Good. Yes.'

Craddock went limp, a lopsided smile on his face. Pumpkinhead rested his forehead against Craddock's and, for a long time, neither of them moved.

Suky sank deeper into her lazy daydream. She remained standing, though the very idea of talking or moving about was ambitious at best. Pumpkinhead began to slowly sway his head from side to side. Suky and the other crow folk moved with him, and she could somehow feel his gloved fingers pressing on Craddock's head, seeping into his thoughts like a cloud of lemon cordial in water. She was in Craddock, the crow folk, Pumpkinhead. All were joined as one.

Suky's mind opened like the petals of a flower and she gave herself to Pumpkinhead. Her strength became his, and Craddock's thoughts dissolved to nothing.

Pumpkinhead gasped, released Craddock from his grip and the spell was broken.

Craddock remained on his knees, his eyes fixed on some unseen spot in the distance.

'There is . . . a book.' Pumpkinhead's words came slow and between breaths. 'He has seen it . . . though I know not where. And there is a witch in the village.' Pumpkinhead's smile stretched across his face. 'I know her of old.'

Suky's mind was almost her own again, and she began to wonder how much of what had just happened was real. A euphoria came over her, along with a clarity and an energy that made her feel reborn. Suky thought she could jump from here to the Moon and back.

'But first, brothers and sisters,' Pumpkinhead said,

raising his arms high, 'we must do right by this man and give him a fair trial. What say you?'

The crow folk cheered and swarmed over Craddock, grabbing his limbs and holding him aloft.

'Let us return him to the barn where we first met,' Pumpkinhead cried. 'I can think of no finer courtroom.'

'Under sea, or over ground, give me sight, give me sound. What once was lost, now is found. Under sea, or over ground.' Faye traced her fingers over her mother's writing in the book as she recited the lines.

'Under sea, or over ground, give me sight, give me sound. What once was lost, now is found. Under sea, or over ground.'

She had left her father with a promise to put the book back in the trunk. To lock it away and never look at it again.

It was a sincere promise and one she intended to keep.

In a minute.

After the birds fell, after the visit from the scarecrows, Faye could no longer deny that something very strange was happening in the village, and it had all started when she found her mother's book.

Magic was in the air. That Pumpkinhead fellow had said it himself.

And a man was missing. Craddock was a grump and a brute, but Faye had been flicking through the book one last time before putting it away when she came across a ritual to find lost things. Her mother's notes in the margin made it clear that this could also be used to find missing people.

Faye had to give it a try.

'*Under sea, or over ground, give me sight, give me sound. What once was lost, now is found. Under sea, or over ground.*'

According to the instructions, the incantation had to be repeated four times. Once facing north, then south, east and west, so Faye shuffled on her bottom as she did so in the confines of the pub cellar.

She swivelled one last time and felt a stinging twinge in her buttock, which she was sure meant she now had a splinter in her bum.

'*Under sea, or over ground, give me sight, give me sound. What once was lost, now is found. Under sea, or over ground.*'

She was done. Faye sat in the candlelight, waiting.

'Now what?' she asked the book. She wasn't sure what she'd thought would happen – she didn't expect a big finger to appear from above and point the way to where Craddock was – but some sort of clue would have been nice.

Faye held her breath, listening for something. Anything.

Then her lungs started to hurt and she gasped in a lungful of air.

'Oh, stuff this,' she said, flipping her mother's book shut, the displaced air snuffing out the candle and leaving her in pitch darkness. 'Bugger,' she said.

Faye put the book back in the trunk, locking it with a rusty old padlock. Magic was no good to her. Dad was right. It was nothing but a fancy. Faye was going to have to find Craddock herself.

17

Funny Turns

'What gets my goat is no one cares.' Faye and Bertie took a path from the village, crossed over the old stone bridge and entered the wood up the track lined with deadly nightshade, purple and yellow in flower. Faye had considered searching for Craddock on her own, but she didn't much fancy being on her lonesome if she came across a creepy bunch of scarecrows again. She wasn't about to ask her dad, not after their last conversation. She found Bertie at a loose end and less than cheerful after spending all afternoon burning dead birds in a brazier, so she invited him along.

He didn't need asking twice.

Bertie ambled behind her with a walking stick, keeping a slow yet steady pace on his uneven legs. Faye waited for him to catch up, her fists bunched, the woodland floor around her scattered with purple violets.

'A bunch of crow folk want him dead or alive, and no one's seen him since last night. A fella goes missing, you'd think people would be calling the police or telling the papers, but nothing.'

'Craddock ain't missing,' Bertie started, a little breathless. 'He's his own man. He comes and goes as he likes, keeps his own company and has little time for friends. He's a miserable old bugger. That's why no one cares, but . . .' Bertie came to a stop by Faye and gripped his walking stick a little tighter. 'You said something last night that made me change my mind. Maybe he is like Poland and France. Maybe if we had stuck up for them sooner, we wouldn't be in this blasted war. And so it got me thinking we should help Mr Craddock, whatever I think of the grumpy old git and his disposition, if you'll pardon my French.'

Faye looked at him, agog.

'What's . . . what's wrong?' Bertie shifted uncomfortably.

'You . . . you listened to me?' Faye's smile gave her dimples. 'You listened to me and you changed your mind?'

Bertie nodded, his cheeks turning red.

'Why, Bertie Butterworth, a girl could go sweet on you with behaviour like that,' Faye said, and poor Bertie didn't know where to look.

They walked in silence for a while.

Faye couldn't recall if Bertie had one leg too short or one leg too long, but either way it had kept him from joining up and doing his bit in the army when he was old enough. He had immediately signed up for the Local Defence Volunteers instead, and even though the rule book said he was too young, they took him on anyway. They knew that whatever he lacked in physical fitness he more than made up for with determination. All his life Bertie had been told by folk there were things he couldn't do, and all his life he had been proving them wrong. Faye found it odd that a fellow like Bertie was so determined to fight in a war against the terrifying might of the Nazi Blitzkrieg yet couldn't muster the courage to ask a sweet girl like Milly Baxter to step out with him. Faye had long ago decided that fellas were odd fishes and best left to their own devices.

'You don't notice birdsong till it's gone,' Faye said.

'You should hear the noisy buggers at dawn chorus over at my place,' Bertie said with a snort, then he blushed again. 'Blimmin' racket they make. You should . . . you should . . . y'know . . . come over one morning.' He mumbled this last, and it went unheard by Faye as a growl cut through the air above. They looked up to find three fighter aircraft flying in formation over the wood.

'Hurricanes.' Bertie's eyes lit up with excitement. 'You can tell by the shape of the wings. They had a thing in the paper on how to identify aircraft by their silhouettes. I pinned it on me wall.'

'Don't seem real, does it? Folks shooting each other with guns and tanks and planes just over the Channel. You really think they'll come here?'

'*They* do,' Bertie said, his eyes following the aircraft as they banked around the clouds.

Above, a bird cheeped. A solo robin's sing-song chatter. Then came the overlapping gossip of sparrows.

'They're back.' Faye gripped Bertie's arm. 'Listen. The birds are back.'

The trees filled with chirps, tweets and cheeps as if they had never been away.

'Ain't it beautiful,' Bertie said, the song bringing a smile to his face.

'There's more. Listen.' Faye angled her head and Bertie did the same. 'You hear that?'

'Er . . . yeah, a robin, I think, and a—'

'The sparrows. They're all singing the same song.'

Bertie shook his head as he listened. 'Sounds like a load of cheeps and—'

'No, listen carefully,' Faye insisted, and sang along in a whisper. '*Under sea, or over ground, give me sight, give me sound. What once was lost, now is found. Under sea, or over ground.*'

'Is that a nursery rhyme?'

'No. It's what they're singing.'

Bertie winced. 'I . . . I don't hear it.'

Faye sang louder now, '*Under sea, or over ground, give me sight, give me sound. What once was lost, now is found. Under sea, or over ground.*'

The sparrows sang back, then with a flutter that made Faye's heart skip, they flew from their perches and flocked in the sky above the treeline. They all swirled in the same direction, back down the path, for about fifty feet in a cloud of wings, then settled on another tree and began singing again.

'Under sea, or over ground, give me sight, give me sound. What once was lost, now is found. Under sea, or over ground.'

'Bloody hell,' Faye muttered, then yanked on Bertie's arm as she followed the sparrows back the way they'd come. 'We're going the wrong way.'

'Faye, I don't hear it. Are you sure?'

To Faye it was as clear as a bell. The sparrows would sing the spell, then move to another tree, wait for Faye to catch up, then repeat the same thing again. 'You must hear it – c'mon, Bertie, surely you hear it now?'

'I'm, well, I'm hearing birds singing, so . . .'

Once again, the sparrows sang and fluttered to another tree further down the path.

'Look.' Faye beamed. 'Look at them. Birds don't do that, do they? It's not normal, it's almost . . .'

'Almost what?'

Faye saw a smidge of confusion on Bertie's face. Either he didn't get it, or he genuinely didn't hear or see what was happening right in front of him. Faye thought back to what her dad said about folk thinking less of her mother because of how she saw the world. *Away with the birds*, he'd said. That made Faye laugh, and she caught Bertie giving her a funny look.

'It's almost . . .' Faye didn't know what to say. Words like *magic* might make Bertie think she was away with the birds, too.

The sparrows took off again, and Faye noticed that the trees were beginning to thin out. The birds were taking them to the edge of the wood.

'There,' Faye said, and they came to a stop. Beyond a field of hops, they could see a cluster of buildings and all the sparrows had come to rest on top of the biggest barn. A pheasant wandered its perimeter like a prison guard doing the rounds.

'That's Harry Newton's farm,' Bertie said. 'You reckon Craddock's in there?'

'I do.'

'Cos a load of birds are making a racket and they landed on its roof?'

'Only one way to find out,' Faye said.

ꞵ

They scurried around Harry Newton's field of hops. Faye creaked open the doors of the biggest barn. The sparrows returned to singing their usual song before flying away.

'Hello?' she called. 'Harry? Anyone?'

'There's a tractor out on the fields,' Bertie said, hobbling behind her. 'Probably Harry. We shouldn't be here, Faye. This is trespassing, strictly speaking, and I know Harry has an old blunderbuss. We'll be picking bits of shot out of our backsides for months.'

'What's that?' Faye slipped inside the gloom of the barn to where something was turned over in the mud and straw. She picked it up. 'Someone's old boot—' she started to say, then the whole world swerved to the left.

Craddock struggled as the scarecrows held him aloft. He kicked his legs wildly and a boot came free, landing in the mud and straw.

'Faye? You all right? You looked like you had a funny turn,' Bertie said as Faye jolted back into the real world. Her eyes darted about her. The boot was on the ground where she had dropped it. What in the blazes had just happened? She tried to recall if she had touched the deadly nightshade while walking here. Doing so could make one feel very ill, but she was sure she hadn't gone anywhere near it.

'I'm fine,' she told Bertie. 'Just went a bit … giddy. That's all.'

Faye crossed the barn to right an overturned hay bale. A whole stack of them had toppled over. She gripped a corner and—

Craddock was thrown by the mob into a pile of hay bales, knocking them over.

The scarecrows formed a circle around him. A kangaroo court. They brought forth the charred body of the jolly scarecrow. Pumpkinhead pointed a finger at Craddock: Guilty!

Faye backed away from the bale. This vision was accompanied by the musky scent of Craddock's fear mixed with the whiff of burned straw. She trod on a hessian sack, blackened by soot. She crouched down and turned it over to find a jolly scarecrow's face smiling back at her.

'Faye …' Bertie stood by the barn door. He had opened it and she could see through to the field beyond. A scarecrow stood alone in the corn.

'It's a scarecrow, Bertie. One that ain't alive, thank goodness.'

'It's wearing Craddock's coat,' Bertie said. A chill prickled Faye's skin.

Faye and Bertie trudged across the field through waist-high corn to where the scarecrow hung on a crude cross. A dead hare lay on the ground before it. As well as Craddock's coat, it wore one of his boots and its head was made from his black poacher's sack. Faye reached out to touch it.

Craddock struggled as the scarecrows tied him to the cross, but he was exhausted, the fight was going out of him. Pumpkinhead stepped closer with the poacher's sack and pulled it tight over Craddock's head. The poacher's screams became muffled. Pumpkinhead placed his hand on Craddock's head and recited bygone words of incantation.

Craddock became still. His head slumped forwards.

Craddock's screams had been so loud they hurt Faye's ears. How could that be? These weren't dreams. She had been there. Watching, listening, unseen. For a few moments, then and now were mixed like milk in tea. Faye shook her head clear and looked to Bertie. He was real, he was here with her. She wanted to take his hand to be sure, but some instinct told her that might be a bad idea.

Instead, Faye took a breath and reached for the sack. She gripped it for a heartbeat, terrified of what she might find beneath it, then clenched her teeth as she whipped it off.

Nothing but straw. Just another scarecrow.

'Faye.' Bertie's voice was muffled by the wind as it whipped around them. The sun was behind the clouds and the only birds were crows. 'I don't . . . I don't think we're going to find him, do you?' Bertie shuffled his feet, edging away from her. What was he frightened of? It was only a scarecrow stuffed with straw. The visions had ended, and they were alone.

And then it dawned on Faye. Bertie was frightened of her. Only a little, but her heart sank as she realised what her father had meant about her mother being an outcast.

'Come on, Bertie,' she said, trying to sound friendly as she wriggled the sack back on the scarecrow. 'Let's go and put the kettle on. I think we still have a few biccies left.'

Bertie's smile returned and they headed back to the village, leaving the new scarecrow hanging on his cross.

18

Constable Muldoon Does Not Care

'His coat, and the other boot.' It was after hours in the Green Man and Faye was giving a statement to Constable Muldoon, his pencil scratching on his notepad. Terrence was putting chairs on tables and sweeping the floor much slower than usual. Faye knew he was lurking to make sure she said nothing too peculiar. He needn't have worried. Bertie's fearful looks earlier today had taught her to keep certain things to herself. Faye didn't want to tell her dad or Bertie about the strange visions she had seen in the barn, and she certainly wasn't about to tell the constable. Muldoon was more moustache than man and not given to any nonsense.

'So this . . .' Muldoon cleared his throat with more disdain than was entirely necessary. 'This . . . *scarecrow* was wearing all of Mr Craddock's clothes?'

'Except the first boot. Is this important? A man is missing.'

'A man as naked as the day he was born, apparently.

Funny no one's mentioned seeing any fugitives in a state of undress.' He caught Terrence's eye and they both chuckled.

'This ain't no joke,' Faye snapped. 'Craddock could be dead.'

'Speaking frankly, if I may, Miss Bright, if Mr Craddock has departed this world, I doubt there are many here who would mourn him.'

'What?'

'With all due respect to the man, he was, and if you'll pardon my use of the vernacular, a miserable old goat who had a particular knack for rubbing folk the wrong way.'

'Are you saying he had it coming?'

'That would not be in keeping with my position as an officer of the law. But yes.'

'Constable Muldoon!'

'That said, I am a consummate professional and will investigate to the best of my abilities. I would also remind you there is a war on.'

'What's that got to do with the price of fish?'

'The duties of war require a ceaseless vigilance, and we must concentrate our limited resources on the very real threat of an invasion by the Narzees.'

'Is that your way of saying you're not going to do anything?'

'Certainly not.'

'It sounded like it. What *will* you do, exactly?'

'We will consider the evidence and proceed from there.'

'Oh, very reassuring, I don't think.'

Constable Muldoon pouted at this slight against his professionalism. 'Thank you for your statement, Miss Bright,' he said, closing his notebook with a snap. 'A good evening to you both.'

Faye stood open-mouthed as Terrence let Muldoon out. 'Night, Constable.'

Faye slumped into the armchair by the fireplace. 'Why does nobody care?'

'Ain't a copper's job to care, Faye. What do you expect him to do?'

'His job? Find out what happened to Craddock?'

'And he will, in time. Just cos you snap your fingers, girl, it don't mean the whole world has to jump.'

'I never said they should, but a man is missing and . . .' Faye bit her lip.

'And what?'

'And I think it's cos of me.'

'What? Don't talk daft.'

'I said his name, Dad. I said it in front of the scarecrows, I told 'em, and they went and grabbed him.'

'You don't know that. Stop talking rot. Calm down a minute and listen.' Terrence sat opposite her and started poking tobacco into his pipe. 'Let me tell you something about Craddock and your mother.'

Faye's anger with Muldoon was forgotten in a moment and she leaned forward. 'Mum and Craddock?' she said with a wince. 'Please don't tell me she was ever stepping out with him because I don't think I could cope.'

'Oh, lor', nothing like that.' Terrence grimaced. 'Nah, your mother had *some* taste. She just ended up with me.' He smiled and became lost in memories as he lit his pipe.

'Dad?' Faye tilted her head to catch his eye. 'Dad? Wake up. You were saying?'

'Yeah, yeah, give me a moment to sort me thoughts in order,' Terrence said, puffing on the pipe. 'When your mother and I were first stepping out, some tinkers came to town and she gave them what little money she had to buy a length of gingham. She spent the better part of a week measuring, cutting and sewing to make herself a dress. Gorgeous, it was. She wore it to the Summer Fair. And she . . .' Terrence faltered for a moment and Faye felt her heart flutter. Dad was a stiff-upper-lip bloke and he only ever got tearful after a few brandies at Christmas. 'Ah, look at me, I'm as soppy as a sack.'

'Don't stop.' Faye smiled and took his hand. 'I like it.'

'That smile.' Terrence sniffed and blinked himself back into the room. 'I knew right there and then she was the girl for me. She could brighten up the darkest day. Where was I?'

'The Summer Fair.'

'Right you are. So, we're at this fair, the sun is shining, we're arm-in-arm, we have a go at the coconut shy and everything's wonderful and I've never been happier. Then along comes Craddock – a younger man then, full of piss and vinegar and more than his share of cider – and he's having a lark with his mates from the cricket club. You wouldn't believe it, but he used to play for the village first eleven. Did you know that? Not half bad a wicketkeeper in his youth, as a matter of fact. Nothing got past him. Terrible batsman, though. He could never—'

'Dad!'

'I'm getting to it, keep your hair on. So, there's Craddock and his gang shoving each other about over by the coconut shy, and there's us minding our own business, holding hands and it's all lovey-dovey, and then that great lummox is a-shoving and a-pushing and he spins round and spills his pint all over your mother's new frock.'

'No.'

'Apple cider. Big orange stain. Looked like a map of Afghanistan my old man used to have on the wall there.'

'Oh my gawd. What did you do? Did you thump him?'

'Faye, when have you known me to be a man of violence?'

'You keep a bloomin' great knobkerrie behind the bar.'

'That's for emergencies only and I've never had to use it.'

'You threatened Finlay Motspur with it only last week.'

'Do you want to hear this story, or don't ya?'

'Did you thump him or not?'

'He was twice as big as me, even then. As you can imagine, this puts me in a very awkward position: defend my young lady's honour and get well and truly pasted by the biggest bugger in the village, or say nothing and move on.'

'Well, you're still in one piece, so you clearly said nothing.'

'O ye of little faith. I took a breath and was about to tell Craddock what a prize pillock he was when your mother steps between us. "Boys," she says, "don't start any trouble." She looks at me and says, "It was an accident, Terrence, I'm sure young Master Craddock is sorry." And she turns to him and smiles. And y'know what he does? He looks her up and down, at her beautiful face, at the frock she made with her own two hands, at her bright smile ... and he calls her a witch and a whore ...' Faye felt her dad's hand tighten in hers. 'In front of the whole village. Can you imagine that? *Now* I was ready to thump him, but your mother—'

'Is this when all his hair fell out?' said another voice. Faye and Terrence turned their heads to find Bertie half in and half out of the saloon bar door.

Terrence gave the lad a steely glare. 'You ever hear of knocking, Bertie?'

'S-sorry,' the boy said. 'I've got that elderflower cordial you asked for, Mr Bright.'

The tobacco in Terrence's pipe glowed red as he inhaled. 'Thank you, Bertie. Stick it on the bar there, will you, lad?'

'Righto.' Bertie hefted a crate of bottles across the room and onto the bar.

'When whose hair all fell out?' Faye asked Bertie, aware her dad was looking at her in a way that suggested she should stop talking right this very moment. 'Craddock's?'

'Me Mum told us. She was there. She said your mum cursed Craddock,' Bertie said, wiggling his fingers like a stage magician for good effect. 'Next day, all his hair fell out. And I mean all of it. Even the down-belows. Arse as smooth as a baby's head, according to Doctor Hamm.' Bertie caught sight of Terrence glaring at him. 'Or not. I don't know. Don't remember, rightly. Night, everyone.'

'Bertie!' Faye snapped, but the lad had fled the pub.

She looked back at her dad, who was getting up out of his chair. 'Oh no you don't. Sit.'

Terrence sat back down again.

'Mum cursed Craddock?'

'She didn't.'

'That's not how Bertie's mum remembers it.'

'I remember it different. I was there, don't forget. Curses and nonsense. None of it matters.'

'It matters cos it sounds to me like a woman can't speak her mind round here without some fella calling her a witch or a whore or accusing her of cursing 'em.' Faye twisted her lips into a scowl.

'I hope you don't think I agree with that sentiment, young lady.'

'I dunno. Do I?'

'I spent enough time with your mother to know that a woman can and should say whatever she likes,' Terrence said, jabbing his pipe at her to make his point. 'But I also know that when someone says something a bit loopy – be they man or be they woman – that very same someone should also prepare themselves for the consequences of their apparent loopiness.'

'So Mum was loopy, was she?'

'Don't twist my words, girl. I said *apparent*. She knew what she was saying, but folks are liable to misinterpret anything they don't rightly understand.'

'Did Mum curse Craddock or not?'

'What matters,' Terrence said, evading the question like a midfielder dodging a tackle, 'is that Craddock could be a nasty piece of work when he wanted, so don't go feeling too sorry for him. Anyway, yes, she might have given him one of her looks, y'know, the ones that turned my barnet grey. But she never cursed anyone. She kept her head high and took me over to the tombola. We won a bottle of sherry.' For a moment, Terrence was still there and he smiled.

'I think I've learned more about Mum in the last couple of days than in the previous seventeen years,' Faye said.

'I reckon I have to take the blame for that.' Terrence lowered his head. His smile faded. 'I don't like dredging up old memories, Faye. This'll sound strange, but … whenever I think of your mum, it makes me angry.'

Faye felt something flutter inside her. 'Me … me, too,' she said. 'I feel like I've been … robbed.'

'We both have,' Terrence said.

'And I don't feel like I should complain, cos there's others who've had it much worse, but I'm cross, Dad, I'm bloody cross that I never got to know my mum.'

Faye was surprised to find her dad's hand gently squeezing hers.

'I was lucky,' he said. 'I got to know her very well, and she would've been so proud of you. You're so much like her.'

'In what way?'

'You're kind,' he said. 'And you're useful.'

Faye couldn't help but smile. 'I'm what?'

'You know what I mean. You help folks out. People think you're poking your nose in, but you just want to do good. She was the same.'

And she was a witch, Faye thought.

'And she didn't take no nonsense.' Terrence heaved himself out of his chair and ambled back to the bar. 'Craddock never said anything to her again, but he would always give a look like he didn't approve of her. I'm not one for vengeful thoughts, Faye, but a fella reaps what he sows.'

'He still don't deserve to die,' Faye said, though she promised herself she would have words with Craddock if and when she next encountered him.

'No. But he can't expect us to care. Not you, not me, not the constable. He's—'

Terrence was cut short by a scream from across the street.

Faye was first to the door and she whipped it open to find Mrs Teach in her curlers and dressing gown staggering through her front door. 'It's one of them,' she cried, pointing up towards the church where a shadowy figure scurried into the shadows. 'One of them scarecrows was in my house!'

19

The Second Death of Ernie Teach

When Ernie Teach was alive, he returned from the garage every day at six on the dot, and Mrs Teach always had a hot tin bath ready for him to scrub himself clean. They had tea together, listened to the wireless – *It's That Man Again* was Ernie's favourite show – and then he would see to his jigsaw and she to her cross stitch. At ten o'clock, they retired to bed and made love with such rampant enthusiasm that even Mrs Nesbitt next door complained about the noise, and she was as deaf as a post. The next morning, Mrs Teach always had to explain to Mrs Nesbitt over the garden fence that the banging was caused by air trapped in the plumbing, and Ernie would always get the giggles, make his excuses and step inside.

Mrs Teach's nightly routine had changed since her Ernie passed away. Now at six she lit a candle for him, the radio remained silent and, instead of cross stitch, she went to bed early, accompanied by a cup of tea laced with gin and read a good book.

On this particular evening, Mrs Teach was some way into a revised edition of *The Sworn Book of Honorius* – a medieval grimoire of some infamy – when she heard the latch on the back door slide open.

Only her Ernie ever came through the back door, as only her Ernie knew how to jiggle the latch in such a way that the sticky door would budge.

Mrs Teach heard the familiar groan of the back door rubbing against the frame as it opened, followed by shuffling footsteps across the kitchen floorboards. Her heart began to race. She put her book down, wriggled into her dressing gown and slippers and crept across the landing. She was about to reach for the light switch when she heard a voice from downstairs.

'After you, Claude. No, after *you*, Cecil.'

Mrs Teach cursed herself for not having the foresight to keep something heavy like a frying pan next to the bed in case of unwanted visitors. She made a mental note to do so immediately after she saw off this intruder, then remembered she had given her old spare skillet away as part of the Saucepans for Spitfires collection.

'Don't forget the diver, sir.'

Whoever this intruder was, they were repeating catchphrases from *It's That Man Again.*

'I don't mind if I do. Sweeeeoooosssh.'

An intruder who was making noises like a radio tuning.

'This is Funf speaking. You are doomed!'

Mrs Teach gripped the bannister and trod carefully down the stairs. He was in the living room. Mrs Teach thought about dashing to the front door and making a run for it, but the more she heard of this intruder, the more she knew his voice.

'I go, I come back.'

It couldn't be him. It simply wasn't possible.

'Ladies and gentlemen, take your seats, please.'

She threw open the living-room door.

The thing she found was shrouded in shadow, hunched over by the wireless, its head jerking from side to side as it inspected the device from all angles while muttering the same thing over and over. 'ITMA, ITMA, Ra-Ra-Ra! ITMA, ITMA, Ra-Ra-Ra!'

Mrs Teach's voice was tight as a drum. 'Ernie?'

The thing spun around, its face revealed in a sliver of moonlight that cut through the curtains. A face of ragged sackcloth and pity, button eyes and wretched straw for hair.

It reached out to her with creaking leather gloves and tufts of hay in its sleeves and said in a mournful voice, 'It's that man again.'

It took a lot to frighten Mrs Teach, so the scream that came from her belly and woke half the village was not only unexpected, but so drenched in terror it sent the scarecrow tumbling back into the fireplace, crashing into the poker stand and sending the drinks cabinet smashing to the carpet.

The scarecrow wobbled to its feet, arms outstretched to her. 'It's that man again. It's that man again!'

'Get out!' she cried, grabbing a poker and bashing it across the back of the scarecrow's head. It howled and scurried from the room into the hallway and slammed into the door, falling back onto the stairs. Mrs Teach darted around it, yanked the door open, grabbed it by the scruff of the neck and tossed it out into the street.

The thing dashed along the pavement as lights began to flick on in neighbouring houses. The door to the Green Man swung open and young Faye was first out, followed by Terrence.

'It's one of them,' Mrs Teach cried. 'One of them scarecrows was in my house!'

There began a shambling pursuit as a few of the Local Defence Volunteers headed off after the fugitive scarecrow. The war had left the village short of athletic males and Faye held out little hope for the success of Terrence, Bertie and a handful of pensioners from the village bowls team who gave chase.

In the meantime, Faye comforted Mrs Teach in the Green Man with words of sympathy and a gin.

'Tinkety tonk old fruit and down with the Nazis,' was Mrs Teach's toast as she knocked it back in one.

'How did it get in?' Faye asked.

'The back door was unlocked,' Mrs Teach replied. 'I'm such a fool. My Ernie used to check it every night and I still haven't got into the habit myself.'

'But why you?' Faye asked, squinting one eye and adjusting her spectacles.

'I'm a woman alone,' Mrs Teach said, fanning herself with a beer mat. 'Vulnerable and in mourning.'

More squinting from the girl. 'So's Mrs Nesbitt. And Mrs Brew. And if you're a no-good scarecrow wanting to put the willies up vulnerable ladies, why not try Miss Moon and Miss Leach on the corner? They're easier targets, surely? The scarecrow would have passed all their houses before reaching yours,' Faye said, sensing she was starting to get on Mrs Teach's nerves. 'It's almost like the scarecrow knew who you were.'

'All I know,' Mrs Teach said, her voice trembling, tears glistening, 'is that *creature* came to my home in the dead of night and tried to ravage me.' Her body shuddered with melodramatic sobs, causing Faye to back off and stop asking annoying questions. 'They must be driven away, the lot of them,' the widow blubbed. 'They're a danger to us all.'

'Just last night you was telling us all to let them be.'

'That was before I had one of them break into my house and try and get up me nightie.'

Faye had the decency to blush with shame and she shut up. That's when they both heard the cries from outside. 'We got it!'

ꝿ

Faye had tried to convince Mrs Teach to stay safe inside, but the widow was having none of it. The pair of them marched out into the street where they found Terrence, Bertie and the other Local Defence Volunteers dragging a thrashing figure to the war memorial. As

Faye got closer, she could see its sackcloth head. It was a scarecrow. A living scarecrow. She would never get used to the idea, and a part of her wanted to take the sack off its head and see what was underneath. But first she had to deal with the creature's captors, who were so excited they had actually caught it that they didn't quite know what they should do next.

'Interrogate the cur,' declared Mr Marshall, the captain of the bowls team, trembling with anger.

'We should give it a bunch of fives,' Mr Baxter the ironmonger said, clenching his fists but not going so far as to raise them.

'Tie it up first,' Terrence said. 'We'll need some rope, though.'

'Or a whistle, maybe?' Bertie asked. 'We should call a constable.'

'First sensible idea I've heard,' Faye said. 'Constable Muldoon just left. If we hurry—'

'No police,' Mrs Teach said in a voice that cut through the confusion and would brook no dissent.

Except from Faye. 'Mrs Teach, we have to—'

'*No* police,' Mrs Teach repeated, not taking her eyes off the scarecrow. 'Stand aside.'

Bertie and the bowls team all looked to Terrence, who in turn looked to Faye, and she got the peculiar feeling they thought she was in charge, which was nonsense as it was perfectly clear it was Mrs Teach who had taken control. Nevertheless, Faye nodded and the menfolk released the scarecrow and backed away.

The creature reached up to her. 'Philomena,' it said.

Surreptitious glances were shared all around. The only person who ever dared to call Mrs Teach by her Christian name was her late Ernie. How could this thing know her so?

Faye looked on as Mrs Teach crouched down, took one of the creature's gloved hands in hers and gently squeezed it, looking into its button eyes all the while. Mrs Teach leaned closer and whispered to the scarecrow. She spoke for some while and it nodded three times in response to questions Faye could not hear. Mrs Teach gave the thing a long embrace and it lay back on the stone steps of the memorial as if readying for sleep.

Once the scarecrow was still, Mrs Teach tugged its shirt open, popping the buttons which clattered on the steps. She thrust a hand into its body, right where its heart would be, and began to pull it apart with her fists, tossing great clumps of straw into the air behind her again and again and again. The scarecrow did not protest as she whipped off its sackcloth head, revealing only straw stuffing, and it was the work of moments for her to take that apart, too, followed by the arms and legs. Terrence, Bertie and the bowls team backed off, shielding their eyes from the floating particles of dust in the night air, but Faye stood her ground, unable to look away. Mrs Teach quickly reduced the scarecrow to naught but baggy clothes and dried strands of corn stalks on the cobbles.

And then it was gone. A gust of wind swept down the street and all that was left were the clothes.

Mrs Teach remained on her knees for some time,

facing the ground in silence, though Faye thought she detected a little sob.

'Job done,' Mr Marshall said with all the certainty of a man who had just opened the larder door but had quite forgotten what he was looking for.

'Quite,' said Mr Baxter, similarly befuddled. 'Well, I must be off.'

'Me, too,' Bertie said, scratching his head as he limped away down the Wode Road.

Faye watched, incredulous, as the men wandered in uncertain zigzags back to their homes. She was left standing by the war memorial looking over the clothes of the late Ernie Teach laid out on the cobbles.

Terrence stayed by Faye's side. She took his hand. 'Don't you go nowhere,' she told him.

'I'm not sure I could anyway,' Terrence said, his face wrinkled in confusion.

Mrs Teach stood, turned to face them, raised her chin and said, 'I am rather tired and I should like to go home now. Goodnight to you, Faye, Terrence.'

'What just happened, Mrs Teach?' Faye asked.

'What do you think happened?'

Faye glanced at her father as if to apologise before replying, 'Magic? Witchery?'

'You're tired, girl,' Mrs Teach replied. 'As am I. We should retire to bed and forget what happened here.'

'I'm not sure I can,' Faye said.

'Me neither,' said Terrence, still open-mouthed in astonishment.

Mrs Teach smiled at him. 'I understand.' She took a

small perfume bottle from her dressing-gown pocket and sprayed a tiny puff in Terrence's eyes. He shook his head, blinking tears. Mrs Teach took his chin, looked into his eyes and commanded, 'Forget.'

Terrence became still and nodded.

'What have you done to my dad?' Faye rushed forwards and took his arm. 'Dad? Dad?'

'He'll be fine.' Mrs Teach remained calm as she put the perfume bottle away. 'The others cannot understand what they saw, so their minds tell them it never happened. Your father is more open to the arcane through his association with your dear departed mother. Come and see me, Faye. Not tomorrow, not on a Sunday. Come for elevenses on Monday. We'll have tea and I'll tell you what you saw.'

'I know what I saw.'

'But you cannot explain it,' Mrs Teach said. 'I can. Monday. Elevenses.' Mrs Teach wiped a tear from her eye as she walked to her front door and stepped inside.

'Dad?' Faye shook her father and he took a deep breath through his nostrils as if waking from a nap.

'Faye?' He looked around at the war memorial and the empty village. 'Have I been sleepwalking again?'

20

Normal Girls

Church wasn't the same without bells. The bells called the villagers to the service. The bells were Faye's purpose and focus on a Sunday morning. And because the bells finished ringing once everyone was inside the church, they gave Faye an opportunity to sneak off before the service started so she didn't have to sit through the boring rigmarole of hymns, prayers and sermon.

No such luck today. No ringing before the service, no ringing a quarter peal for her mother later that day and no escape from the service.

'Oh, come on, Dad. Let me skip just this once.'

'If I have to suffer, then so do you.'

He hadn't mentioned anything about the events of last night and Faye didn't dare bring it up. Over breakfast he said he'd had his best night's sleep in years. He was happy and full of energy and Faye didn't want to set that off balance.

'You're coming to church,' he told Faye. 'Wear a nice frock for once. Be normal.'

'Normal?' Faye snorted. As if anything in this village could be normal ever again. 'This is not normal.' Faye stood before the hall mirror in her Sunday-best floral-print frock, which she outgrew last summer and had a hem that was now way above her scuffed knees. 'I can't wear this,' she told him. 'I look like an overgrown seven year old.'

Dad stood next to her, adjusting his tie. He made several attempts to tell her that she looked fine, but in the end, he could only pat her on the shoulder. 'There's one of them clothing exchanges in the church hall after the service,' he told her. 'Maybe you can get something nice there?'

'Can't I just wear my dungarees?'

'In church? Certainly not.'

'How about my ARP uniform?'

'Oh, and I suppose you want to sit there with a tin hat on your head, too?'

Faye beamed and nodded.

Terrence shook his head and scruffed her hair. 'You're a funny old fish, aren't you?' he said with a smile. 'When you arrived, your mother and I were over the moon. A lovely little girl, we said, who'd wear dresses, play with dollies, have her hair in bunches or pigtails. Look at you now. You're more likely to end up in pig muck.'

Faye shrugged. 'Least I'm handy around the pub.'

'Tell you what,' Terrence said, raising a finger. 'I'll

let you wear your ARP uniform – minus the tin hat – if you wash the pub windows this morning.' He extended his hand and Faye shook it.

'You, dear Father, have got a deal.'

And that's how Faye found herself in church in her ARP bluette boiler suit. It was far too baggy for her, and it got her some funny looks as she took her seat, but at least no one could see her knees. She sat next to her dad in the pews by the porch of the north transept. The door had been left open and a draught crawled around her ankles. Only a church could be so cold on such a lovely summer Sunday. Faye folded her arms and crossed her legs to keep warm as the Reverend Jacobs gave a patriotic sermon on 'being vigilant'. On cue, Faye's bottom started to go numb and she fidgeted to get comfy.

Miss Moon hammered the keys of the church organ and everyone stood to sing 'Jerusalem'. Miss Moon's playing slowed to a crawl after the first verse, as did everyone singing along with her. She had to cough to wake Miss Leach, who had nodded off on sheet-music duty. Miss Leach jolted awake, turned the page of the organ music and the hymn resumed its regular pace.

As Faye sang, she looked around the church in idle curiosity. The old flags from the Great War, the tatty carpets around the altar, the stained-glass windows, the strange shadowy figure skulking by the porch door.

She gave a little yelp, dropping her hymn book in fright.

The singing faltered as some of the congregation turned and stared at her. Her father shook his head in disapproval and the singing returned to its usual volume as Miss Moon hit a few bum notes before getting back on track. Faye grimaced in apology, crouching to pick up the hymn book. As she did so, she caught sight of a long shadow creeping around outside. It wore a dress and a summer hat.

One of the scarecrows? The one who wanted Craddock? Suky?

Without daring to look at her father, Faye slipped from the pew, through the transept porch and out into the sunshine just in time to see the shadow hurrying around the back of the church.

Faye, wobbly legs telling her to turn back and heart thumping, took off after it. Like the LDV men last night, she wondered if she would know what to do with a scarecrow if she caught one. Drag it before the village congregation as proof that she wasn't losing her mind? Confront it about Craddock and demand to be taken to him? Faye told herself she would know when she caught it. And that would be any second now as she could hear the thing whispering by the entrance to the vestry.

Faye leapt around the corner, hands like claws, ready to grab. 'Gotcha. Oh.' She stumbled to a halt.

'Faye Bright, what the bloody hell are you doing?'

It was Milly Baxter in her Sunday-best summer frock and straw hat. She was with Betty Marshall, also resplendent in a pretty dress. Both were leaning towards one another, cigarettes on lips, a lit match between them.

'Oh, sorry,' Faye said, taking a step back. 'I thought you were ... Well, not you.'

'Don't you dare snitch, Faye Bright, or I'll get my brother to duff you up,' Milly declared, shaking the match out.

'In't he fighting in Malta?' Faye asked.

'Yes, but he'll do it when he comes home. I have a list.'

'Don't tell my mum and dad,' Betty Marshall begged, hiding the unlit cigarette behind her back. 'They'll half kill me.'

Milly gave Faye the side-eye. 'What are you doing out here anyway?' she asked. 'You look as guilty as we do.'

'Nothing. I thought I saw ... Don't matter.'

'Thought you saw what? A scarecrow?' Milly grinned.

'What do you mean?'

'Word is you're telling everyone that scarecrows are coming to life and stealing babies at night.'

'What? I never said that.'

Betty added, 'I heard you took Bertie Butterworth out to the woods to turn him into a scarecrow.'

'Like anyone would know the difference,' Milly cackled, and Faye resisted the urge to thump her for being rude about Bertie.

'Maybe you pair need to get your ears cleaned out,' Faye told her, 'cos everything you're hearing is wrong.'

'That so?' Milly looked up and down at Faye's ARP uniform and snorted. 'Like your outfit.'

Betty giggled. 'Proper Sunday best.'

'Oh, shut your cakeholes,' Faye said, stuffing her hands in her pockets and turning back for the church porch. That's when she spotted someone cross the road to Perry Lane. Miss Charlotte. And she was pushing a wheelbarrow. She was out of sight in moments, but they all saw her.

'That one's off her rocker an' all,' Milly Baxter said, scratching a new match to life and lighting her cigarette. 'You two would get on like a house on fire.' Faye ignored their silly giggling and walked away.

ꞵ

Faye didn't dare go back into the church. From the sound of it, the service was as good as over. She could hear them singing 'Abide with Me', and Reverend Jacobs *always* ended with 'Abide with Me'. She leaned against the lychgate as the congregation slowly filed out into the summer sun. Bertie was one of the first to emerge and came limping over to her.

'Not the same without bells, is it?' he said with a *tut*.

'Definitely not.'

'Nice service, though,' he said.

'It was the same as last week's, and the week before.'

'Even so, shame you missed half of it. What happened?'

Faye briefly wondered if she should tell him the truth. That she was jumping at shadows and how she had discovered that Milly Baxter was a two-faced cow. 'I don't like that song "Jerusalem",' Faye said in the end. 'I walked out in protest.'

'Why?'

Faye thought for a second. '*Builded* ain't a proper word. *And was Jerusalem builded here?* I mean, what sort of half-arsed question is that?'

'It's just an old word, ain't it? Hymns have all sorts of old words we don't use any more. Words we forget.'

'That ain't all we forget. Look at 'em. Mr Marshall there. Mr Baxter, too.' Faye nodded at the happy congregation chatting away on the church steps. She wasn't a vindictive person, but the temptation to snitch on Milly Baxter and Betty Marshall as they mingled with their parents was almost irresistible. 'You'd never think they saw a straw man torn to pieces last night.'

'Saw a what?' Bertie flared his nostrils when he was puzzled.

'One of them crow folk. Last night,' Faye said, but Bertie's nostrils only got bigger. The bigger the nostrils, the greater the confusion. *You could stick corks up them*, Faye thought to herself. 'He nearly gave Mrs Teach a heart attack, and you and the rest of the Old Contemptibles chased after it and ... and you haven't got a clue what I'm going on about, do you, Bertie?'

'Yeah, yeah, no, er ... I remember ... there was an intruder ... or a burglar ... or something, and then we chased him off and ...' Bertie's eyes rolled skywards as he tried to recall. 'I'm a bit knackered, to be honest. Long day yesterday. And I haven't had me breakfast.'

'Where's Mrs Teach? She'll remember.' Faye scanned the dispersing congregation.

'Didn't see her this morning,' Bertie said.

'That's not like her,' Faye said. 'She's usually front row on a Sunday, first with a few pennies in the collection box.'

'Maybe she's poorly?' Bertie ventured. 'She had a hell of a fright.'

'Maybe,' Faye said as she saw Milly and Betty skipping off with their fathers and mothers. Normal girls with normal parents off to their normal homes. 'Bertie, if I ask you an honest question, will you give us an honest answer?'

'I'll do my best. Is it about Spitfires, Hurricanes, tanks or bombers? I, well, I don't want to blow my own trumpet, but I'm becoming something of an expert. Did you know—'

'Do you think I'm off my rocker?'

Bertie's nostrils became so big she could see his brain. 'No,' he said.

'You took your precious time answering.'

'Sorry, I don't mean any disrespect, Faye. You said some funny things yesterday. Funny ha-ha and funny peculiar. I'm still your friend, though.'

Over Bertie's shoulder, Faye spotted Miss Charlotte crossing the road from Perry Lane, returning from wherever she'd been with an empty wheelbarrow.

'What about her?' Faye asked.

'Miss Charlotte?' Bertie lowered his voice. 'Oh, I'm not sure there's even a rocker that she was ever on in the first place. She's a wise soul, but not like normal folk. She scares me a bit, truth be told.'

Faye almost told Bertie about finding Miss Charlotte

in the altogether with a toad on her belly, but if he was as sketchy on the birds and the bees as he made out, then she wasn't sure he was ready for the image of a naked witch in the depths of the woods.

'There's me dad,' Bertie said, waving goodbye. 'Must rush.'

'Me, too,' Faye said, hot on the trail of Miss Charlotte – for exactly two steps before she found her father blocking her way.

'And where the bleedin' heck did you go, young lady?'

21

When I'm Cleaning Windows

Dad grumbled all the way home. 'What am I supposed to tell people, eh? When you go dashing out of the church in front of everyone like that?'

'Tell 'em I've got me monthlies.' Faye gave him a wicked grin as they headed along the Wode Road to the pub.

'Will you keep it down?' Faye's father was less squeamish than most men about periods; he had been her only parent through the puberty years, after all. Even so, to speak of it at any volume louder than a shameful whisper behind closed doors after dark with the curtains closed was more than he could take. 'Tell me the truth. What were you playing at?'

'I thought . . .' Faye trailed off, kicking at a stone as they walked. 'I thought I saw something.'

'Saw what? Have you been looking at your mother's book again? It'll only fill your head with nonsense. I told you to put it away.'

'I did, I swear. It's under lock and key, but that don't stop strange stuff from happening.'

'Such as?'

'What do you remember about last night?' Faye was careful not to give her dad too many details. 'With Mrs Teach?'

Terrence opened his mouth, frowned, then closed it again. 'Well, er ...'

'You don't remember, do you?'

'I do, I do. It's just a bit fuzzy is all. What ... what did happen?'

Faye considered telling him, but the thought of explaining that a straw version of Ernie Teach had invaded the poor woman's home and was torn apart by her was exhausting enough. 'Nothing. It don't matter. I'm jumpin' at shadows. Being daft. I keep seeing stuff that probably ain't there and it's driving me mad. I'll stop it. I promise.'

'I warned you about this, didn't I?'

'Yes, you did, Dad. *Consequences of apparent loopiness*, you called it.'

'You're not loopy,' Terrence said as they came to a stop under the Green Man sign. He sorted through his keys to open the door. 'You're just like your mother. You've got an imagination. You notice stuff other people don't. The trick is to keep it to yourself.'

'I will,' Faye told him. 'Cross me heart and all that. No more flights of fancy. I shall keep me head screwed on and me feet on the ground.'

'Good,' Terrence said, unlocking the pub door. 'Now get up that ladder and wash those windows.'

After a cuppa and a spot of jam on bread, Faye changed back into her dungarees and clambered to the top of a ladder to wash the pub windows. Every now and then her thoughts drifted back to last night and Mrs Teach's promises of answers at elevenses on Monday. Was that an appointment Faye would keep? Or would it be simpler just to put all this nonsense behind her? There was a war on. Enough to worry about as it was without strange fancies pecking at her brain. There was a calm simplicity in applying suds to glass. A pleasant satisfaction in getting them squeaky clean. It was tempting. An ordinary life where she could still be useful. Bread and jam and church on Sunday.

Faye caught sight of Charlotte Southill again. Dressed in gumboots and a summer frock, pushing a wheelbarrow with two grey sacks up Perry Lane, a shortcut that folk took through the village when they didn't want to be seen.

'Just what the hell are you up to, then?' Faye muttered to herself. The quiet life had its allure, of course, but Faye's curiosity fed something in her that she couldn't get elsewhere.

Faye tried to put Charlotte out of her mind, but twice more that afternoon she spied her going back and forth. Bags full when coming from her cottage, bags empty when returning from the edge of the village. Faye finished cleaning the last window, hurried down the ladder, poured her suds down the drain and got on her bicycle in pursuit. She couldn't help herself.

Faye lost her at the top of the lane and ended up doing

almost an entire circuit of Woodville. It was by the duck pond that she first noticed a line of black dust. She wondered if it was something dangerous, like gunpowder, so she dabbed her finger in and gave the stuff a sniff. Coal dust, ashes from a bonfire and another ingredient she couldn't quite pin down. She followed the line of dust and was astonished to find it circled the entire village. Faye was almost back where she'd started by the duck pond when she turned down the Wode Road and found Charlotte. She was inside the wall of Saint Irene's graveyard, carefully pouring the dusty contents of one of her sacks in a thin line that ran parallel with the old stone wall. Once the first sack was empty, Charlotte tossed it back in the wheelbarrow and wiped her brow, leaving a charcoal smudge on her forehead. The gumboots were a bit dress-down compared to Charlotte's usual get-up, but her white hair was tied back in a neat bun and her scarlet lipstick was red as a poppy.

Faye watched as Charlotte reached into a patchwork pocket sewn onto her frock, took out a hip flask, had a quick swig, then started with the next sack.

'Morning, Miss Charlotte.' Faye parked the bike and sauntered over like she always took a cycle through the church graveyard. 'Lovely day, ain't it?'

'I know you've been watching me, girl,' Charlotte said, not looking up from her work. 'You would make a terrible spy. What do you want? I'm busy. And no tedious questions about your mother.'

Charlotte's rudeness made Faye blush, but she reckoned that meant the gloves were off. 'What the blinking flip are you doing, if you don't mind me asking?'

'I do.'

'Do what?'

'Mind you asking. Go away.'

'I have every right to be here. As much right as you and your wheelbarrow and them sacks of whatever that is,' Faye said. 'And your goat ain't here to spook me.'

'He's not my goat.'

'I'll ask again: what are you up to?'

'You wouldn't understand.'

'Is this about them scarecrows?'

Charlotte said nothing and continued to shake her bag, backing away from Faye. The black powder poured out, glistening when it caught the light.

'Coal dust?' Faye asked, matching Charlotte step-for-step. 'Ashes? What you been burning?'

'Good grief, you're like a little child,' Charlotte muttered. 'Leave me in peace.'

'One of the scarecrows came back last night,' Faye said.

Charlotte didn't look up but made a noise at the back of her throat that suggested Faye wasn't telling her anything new. This was the first time Faye had mentioned scarecrows to anyone and not immediately been ridiculed. She was so used to getting the cold shoulder that she wasn't entirely sure what to do next.

'A proper living and breathing scarecrow,' Faye persevered, waiting for Charlotte to call her a fool. 'That's what they are, aren't they?'

'So it would seem,' Charlotte replied, and Faye wanted to clap her hands in delight.

She restrained herself and angled her head to catch Charlotte's eye. 'I reckon it was Ernie Teach.'

'Ernie Teach is dead.'

'Then someone needs to tell him as it didn't stop him last night.' Faye adjusted her specs, then put her hands on her hips. 'Ain't no doubt in my mind the scarecrow that woke up half the village last night was definitely Ernie Teach.'

Charlotte stopped shaking the bag. 'What makes you so sure?'

'He went straight for Mrs Teach's house *and* he called her Philomena,' Faye said, getting more excited. It was such a relief to share this with someone who didn't just stare at her like she was a cow dancing the jitterbug. 'No one was ever allowed to call her that except him, and how would some scarecrow know her name, anyway? I don't know how a dead fella like Ernie Teach gets inside the body of a dusty old scarecrow, but considering all the peculiar goings-on we've had here these last few days, it makes as much sense as—'

'Be quiet.' Charlotte dropped the bag, raised her fingers to her lips and Faye shut up.

Faye waited for the ridicule, to be told that she was a silly little girl, but Charlotte wasn't looking at her, rather at something behind her.

'It's perfectly safe.' Charlotte's voice was gentle.

Faye turned to face the trees on the other side of the church wall.

Her heart began to thump as a shadow peered out from behind an oak.

'You can show yourself,' Charlotte said. 'I won't hurt you.'

The figure shuffled from behind the tree. It wore a black cloth sack on its head made to look like a blackbird, complete with an orange beak.

A scarecrow.

22

Black Salt Burns

Faye was rooted to the spot. It was one thing to convince everyone else that these scarecrows were real, but to be so close to one in broad daylight brought its own special kind of fear. Its blackbird head didn't help Faye's nerves much, either. It kept twitching and darting from side to side. It was unnatural. Inhuman. Straw given life.

'Come closer.' Charlotte beckoned the blackbird scarecrow towards the wall. Faye watched as it hesitated, as if expecting some kind of trap. 'I promise, I won't hurt you,' Charlotte said gently, as if speaking to a child. The scarecrow shuffled nearer to the wall. 'Stop.' Charlotte pointed to the long trail of black dust on her side of the wall. 'See that?'

The blackbird scarecrow peered where she was pointing.

'Black salt,' she said, waving it closer. 'Come. Hop over. Careful now.'

The blackbird scarecrow did as it was told.

'That's it. Don't cross the line, not yet,' Charlotte told him, then added, 'Your kind may not cross this. I have protected the village, do you understand?'

The blackbird scarecrow stared at her with little sign of comprehension.

'A demonstration, perhaps,' Charlotte said. 'Come forward, just a little, yes, that's it. A little bit more … a little bit more …'

The blackbird scarecrow inched its slippered feet across the line. Faye watched them blacken. A small spiral of white smoke puffed up from each foot like the first wisps of a bonfire. The blackbird scarecrow quickly drew its feet back.

'You see?' Charlotte glared at it, her voice harder. 'Cross this and you will burn. All of you. Go away and do not come back. Understand?'

The blackbird scarecrow looked up at Charlotte. It had crossed stitches arranged in squares for eyes and it did not appear to be breathing.

'Go and tell your master,' Charlotte said. 'He will know what this means, and if he's half as clever as he thinks he is, he will stay away.'

The scarecrow remained where it was.

'Maybe … maybe it don't speak English?' Faye found her voice, though she was still breathless and awed.

Charlotte shot Faye a silencing glare, then raised her chin, closed her eyes and muttered under her breath. Faye couldn't make out the words, but there was something in their rhythm that reminded her of the rituals in her mother's book.

Light flashed, leaving streaks of green and purple on Faye's retinas. Heat brushed her cheeks as a section of the black salt burst into flame.

'Go. *Shoo!*' Charlotte jolted forwards and the blackbird scarecrow vaulted back over the wall and fled like a startled child. It ran in zigzags between the trees before vanishing from sight. Charlotte muttered more words and the flames guttered into white smoke.

Faye was half blind and giddy. If her mind wasn't playing tricks, she had just seen an actual witch do some actual magic. 'What's . . . what's black salt?' she asked, half afraid to know the answer.

'Two parts salt, one part coal dust and ash,' Charlotte said, picking up her black bag. 'I've had to burn a lot of coal and wood to create the ash I need to protect the whole village.'

'From the scarecrows?'

'It's not the scarecrows that worry me,' Charlotte said as she replaced the burned black salt with a fresh line.

'Then who?'

'That doesn't concern you.'

'There's something *worse* than scary-arse crow people that have heads like blackbirds and pumpkins? And you're telling me I shouldn't be concerned? Pardon me, but I think I have a right to know.'

'If you knew half the things I know, you would never leave your house of a morning.'

'And that's supposed to reassure me?'

'I wouldn't expect you to—'

'Yes, yes, I wouldn't understand. Fine, but you're a witch, aren't you? A proper witch that can do spells and stuff. That was magic just then, weren't it?'

'Don't pretend you don't know,' Charlotte said with a sneer. 'Your mother was the same. All smiles and innocence.'

'My mum? So my mum was definitely a—'

'I said no tedious questions about your mother.'

'You started it.'

'Do me a favour and stop meddling in things you don't understand, little girl.'

'I'm seventeen.'

'Yet you act like a child, prodding, poking, breaking, whining. For all I know *you* started this mess . . . or her.'

Charlotte nodded towards the church. Faye spun to find Mrs Teach moving between the stones with a small bouquet of blue and pink hydrangeas clutched to her breast.

Charlotte and Faye ducked down and hid behind a gravestone.

'I reckon she's a witch, too,' Faye said in an excited rush. 'She took that scarecrow last night and reached into its stuffing and—'

'What scarecrow last night?'

'Weren't you listening to a word I said? Ernie Teach came back as a scarecrow last night and Mrs Teach pulled all its stuffing out.' Faye wondered if this might be the most ridiculous thing she had ever said, and she waited for Charlotte to pour scorn on her, but it didn't come.

'That two-faced cow.' Charlotte's voice dropped to a shocked whisper. 'She lied to me, right to my face.'

'About what? Is she a witch like you? Does she—?'

Charlotte pressed a finger to Faye's lips to silence her.

They watched, unseen, as the widow found her husband's gravestone and placed the flowers on the ground. She stood in silence for a moment, covering her eyes with her hand, her body trembling with sobs.

Faye removed Charlotte's finger from her lips. 'This ain't right. Spying on a widow's grief.'

'Her grief is half the problem,' Charlotte said.

'Don't be so cruel. It's normal for people to cry when their loved ones die.'

'Yes, we cry, we grieve, we move on. Not her, though, not Mrs Teach. Oh no, she always has to get her own way, whatever the cost.'

Mrs Teach let out another sob and blew her nose on a white hankie.

Faye flushed with shame. She wanted to look away but couldn't. Mercifully, Mrs Teach hurried back home, wiping the tears from her eyes.

Faye didn't speak till she was sure she was gone. 'Are you saying that Mrs Teach brought her Ernie back from the dead as a scarecrow?'

'No one has that power,' Charlotte said, sounding only half certain of it. She stood and Faye followed as they made their way through the stones to Ernie's grave, where the hydrangeas lay. It was one of many stones, but the words were freshly carved and the pain of grief still raw. Everyone in the village had gone to Ernie's funeral.

'Then who – or what – was inside that scarecrow?' Faye asked. 'Where did all these crow people come from?'

Faye looked at the other stones, some hundreds of years old, and wondered about the lives of those who had lived and died here, and there she saw something that made the hairs on her neck tingle.

'Miss Charlotte,' she said, her words barely a whisper. 'Miss Charlotte, look.' Faye hurried to a stone behind Ernie's, one faded and covered in moss, but the words were still legible:

Susannah Gabriel
Born 1868, died 1890 in God's Grace
Our 'Suky'

23

Jumbly Thoughts

The crow folk danced as a latticework of wispy clouds drifted across the sun and the air grew chill. Suky sat alone, away from the dancing. She did not feel the cold as she used to. She did not feel it at all. Old thoughts pressed at her mind. Did she ever feel the cold? The warmth of an embrace? One question came to her over and over. She had tried to ignore it in all her happiness and freedom, but it would not go away, and it was a question she knew she could not answer.

Was there a time before this?

She had asked the birds, but they did not understand.

Suky did not want to defy her Pumpkinhead, but the birds had come and spoken to her this morning and she could not help but listen. They had told her how so many of their brothers and sisters had cried in fear before falling from the sky and dying over the village; they had told her how they helped a girl and a boy lost in the woods; they had told Suky she was pretty and that they were glad she wasn't stuck in a field any more.

Suky could not be sure how she understood their twittering. It just came to her mind like a song she knew the words to. They didn't stay long – they were afraid of Pumpkinhead – but they promised to come back, though they still could not answer her questions.

She didn't want to ask the others. Some were playing horns and clacking sticks as the rest danced in circles. Most looked mindless to Suky, or confused as if they had woken from a slumber.

Pumpkinhead led the dance, striking his cowbell faster and faster. The band's tempo increased and the dancers began to whirl like falling sycamore seeds. Pumpkinhead's zigzag smile widened as the dance became a kind of frenzy. He beckoned her to join.

Suky smiled politely and shook her head while sitting on her hands. She had little joy for dancing.

Pumpkinhead's smile narrowed. He began to move around the dance towards her. Suky could not help but be thrilled that he would be with her soon. She had no heart to beat or skin to tingle, but somewhere in her mind she felt a flush of joy at the thought of spending time with her Pumpkinhead. The dancers had their own rhythm now and they continued to twirl as Pumpkinhead tossed the cowbell and stick away and sat next to Suky on the old stone steps.

'Are you troubled, my sister? Why not join the dance?'

'I ain't much in the mood for dancing and cavorting and such,' Suky said. 'I am content to sit here and sort through my jumbly thoughts.'

'And what jumbly thoughts are they, sister Suky?'

He called her by her name. She felt the memory of excitement and blushing.

'Confused thoughts. Childish thoughts. I'm being a silly blabber and I shan't bother you with them.'

'But you must.' Pumpkinhead took her gloved hand in his. 'We are the crow folk, we share our thoughts and dreams. It is no bother. Please. Tell me.'

Suky watched her brothers and sisters dancing for a moment longer. A voice in her head told her that a problem shared was a problem halved. It troubled her that such thoughts arrived in her head like an echo from another place, another Suky.

'If we are indeed named the crow folk,' Suky started, 'then why ain't we friends with the crows and other birds? Why do we fear them so?'

'We do not fear them, Suky.' Pumpkinhead bristled at the suggestion. 'They fear us.'

'Sorry.' Suky dipped her head. 'I din't mean nothing by it.'

'No, no. It is a good question.' Pumpkinhead craned his head up to the sky, scanning for birds. 'There was a time when we were friends with the birds, especially the crows, ravens and jackdaws. We danced with them as your brothers and sisters do now. We sang songs, told stories and watched over the land, spirits and guardians together. Then men came. They grew their crops and wanted it all for themselves. They drove a wedge between us. They changed us. Deformed us. Made us hideous to scare our old friends and now they scatter at the very sight of us.' Pumpkinhead turned back to Suky. She felt his eyes upon her. 'But that is not what troubles you, is it, sister?' he said. 'Tell me. Tell me the truth.'

'I have these memories swishing about in my head,' Suky said, squeezing his hand. 'Thoughts of another time. Another me. They're as distant and thin as clouds in the sky, but I feel them there all the same, like scraps of a dream. What does it mean, my Pumpkinhead?'

Pumpkinhead glanced over at their brothers and sisters as they danced, then he turned back to Suky, his voice low. 'You are not like the others,' he told her. 'Your mind is fast and canny as a fox's. I like that. What does it mean? It means I can trust you to help me make all our lives more content.'

'How can we do that? We can't do nothing but dance all day. We must have a home, a place to rest our weary bones – not that we has bones as such – but a home all the same. Otherwise, what is the point of us?'

'I have had some thoughts about that,' Pumpkinhead said, gesturing at the abbey, then at the wood surrounding it. 'This place still has some of the old power.'

'You mean the thing what made us what we are.'

'I speak of magic.'

Suky hesitated. 'I don't rightly believe in magic.'

'And yet here we are.' Pumpkinhead spread his arms wide. 'What more proof do you need?'

'I believe in you,' Suky told him. 'I believe in us crow folk here and now, and if you reckon it's magic what brung us together, then yes, I do believe in it very much.'

'Very good, sister, very good. There's hardly any magic left in this realm, which makes it all the more precious, and it's what keeps us thriving and together. There is a book . . .' he began, then stopped as if he had said too much.

'What sort of book?' Suky asked. 'A magical book?'

'Yes, yes.' Pumpkinhead leaned closer to her, excited, like a boy with a secret. Suky had never seen him like this. 'A book of spells, my sister, with words and pictures of magic and ritual and power. It is in the village somewhere. I can feel its strength, even from here. If we could find it, we could use it. Imagine. Our brothers and sisters working together with magic to create a haven. A place of our own where we will never be disturbed. You want that, don't you, Suky?'

'Yes. Yes, I do,' Suky said. 'Who has this book of spells? Where will we find it? And how do you know it's here?'

'Someone has been using it,' Pumpkinhead said. 'A witch of great power has been reciting its words. When she does so, the book sings to me, sister Suky, like a bird in a cage, and I want to free that bird and make it fly high. I want magic to soar and do wonderful things for us.'

'Like singing songs with the birds again?'

'Yes, yes, if you like.' Pumpkinhead patted Suky's hands at her simple thought. 'But that will be just the start. For too long have men and witches jealously guarded the secrets of magic. If we could find that book, we would be free.'

'And make peace with the birds?'

'Peace. Yes, Suky. For so long have I yearned for peace.'

'Then we should toddle off to the village and ask them for it.'

'You have seen how they react to us,' Pumpkinhead said mournfully. 'They have no clue of the book's power. If they did, they would surely destroy it, and with it any hope we have of happiness. I don't need to tell you what that would mean for you, me, our brothers and sisters.'

Suky watched the other crow folk as they spun to the beat. 'No more dancing and cavorting and such,' she said.

'No more dancing, no more you, or me. You have to understand, Suky, the likes of us confuse and befuddle the people in the village. They have not come across our kind in their memories, and they recognise us only from their nightmares and shadows.'

'We can't . . . share it with them like good children?'

'I am all for sharing, but the truth is most humans have little comprehension of magic. And once they fathom there is magic to be had, they will want it all for themselves. That's what humans are like. They are jealous and greedy and they never know when their bellies are full. They will take and take and take until there is no more. And we must not let that happen, Suky.' Pumpkinhead squeezed her hand in his. 'Never forget we have every right to live and be as we please. I shall make a promise to you now. Once we take possession of the book, we will have a home, we will be a family and we will be happy.'

'Master. Master!' A cry echoed around the stone walls, bringing the music to a faltering end. The dancing stopped and all heads turned to see the blackbird scarecrow come flapping from the wood and into the ruins of the abbey.

Pumpkinhead's hand slipped from Suky's as he stood. 'What news, brother?'

'The village,' the blackbird scarecrow said, all jittery with his arms flailing back and forth as he hurried to kneel before Pumpkinhead. 'The village is . . . it's . . . I saw . . . and brother Ernie—'

Pumpkinhead rested his hand on the blackbird scarecrow's head. 'Calm yourself, brother. Speak only the truth. What of brother Ernie?'

'He is gone,' the blackbird scarecrow said.

'Gone?'

'The witch spurned him and he was torn to pieces and he is now but straw on the wind.'

Suky's hand went to her mouth. Around her rose wails of sorrow. Pumpkinhead's eyes narrowed.

'And there's more,' the blackbird scarecrow said. 'The village is protected by black salt, brother. We cannot go in. It burns, brother, it will burn us all. I was warned off by the white-haired witch. *Go away and don't come back*, she said with flames. And she said you would know what this meant.'

Pumpkinhead nodded and embraced the blackbird scarecrow. 'Thank you, brother. You are brave to bring us this news.' He turned to the others. 'Did you hear that, brothers and sisters? They mean to frighten us with witchcraft. We cannot let them do this. We will not let them drive us away. Brothers and sisters, I just made a promise to sister Suky, and I make this promise to you, too. We will have a home, a family. We will be happy.'

There were cheers from the crow folk. Suky stayed silent.

'We must stand together in the face of witchcraft,' Pumpkinhead said. 'We cannot wait for them to attack. We must be decisive. We must—'

'No more hurting people,' Suky blurted, then covered her mouth with her hand. Pumpkinhead was staring at her, and she prickled with a little fear and shame, but she continued all the same. Suky lowered her hand and spoke some more. 'That Craddock was a bad man and we did what we did, and none of us took pleasure in it, and it's in the past. But I want no more people hurt on our account. Promise me, my Pumpkinhead.'

And then she saw it. A little flash of anger in her Pumpkinhead's eyes, a tiny blister of frustration. A blink and it was gone.

'We cannot trust them, sister Suky,' he said, his smile back in place. 'You saw how quickly that woman gave up Craddock to us. They betray their own kind, and they will destroy us.'

'I don't like it when we fight,' Suky said, another memory bubbling to the surface, one from another life. 'We must parley with them. Make peace.'

There were murmurs of agreement around her, and she could see Pumpkinhead's eyes dart to spot each dissenter as if remembering them for later.

'Yes, yes, parley. Sister Suky is right,' Pumpkinhead said, all sincere. 'But how, my sister? If we can't go into the village, how can we talk?'

'It's easy as pumpkin pie, my Pumpkinhead,' Suky said. 'We bring them to us.'

24

Smoke Gets in Your Mind

'We need to prove that scarecrow Suky and graveyard Suky are one and the same,' Faye said. 'And if we can find out who this Suky is, then we might figure out where she came from and why she's come back as a scarecrow.' Faye and Charlotte were marching around the side of the church. Faye was thrilled to be walking side by side with a proper witch and talking about living scarecrows. It meant she wasn't half as barmy as she'd thought she was this morning. It also meant she couldn't tell anyone else about what was happening, otherwise they would think she was completely barmy. She would worry about that later.

'Where are you taking me?' Charlotte asked as they left the church graveyard.

'Here's the thing, I know who she is,' Faye said, tapping the side of her head. 'It's up here somewhere, I'm sure of it. I just need to shake it loose.'

'I'm not sure we have time for that.'

'Exactly.' Faye turned up a path towards the vicarage

cottage. The thatch on the roof had seen better days, but the garden with its herbaceous borders was a riot of peonies and lupins in purples, pinks, yellows and oranges. Bees buzzed all around them, and somewhere a chicken clucked as she announced the laying of an egg. 'The parish records have every birth, marriage and death in this village since the year fifteen-something-or-other. She'll be in there, we'll find her.'

'Very good,' Charlotte said with a grin. 'I quite enjoy putting the willies up Reverend Jacobs. He fondles his cross whenever he sees me.' Charlotte increased her pace and overtook Faye. She strode along the gravel path to the front door of the cottage and knocked like a debt collector.

As they waited, Charlotte stuffed her clay pipe with tobacco and struck a match to light it, puffing it into life.

'A pipe?' Faye frowned. 'Now? Bit rude, ain't it?'

Charlotte gave her a wink as she lit and sucked. She raised an impatient fist to knock on the cottage door again when it swung open. Reverend Jacobs' smile vanished immediately and, as predicted, his hand darted to the silver cross around his neck.

'M-miss Charlotte.' He forced a grin, looking to Faye and wondering what devilry had brought these two together. 'How can I help you on this fine—'

'We need to see the parish records,' Charlotte demanded between sucks of her pipe.

'Please,' added Faye, giving Charlotte a glare of disapproval. 'Where are your manners? Sorry,

Reverend. I think they're in the vestry. Would it be possible to—'

'Ah.' The vicar stretched his lips. 'Technically you need to make an appointment with the sexton and that would be for Mondays, Wednesdays and Thursdays between the hours of—'

'Not good enough,' Charlotte snapped, getting another look from Faye. 'We need to see them now.'

'Really.' Faye shook her head. 'What are you like? My dad always told me that good manners cost nothing. How did your parents bring you up?'

'My mother drowned not long after I was born and my father died in agony when I was four.'

'Well . . .' Faye faltered. 'That's still no excuse for rudeness.' She turned back to the reverend. 'Would it be possible to quickly let us in now?'

'I'm afraid I'm rather busy,' he said, moving to close his door. 'Frightfully sorry, but I have to—'

He found Charlotte's gumboot jammed between the door and the frame. She took a long drag on her pipe, the tobacco embers glowing red and white. Slowly and deliberately, she exhaled smoke over the vicar's face. Faye stiffened, recognising the warm and sweet honey scent of Charlotte's tobacco. It was the same blend that had made her feel so woozy in the Green Man the other night.

'Good Reverend,' Charlotte said, nice as pie. 'I wonder if you could kindly spare just a few minutes of your precious time to open up the vestry and leave us to look through the records? We should be forever in your debt and your place among the angels would surely be assured.' She turned to a stunned Faye. 'Polite enough?'

'Just a few minutes, you say?' Reverend Jacobs' words slurred into one another and his eyelids were heavy. 'I'm-I'm-I'm sure that won't be a . . .' He trailed off and looked around as if surprised to be there. 'I say. What was I—'

'The keys, Reverend, if you please.'

'Hmm, yes, of course, keys, keys, keys,' he said, and ambled back into the cottage to find them.

Faye drew closer to Charlotte and hissed in her ear, 'What the hell are you doing? What's in that pipe?'

'My own special blend.'

'I bet it is. You used it on me at the pub the other night, didn't you? What is it? Some sort of magic baccy? You can't do that to people.'

Charlotte said nothing, blowing more smoke over Faye's face.

'Stop it.' Faye recoiled and waved it away.

The jingle of keys came from inside the cottage and Charlotte raised a finger. *Shh.*

'Here we are,' Reverend Jacobs said, holding a ring of half a dozen black iron keys aloft and sliding them around one by one. 'Now, which one is for the vestry?'

'This one.' Charlotte snatched the keys from him.

'Ah, splendid. Do you need me to open up for you?' the vicar asked.

'We'll take it from here, thank you, Reverend.

You're too kind.' Charlotte gave him a wink and reached for the door. The vicar stepped back, clutching his cross again as she pulled the door shut.

'Just pop them through the letter box when you're done,' he called from inside, but Charlotte was already striding back towards the church.

'You can't go around messing with people's minds with your strange tobaccy,' Faye insisted as she caught up with Charlotte.

'No? I promise never to do it again.'

'Why don't I believe you?'

'Believe what you like,' Charlotte said, pipe clenched between her teeth as they came to the vestry door around the back of the church. She slipped in the old iron key, unlocking the door. 'I do.'

ꟹ

The vestry, also known as the sacristy, was a dark and chilly room all year round. Located to the rear of the main altar, it was where the candles, vestments, holy oils, hangings and altar linens were stored on teetering shelves. As Charlotte and Faye stepped in, a shaft of daylight revealed a stone washbasin for the linens against one wall and, at the back of the room, an oak trunk the size of a child's cot. The parish chest.

'Hold this.' Charlotte handed Faye the still-smoking pipe. The girl held it at arm's length as Charlotte picked another key and crouched down to open the padlock.

'Where do we start?' Faye asked.

'The headstone said Suky was born in 1868 and died

1890, yes?' Charlotte tossed away the padlock and flipped up the lid.

'S'right.'

Charlotte began sorting through the registers stacked in the trunk. The older records were parchments bound with ribbons, the more recent ones green leather books with yellowing pages. She checked the spines for dates. 'Here,' Charlotte said, hefting one out and placing it on a table, sending dust spiralling into the air.

Faye opened the door wide to let more light in and peered over Charlotte's shoulder as she leafed through the pages.

'It's all teeny-tiny, squirly-whirly writing,' Faye said. 'How can you make head or tail of it?'

'Experience,' Charlotte said, tossing one register back in the trunk and picking out another. 'When you're as old as I am . . . Ah, excellent.'

'Found it?'

'Births, marriages and deaths 1850 to 1900. Yes.' Charlotte flipped the book open and a flurry of paper particles swirled in the air. 'Oh, bugger.'

'What?'

Charlotte held the register open. Most of the pages had been nibbled down to the spine. Faye peered into the trunk to find a pair of mice huddled in the corner in a nest of yellow paper.

'Is this your doing?' she asked them. They shuffled back at the noise and there was a rustle as a tiny pink nose peeked out from the nest, followed by two more baby mice. Faye looked to Charlotte. 'We should probably tell the vicar he needs a new trunk. This one's occupied. Why . . . why're you looking at me like that?'

Charlotte was fixing Faye with narrow eyes as she propped up one arm on her elbow and tapped her lips.

'You said something earlier,' Charlotte mused. 'Something about you knowing who she was, but it just needed shaking loose.'

Faye wasn't sure she liked Charlotte's tone. 'What're you going to do to me?'

'The human mind is a mess of stuff and nonsense. I can sweep all that away and help you find what we need.'

'H-how?'

Charlotte tapped her pipe on the edge of the washbasin, emptying ashes into its bowl. 'I shall require a different instrument,' she said, reaching into her pocket and bringing out a tobacco tin. Inside, dividers separated six different blends. She took a pinch of a dark brown shag and began to stuff it into her pipe.

'You ain't messing with my brain with that.' Faye backed away and raised a warning finger.

'It won't do any harm, I promise,' Charlotte told her through clenched teeth as she lit the pipe. 'It will merely relax you for a short while, clear your mind.'

'I might not want my mind cleared,' Faye said, finding herself backed against the vestry wall and on the wrong side of the door.

Charlotte's voice was soft, seductive. 'Do you want to find out who these crow folk are, or not?'

'I do,' Faye said as Charlotte took a drag on the pipe. 'But will I be me again, after?'

'Of course,' Charlotte said, gently blowing smoke over Faye's face. It had the zingy scent of oranges and Faye let it sink into her lungs.

'Tell me.' Charlotte's voice was a seductive whisper, both close enough to make the hairs on Faye's neck stand on end, and so far away that Faye's mind had to stretch to find it. 'Tell me about Suky Gabriel.'

Faye felt all extraneous thoughts fall away like leaves off a tree in autumn. Words came easily. 'I don't exactly know a Suky Gabriel, but yes, yes, that's it, I know Bertie Butterworth's mum was a Gabriel, yes, Patricia Gabriel – God rest her soul – and her sister Shirley – she's dead, too, but she was a grumpy old moo and no one had much time for her – Shirley had an aunt or a cousin or something who died young and who no one talked about because of some bad bit of business – illegitimate child or some such, terrible scandal, they reckon – and so anyways I think that must be our Suky and what time is it?' Faye gasped for air as her mind began to clutter up again.

'A quarter to two,' Charlotte said, without checking her watch.

'We need to go to the pub, right now,' Faye said.

'Why?'

'On Sundays we're open noon till two. If we're quick, we'll catch him.'

25

Bertie Begs for Mercy

The saloon bar doors of the Green Man crashed open, revealing Faye and Charlotte in silhouette. They made a peculiar pair. Charlotte, slender in her boots and summer frock, face smudged with charcoal, and Faye in dungarees, fists bunched as she glared through her specs like a hunting dog with a scent. Her mind was still tingling after her experience with Charlotte's tobacco. The floor tilted beneath her feet like the deck of a ship in a storm, and the light coming through the windows had a spectral glow to it. Apart from that she was fine.

'Where the bloody hell have you been, young lady?' Terrence said to Faye as he cleaned a pint glass behind the bar. 'I've had a rush on.'

Faye and Charlotte surveyed the room. There was one drinker in the pub.

'Course they've all gone *now*,' Terrence protested. 'Lunch is over.'

Faye ignored her dad and made for the lone drinker.

Poor, unsuspecting Bertie was sitting snug in the armchair under the old photo of the hop-pickers He was enjoying a quick half of cider while reading *The Beano* with a frown of concentration normally reserved for the likes of *War and Peace.* The look on his face as the two women caught him in a pincer movement was one of bafflement and shock. He clutched *The Beano* to his chest for protection.

'Er ... hello?' he said, eyes darting from one woman to the other, wondering what exactly he had done wrong.

'What do you know about your great-great-aunt Suky?' Faye got straight to the point, her speech only a little slurred. She could feel her mind filling up again with all kinds of day-to-day nonsense as it recovered from the effects of Charlotte's tobacco.

'Who?'

'Your mum's sister Shirley had an aunt – or she might have been a cousin – who died young and is buried at Saint Irene's. What do you know about her? What did she look like?'

Bertie's face crinkled in confusion.

'Think, Bertie, this is important,' Faye said.

'He doesn't know,' Charlotte said.

'He must. Bertie, you remember the crow folk from the other night, right?'

'The gypsies?'

'They weren't gypsies, Bertie,' Faye said, daring to glance over at her father who was giving her one of his looks. 'They were ... dressed like scarecrows.'

'Oh.' Bertie smiled like he'd worked out a difficult sum in his head. 'Yes, that lot. Queer bunch.'

'And you remember one of them was called Suky . . . ?'

More crinkling. 'Was she?' Bertie shrugged. 'I don't remember.'

'You must. She was the one who looked like a rag doll and told us she wanted Craddock.'

Bertie slowly shook his head.

'She raised up off the ground like she was hanging on a hook,' Faye persisted, but Bertie was still blank.

'She had a face made of sackcloth and buttons for eyes.'

Bertie bit his lip. *Nope.*

'She had a red gingham frock and a shawl on.'

'Oh, that one.'

'Yes.'

'She was called Suky?'

'Yes.'

'And I had an Aunt Suky?'

'Yes!'

'Did I?'

'Yes, don't you remember?'

Bertie scratched his head. 'Sorry, Faye, Miss Charlotte. I'd love to help you, but Mum knew all that stuff and she took it with her when she passed away. Dad might know, but he's out on the farm, and he's expecting me back in a minute. I could ask him, but it weren't no secret he didn't much care for Mum's side of the family, so I don't reckon he'll be much help, either.' Bertie gripped his *Beano* tighter. 'Please don't be angry.'

A dead end. Faye's mind had all but returned to its usual overstuffed self.

'Faye, floor needs sweeping and there's glasses need cleaning,' Terrence said.

And they were so close. Faye glanced down at Bertie, still using his copy of *The Beano* as a shield. Oh, poor Bertie. She never meant to frighten him.

'We could . . .' Charlotte nudged Faye as she took the pipe from her mouth, pointing its stem in Bertie's direction. 'Same blend.'

'What? No. He said he doesn't know.'

'He might be lying.'

'Bertie don't lie. Leave the poor lad be.'

'Faye, the floor,' Terrence said.

'I'll just slip off now, if it's all the same to you,' Bertie said, crouching as he ducked under and around Faye and Charlotte.

'It's not worth a try?' Charlotte asked.

'Faye.' Terrence was getting angry. 'Faye, will you listen to me? Remember what we said this morning about keeping your head screwed on?'

Faye ignored them all. She was looking straight ahead with a faraway expression.

'Faye?' Charlotte asked. 'What is it?' Charlotte followed Faye's gaze until she saw the same thing. 'Well, well, well . . .'

'What?' Bertie asked, one hand on the saloon bar door in case he had to do a runner.

Faye stepped closer to the photo of the hop-pickers hanging above the armchair. It was an old sepia photo, faded by time with the title *Hop Picking at Newton's Farm, Summer 1890*, of a group of twenty or so people gathered around a gypsy caravan and their crop of hops. Some were gypsy folk who helped with the hop picking in the summer, though most were locals of all ages, from toddlers to an old chap with a walking stick. Men stood with their arms folded, faces stern as they probably had to keep still for some time for the old camera. One held a wicker basket on his head, which must have made his arm ache. And there, at the front, was a young woman kneeling by the hops, holding a jug of water. She wore a familiar gingham frock and a shawl.

'That's her,' Faye said. 'That's Suky.'

'She's been watching us all this time.' Charlotte smiled. 'We know who she is. Now what?'

Faye hesitated. 'If she's the same Suky, if she was a living, breathing woman, then what does that make the rest of them? We need to find her and—'

'*FIRE!*' A cry came from outside. 'Fire. The barn is on fire, come help!'

[illegible]

[illegible]

[illegible]

[illegible]

[illegible]

26

Fire!

Faye and Charlotte barged past Bertie and dashed out into the street to find Ruby Tattersall calling for help, her face sweating and her bib and braces streaked with soot. Ruby was one of a dozen or so girls who had come from London to do her patriotic duty in the Women's Land Army, helping on the local farms while the men were away fighting. Ruby stood out in Faye's memory from all the other Land Girls because she was frightfully posh and had blotted her copybook in her first week by trying to milk a bull. Since then she had been a quick study and Harry now said he couldn't keep the farm going without her. She had an empty wooden bucket in one hand and was frantically waving for folk to help. 'Harry's barn,' she said, her voice choked from the smoke, 'it's on fire. We need more buckets.'

Faye started to move but found Charlotte's bony fingers gripping her arm.

'Something's not right,' Charlotte said.

'That barn is Harry's livelihood.' Faye wriggled free

of her grip. Around them, villagers were hurrying after Ruby with buckets and pails. 'Call the fire brigade and the LDV.'

'Don't go beyond the black salt,' Charlotte warned, but Faye was already running around the back of the pub where she grabbed her window-cleaning bucket. By the time she was back in the street, Terrence already had an old wooden pail and their big saucepan and Bertie was limping after him dragging a tin bath. Charlotte had vanished. Faye hoped she was heading for the telephone box by the post office, but something made her doubt it. Someone somewhere started ringing a bell and Faye put the thought aside as she hurried up the street and past the church and the pond where the white smoke could be seen between the trees, spiralling up into the blue sky.

ꞵ

Faye arrived breathless at the barn and immediately wondered if Ruby had been exaggerating. The barn was upright, solid, still in one piece with just a bit of smoke coming out of the back. It didn't look that bad.

Then Faye heard the crackle of wood burning. She ran around to the front to find the doors blazing, orange flames clinging to black timber and spreading fast. The heat pressed against her face. 'Oh, bloody heck.' She glanced back to see half the village staring gormlessly at the smoke.

The Local Defence Volunteers and the Air Raid Precaution wardens were the ones who had been trained to put out fires, but they were nowhere to be seen. Apart from Faye, of course, but she didn't much fancy facing this alone.

Poor Harry looked lost as one door fell away from the barn, landing on the grass and fanning the flames.

Faye's second fire in as many days. She looked to the sky, wondering if a murmuration of birds would come to the rescue like yesterday. But as the flames grew in intensity, she realised that all the birds in the world might not be able to put this out.

'Form a chain,' Faye cried, reckoning that if no one else was bothering to take charge then she had to. 'Start at the pond and keep the water coming. Dad, you at the front. Ruby, you and Bertie get to the pond, and everyone else in between. Come on, you lot, move your arses.' She clapped her hands and folk jolted into action. In minutes, buckets full of pond water were being passed from villager to villager, to Terrence and then to Faye, who hurled the contents onto the base of the flames where it hissed. There weren't enough of them to stretch from the pond to the barn and folks were running back and forth with buckets, sloshing water onto the grass, and Faye was often left waiting for a bucket to come to her, and when it arrived, it was usually half empty.

Faye's skin prickled as the flames climbed higher. Tiles popped, the roof began to sag and beams started to bend. They were losing the fight.

'More water,' Faye hollered, the smoke catching in her throat and stinging her eyes. 'Keep it coming.'

Mr Paine arrived in his ARP helmet and joined Faye in geeing everyone along. A few of the uniformed Local Defence Volunteers appeared, led by Mr Marshall. They hurried into position with their now-repaired pump. As a handful of them unravelled the hose, the others joined the line and the buckets came faster and fuller now.

Shadows swept across the grass and caught Faye's eye. She took a moment to look up.

Birds. Hundreds of them, more than she had ever seen, gathering high above and circling like water in a drain.

'Dad, look,' Faye cried. 'Everyone. Up there.'

People kept passing buckets at first, but one by one they started to look up, nudging each other, pointing into the sky as the birds swirled above, a black sheet on the breeze.

'I saw this yesterday,' Faye said. 'The birds, they're going to put the fire out.'

Terrence shielded his eyes against the sun. 'What are you on about, girl?'

'You watch, they'll circle, then come down and—'

There was a crack of wood and the mournful groan of nails bending.

Faye was shoved aside by her dad. 'Look out!' he shouted as the barn wall closest to them came crashing down, wreathed in white smoke. The displaced air threw grit and ash in their faces as they leapt clear. Faye's specs tumbled to the ground and everything became a blur. Sweat soaked the back of her shirt and ran down her forehead and into her eyes. She scrabbled on her elbows to where her glasses had landed and wriggled them onto her nose.

'Get back,' Terrence yelled, waving people away from the fire.

'No, Dad, you wait and see,' Faye said, clambering to her feet. 'The birds, they'll—'

As she spoke, the birds broke apart and scattered, flying in every direction away from the burning barn.

'No, come back, come back,' Faye called after them. Through her smudged lenses she watched as the sky emptied and the fire in the barn raged unchallenged. Nothing could stop it now. Faye staggered away from the heat, holding her dad's hand as they propped one another up, unable to speak until they coughed the smoke from their lungs.

'Something must have scared them,' Faye managed. 'Something . . .' Faye sensed shadows shifting in the surrounding woods.

The crow folk were here.

[illegible] together and [illegible] ever. She [illegible] [illegible]

[illegible]

Now that you [illegible] and [illegible]

As [illegible] in each direction, away from the [illegible]. [illegible] have [illegible] [illegible]

[illegible] and simply [illegible] [illegible] the [illegible] [illegible]

[illegible]

[illegible]

27

Suky's Parley

The fire had been Suky's idea.

The others were afraid after what had happened with Craddock and their jolly brother. Flames catch quickly when you're made of straw, but Pumpkinhead liked the idea and that was enough. He had boasted that he could put out any fire. His bluster troubled Suky for reasons she couldn't quite fathom, but after his snapping and short temper she oh-so wanted to impress her Pumpkinhead. She put her troubling thoughts aside and volunteered to start the fire. She used the bottom of a broken bottle she found by the abbey, angling it in the sunlight to direct a beam that would set the barn alight.

Something tickled at the back of her mind as she held the glass steady. A memory or a dream, she couldn't be sure, but she had done this before. She had started a fire that got her a spanking and no supper for her troubles, that much she could remember.

As soon as the flames caught, Suky hurried to safety. It had been a dry night, but it still took a while for the barn to kindle. When it did, the crow folk retreated into the wood and waited, peering out from behind the trees.

The farmer was the first to see the black smoke and for too long he tried to put it out himself. The crow folk watched as he called on a handful of girls to help, but they were too few. He sent one into the village to raise the alarm as the flames continued to crawl and smother the barn. After some time, the people came in their droves and passed buckets along a line in a vain effort to quench the fire, but they were too late. The barn roof was already caving in and the flames licked higher. One wall came tumbling down.

'Now,' Pumpkinhead said.

At Suky's signal, her brothers and sisters stepped out of the wood and formed a circle around the villagers and the blazing barn. The villagers didn't notice them at first, and it gave Suky a peculiar thrill when they dropped their buckets, nudged their neighbours and began to wail warnings to one another. They gathered into a protective group before the crackling barn.

Pumpkinhead raised his hands. 'Good people of Woodville, listen to me . . .'

The villagers weren't having any of it, and some of the men began to roll up their sleeves, clenching their fists.

Pumpkinhead brought his gloved hands down from around his head and clapped them together. The air shifted, the angry men stumbled back and the fire . . .

. . . died out.

The crackle was silenced and the heat was gone,

replaced by a muggy dew in the air that whiffed of charred wood. The barn was a burned shell, wreathed in smoke. Blackened beams glowed white and orange in places, but the flames were dead. Pumpkinhead had told Suky and her siblings that he could put out any fire, and while she had never doubted him, to see it happen was a thrill nonetheless. Though something about it still troubled her.

'Sister,' Pumpkinhead muttered as he stepped to one side.

Suky dismissed her uneasy thoughts and broke ranks with the other crow folk, pulling her shawl tighter as she approached the villagers. They huddled closer together and Suky could see their faces better now, a blend of fear and defiance in equal parts. She stopped some distance from them, giving herself enough time to turn and run if they came for her. She called to them, 'We wants to parley.'

The villagers shared confused looks and Suky began to wonder if they could even understand her until a young woman in dungarees marched forward, glistening with sweat, her spectacles misted, her face furious.

'You did this?' She pointed at the barn with rage in her voice.

'Begging your pardon, but yes,' Suky said. 'You've gone and warned us away from the village with your shouting and hollering, you've threatened to burn us with your black salt; we cannot enter without great risk and harm to our good selves and we needs to speak to you all. I wants to make peace.'

'You want to make peace by burning down our property?'

'I ask you, if we don't stop hurting each other, where's it all going to end?' Suky said. 'I hads to get your attention and this was the only way. I'm sorry. I just wants to speak.'

The young woman in the specs folded her arms. 'Then say what you've got to say and make it fast and make it good.'

'We are the crow folk,' Suky said, struggling to find a way to match the words she was speaking with her thoughts. 'We ain't after no trouble, we ain't after no fight, we just wants to live in peace and harmony with a little dancing and cavorting when the mood takes us.'

'Peace and harmony? You got a funny way of showing it.' The girl with the specs glanced around at the other villagers who shared angry looks. 'Where's Craddock?'

Suky looked to Pumpkinhead. He nodded.

'Craddock is gone,' she said. 'Punished for his crime.'

It took a moment for the girl in the specs to find her voice. 'And what crime was that?'

'Murder most horrible,' Suky said. 'He killed our jolly brother with fire.' That troubling thought niggled at her again, but she put it aside. 'And another brother of ours was torn to pieces by one of your number, but we are willing to forgive and forget all that and put it behind us.'

'And what if we don't?'

'Then we all carry on hurting each other, day after

day, year after year. And none of us wants that, do we? What's your name, young missy?'

The girl in the specs hesitated. She knew what names were worth. 'None of your beeswax,' she said, then added, 'Why do you come here bothering us anyway?'

'You done made us,' Suky snapped, finding herself more than a little miffed by the question. 'You stuffed us with straw and hung us from crosses in your fields. You laughed at us, joked about us with your friends, looked up our skirts, threw balls at us and called us Aunt Sally—'

'No.' The girl raised a finger. 'We might've made scarecrows, but never any like you. What do you call yourself? Suky, isn't it?'

Suky nodded.

'But that's not your real name, is it?' the girl in the specs said. 'Your real name is Susannah Gabriel. Is that right?'

Suky's mind rushed with memories of her mother calling her name, teachers, her father. *Susannah. Susannah. Susannah.* She hated the name. Hated, hated, hated it. Susannah was always being told off, always getting the blame, but Suky could be whoever she wanted to. Suky fell in love with a boy, Suky ran away to the wood, Suky felt his warm hands on her skin, Suky's heart fluttered as she kissed him.

'Silence!' Pumpkinhead's voice shattered her memories, and Suky felt giddy as he stepped forward. 'Enough of your lies. Where are your witches?' His question echoed across the field. 'The venerable Mrs Teach. Is she here?'

'She's at home, resting,' the girl said. 'Poor love nearly had a heart attack the other night when one of you lot came for her.'

'Oh, really? That's what she told you?' Pumpkinhead's zigzag smile creaked into a smirk. 'Your witches have a book. A book of magic. Give it to me and all this will go away. You have till sundown tomorrow. Deny us what we ask, and . . .' He clapped his hands once more, the air shifted and the flames raged again. The heat bloomed and what little was left of the barn's roof collapsed in on itself. 'Brothers and sisters,' he cried to the rest of the crow folk. 'Retreat!' On his word, the crow folk hurried back to the wood. Suky felt him take her hand and pull her into the shelter of the trees, his soothing voice saying over and over, 'Lies, Suky, it's all lies, don't listen to them.'

More cries from the villagers rose behind them, but one cut through all the others and Suky wondered what it meant.

'Faye, Faye, they got your dad!'

28

Into the Wood

As the flames consumed the barn, villagers ran to save themselves, but Terrence kept throwing water on the blaze. He was alone when four of the crow folk bundled into him in a rugby scrum. They pinned him to the ground as they took a limb each before carrying him off into the woods, thrashing and cursing against the backdrop of roiling flames.

Bertie was the first to see. 'Faye, Faye, they got your dad!'

Faye had never much been one for running, but she gave chase like Jesse Owens at the Olympics when the crow folk took her father.

Bertie tried to keep up with Faye, though his uneven legs were no match for hers. 'Faye, be careful,' he called after her, but his voice faded as she plunged into the wood.

Faye's chest burned and she had a stitch in her side, but she kept running. The fire threw long, swooping shadows and the trees shifted like dancers at a ball.

The whoops and cries of the crow folk echoed around her, their wild, waving arms blending into the shadows. The ground moved under her feet, the sky above twisted and the clouds smudged like a watercolour left in the rain.

Faye lost sight of the crow folk.

'Dad,' she cried again and again. 'Dad, I'm coming!'

'*Dad! Dad!*' came the mocking replies of the unseen crow folk, followed by cackles and caws of laughter.

A twig snapped close by and Faye whipped around, losing her balance and tripping on a root. She fell hard on the ground but picked herself up pronto. She left no footprints and the glow of the barn fire was lost in the thick of the trees. There was no path here and the canopy above was so dense that only dappled light fell around her.

'Dad!'

Again, the mocking voices came. '*Dad! Dad!*' The words ricocheted off the tree trunks around her. No sign of her father, no sign of Bertie, no way of knowing the path home. Panic began to scratch at her, so she ran. The direction didn't matter. She ran and ran, calling after her father, 'I'm coming, Dad, I'm coming.'

ꞵ

The woodland around the village could be unforgiving to those who lacked direction. Smaller creatures followed their noses and birds flew above the canopy, but when humans got lost they would choose a direction and follow it, change their minds, turn back, choose another direction, follow that, change their minds again and again and again until they either wound up back where they started, or were spat out in a strange place wondering how on earth they had got there. Sometimes, there was no way out. In the freezing rain and the snow more than a few had died, lost in its labyrinth, only to be found later in the thaw. In the heat of summer, some wilted for want of water during the day and made a feast for hunters at night.

This girl was lost and alone and zigzagging deeper and deeper into the wood and she would not stop. But the wood knew someone was watching over her. Someone was always watching over her.

❦

Faye was not panicking. Definitely not. She, Faye Bright, did not panic.

Ever.

Much.

It had been some time since she last heard the cries of her father or the crow folk, but she followed their echo in a straight line. She would continue on this course until she found them. And if she came to the edge of the wood, she would go back the way she'd come, looking for clues. She would not give up. Not on her father. Not now. Not ever.

Blimey, her mouth was dry and her head was pounding.

The stream that came off the River Wode had to be nearby – she could hear its trickle – but she didn't want to risk veering off the path and so carried on with a dry mouth. Her run became a jog, which became little more than a walk with flailing hands and heavy, flappy feet. The pain in her head moved behind her eyes, her thoughts sloshed around in her skull, her heart threatened to pop from her chest. Faye's lips were dry and flaky and she was wheezing with every step. She had to stop.

Faye could no longer hear the stream.

She could go back and try to find it. Or she could carry on. Her legs ached, her lungs burned. She hadn't noticed it when she was running, but now she had stopped she felt the weight of her legs. She tried running again but her body protested. It wanted rest. It needed water.

Faye thought back to her last proper exchange of words with her father. Before the fire, in the pub. He was angry at her. No, not angry. Disappointed. She had promised to keep her head screwed on, and there she was gallivanting about with a witch looking for clues about strange scarecrow people.

'Oh, Dad, I'm sorry. I'm . . . I'm coming, I promise, I promise, I . . .'

Faye leaned forwards, hands resting on her thighs. She could sit for a while. Just to catch her breath.

She fell back onto her bottom, noticing a few bright red cherries on the ground, dropped by some squirrel in a hurry to get home. She snatched them up and chewed on them, the flavour bursting across her tongue, but it wasn't enough. Faye needed water. Lots of water.

And rest. Just a quick break. She could …

She could …

She could …

She could lie down among the sticky sycamore leaves and sleep …

Just …

For a bit …

ᛒ

Faye's mind wandered in the dark. It took her to last summer, before the war, when no one had a care in the world. Memories came and went in a flash. Pulling pints in the Green Man. Eating strawberries and cream. Helping with the hop picking. Then, after summer, listening to Mr Chamberlain on the radio. War came, evacuee children with little cardboard suitcases and gas masks huddled in groups; everyone had a uniform now and so many of the young men left the village to fight. Though not much else changed. Faye helped harvest the squashes on Ernie Teach's allotment. He gave her cloudy lemonade, the taste sharp and refreshing. Weighing and measuring the pumpkins for the harvest festival. Ernie carving eyes and a smile in one and fixing it as a head on his scarecrow.

ᛒ

Faye jolted awake. She had only closed her eyes for a moment, she was sure, but somehow the trees were full of birdsong.

Ernie Teach's scarecrow had a pumpkin for a head.

Lots of scarecrows had pumpkins for heads. It didn't mean a thing, but Faye recalled its dusty dinner jacket and scuffed top hat being awfully like the outfit of the one that had just kidnapped her father.

Jays screamed at her, magpies cackled and crows cawed. The birds were insistent she get up.

'All right, all right, I'm not stopping, I'm not.' Faye heaved herself up onto her hands and knees. 'Yes, yes, I'm . . .'

On every twig of every branch of every tree sat a bird.

And every single one of them was staring straight at Faye and singing in unison. Faye felt a tingle at the nape of her neck. The air was charged like a storm about to break.

'Hello,' Faye said, getting to her feet.

The birds fell silent.

'You were supposed to help. You were supposed to put the fire out.'

Some of the birds shuffled guiltily.

'Yeah, you should be,' Faye said. 'But you help me find my pa and you can redeem yourselves.'

The warbling resumed, a debate in chirps and twitters.

'Yeah, yeah, all right, give it a rest.'

As one, the birds fell silent again.

'You're a peculiar lot, aren't you? Escaped from a circus, did ya?'

As one, they flapped into the air and moved further down the path before settling in new trees, waiting for Faye.

'I should follow you, then, should I?' The birds remained silent. 'Just let me get my breath.'

The birds began cheeping again, irritated and impatient.

'Fine, right, yes, hold your horses.' Faye staggered after them and, as before, they flitted from tree to tree, waiting for her to catch up before moving on again, leading her through the wood. 'Thank you, thank you,' Faye managed between gasps of air. 'I'm coming. Dad, I'm coming, I'm . . .'

Faye stumbled out of the treeline and into a field. Above her, the birds dispersed silently into a sky with stars peeking between sheets of grey cloud.

'Why's it . . . ?' Faye panted. 'Why's it so dark?'

By rights, Faye should have come out of the other side of the wood by Farmer Dell's brassica field, but she was back where she started by Harry Newton's barn. Bertie sat alone on his upturned tin bath by the smouldering remains.

'Why?' Faye called after the birds. 'Why did you bring me back here? I didn't want to come back here. I wanted to find my dad.'

Bertie jolted upright when he heard her. 'Faye, where have you been?' He hobbled over to her as fast he could. 'We thought they'd got you, too.'

'What . . . what time is it?'

'It's after eleven,' Bertie said. 'You've been gone hours.'

'Hours? That don't make sense. I was only . . .' Faye grabbed Bertie's arm. 'My dad. Have you seen my dad?'

'Faye, listen, please. Miss Charlotte says—'

'I don't care about her. Have you seen my dad?'

'She says you're to get the book and go to her cottage immediately. Mrs Teach is there, too.'

'Mrs Teach? With Charlotte?'

'Right away, she said. She made that very clear. "*No matter how much that girl stamps her feet, you send her straight here with the book. Don't you let me down, Bertie Butterworth,*" she told me. And I'm inclined to listen to her.'

'I don't stamp my feet,' Faye said, catching herself with a foot raised in the air. She gently lowered it again. 'What book?' Faye asked, though she knew the answer.

'I don't know, but she said it in a way that made it sound like you would know, so I didn't ask her for any more details because ... Well, I'll be honest, because she scares the willies out of me. We're all scared, Faye, what with the fire and the crow folk and the birds. No one knows what's going on so they've all gone home, closed their curtains and put the kettle on. Do ... do you know what's going on?'

There was something in Bertie's tone that saddened Faye. He couldn't quite bring himself to accuse her of causing all this madness, but the insinuation was there.

'I had nothing to do with this, you know that, don't you, Bertie?'

He nodded and took a step back. 'It's just ... Milly Baxter and Betty Marshall said you spooked them outside the church earlier today and put a curse on them and—'

'What? Fibbers.'

'A-and you've spent all day with Miss Charlotte going around the village asking about dead people and then them crow folk show up and burn the barn and now, well, tongues are wagging.'

'Are they now?'

'N-not mine,' Bertie protested. 'I ain't said nothing.'

'Do you believe them, Bertie? Do you really think I put a curse on Milly Baxter?'

Bertie scratched the back of his head. 'Course not. Will you go to them, though? Miss Charlotte and Mrs Teach, that is?'

'Yes.' Faye started marching towards the village. 'I need them to help me find my dad. We can't let what happened to Craddock happen to him, too.'

'Good, cos that's the thing about the book, Faye. You've got to take it to Miss Charlotte. She said . . .' Bertie took a breath and bit his lip as he hurried after her. 'She said it was the only way to save your pa.'

29

Three Witches

Bertie was friendly enough when he bade Faye goodnight, but there was something different in the way he spoke to her now. He was scared of magic, strange books, birds and now her, and he couldn't get away from Faye quick enough. It broke Faye's heart to see him so, and she wanted to reassure him that he had nothing to fear from her, but what mattered to her most now was getting her dad back safe. And to do that she had to keep an appointment with a pair of witches.

Returning home to an empty pub wasn't easy. Faye half expected her dad to pop up from behind the bar and start making jokes, but it remained dark and cold. She went straight to the trunk in the cellar, unfastened the rusty padlock and retrieved the book. She couldn't resist a quick look through its pages, hoping that some solution would present itself, but its words and sketches remained a mystery to her. The witches would know. She imagined them flicking through the book, finding just the right ritual, saying a few magic words and her dad would walk through the door again. She snapped the book shut, stuffed it in her satchel and closed the trunk.

ꝭ

It was past midnight when the three of them gathered at Charlotte's cobwood cottage. Faye arrived red-cheeked and breathless from cycling, then trudged through the undergrowth down the narrow woodland path. She had her satchel strapped over her shoulder, her mother's book safely tucked inside.

As Bertie promised, Mrs Teach was already at the cottage, teacup and saucer held daintily.

Charlotte offered Faye a cup of elderflower gin and a chair by the stone fireplace. A pot of stew bubbled over the flames. Faye took the gin and gulped it down. She was so knackered she reckoned if she took a seat she might never get up again, so she stayed standing, arms folded.

'You're both looking very chummy,' she started. 'I thought you two couldn't bear the sight of each other?'

'Needs must when the Devil drives,' Charlotte said, stirring the pot.

'The Devil?' Mrs Teach chortled. 'Oh, hardly. One of his minions, at the very best.'

'Right.' Faye's pointing finger swept across the room from one woman to the other. The gin had put a fire in her belly. 'You two had better start giving me some blimmin' answers right now. Who are these scarecrows? Why are they named after dead people in Saint Irene's graveyard? Why have they taken my dad? And why did they specifically ask for you?' This last was aimed at Mrs Teach, who choked on her tea. She placed the cup and saucer down with a clatter as she cleared her throat, waving Faye away.

Faye turned on Charlotte. 'And why didn't you help with the fire?'

'I told you not to go,' Charlotte said, stuffing her pipe with tobacco. Faye tensed, wondering what strange smoke would come from it. 'It was clearly a trap.' Charlotte struck a match and puffed on the pipe. The tobacco was a regular blend from the smell of it, and Faye allowed herself to relax a little.

'Why? Why was it clearly a trap? What are you seeing that I ain't?' Faye snapped. 'And will you just stop it with the mysterious witchy woman act. Speak plainly and truthfully, or I swear I shall empty that pot of stew over your blimmin' head.'

'Young lady,' Charlotte said between puffs as she lit her pipe, 'have you ever considered *not* flying off the handle at the slightest provocation?'

Mrs Teach brushed her skirt. 'Now, now, Miss Charlotte, she's still a tyke. Let her have her little tantrum.'

Faye ground her teeth and balled her fists. 'Perhaps, ladies,' she chose her words carefully, 'the two of you should stop being so snooty and treat me like a grown-up?'

'We will when you act like one.' Mrs Teach's smile fell short of her eyes as she poured herself another cup of tea.

Faye took a step forward, but a smoke ring got in her face and Charlotte followed in its path.

'We will solve nothing if we continue like this,' Charlotte said. 'To answer your question and to speak plainly and truthfully, when the alarm was raised for the barn fire, I saw no value in walking into a confrontation of the crow folk's devising. Instead, I sought counsel with Mrs Teach. We have agreed to put aside our differences for the moment and solve our little problem. And yes, Faye, I am a witch. I have never pretended otherwise.'

'And I've been practising the craft since I was a child,' Mrs Teach said, adding a splash of milk and two lumps of sugar before stirring them into her tea. 'My nana said I had the gift and showed me a few things, though I rarely dabble these days.'

'What did I say about lying?'

'I'm telling the truth, Faye, though I must confess this past week has been rather extraordinary. And finally, young lady, we come to you.'

Both heads turned to Faye.

'What? I ain't no witch,' Faye protested.

'You brought the book?' Charlotte asked, reaching out.

Faye glanced down at the satchel hanging at her waist. 'It was my mum's.'

'We thought it was lost,' Charlotte said.

'She told us she was going to burn it,' Mrs Teach added.

'Who did?'

'Your mother.'

'You knew my mother?' Faye tried to imagine the three of them together and a little of the old anger flared. Then she wondered how Mum had put up with the pair of them. 'Did you know her well?'

'Not nearly well enough, it seems,' Mrs Teach said. 'She promised us she would get rid of the book, a promise she clearly broke.'

'But we'll use it, right?' Faye looked from witch to witch. 'We'll open it up, find a spell to send these crow folk on their way and get my dad back, yes?'

Charlotte and Mrs Teach shared shifty glances.

'Then what *are* you planning to do with it?' Faye asked, her eyes darting from the satchel to the fireplace. Charlotte and Mrs Teach said nothing in such a way that it confirmed Faye's worst fears. She clutched the satchel tighter. 'You are not flippin' well burning it.'

'Faye, petal, calm down,' Mrs Teach said. 'You have to understand who we're dealing with here and why we must defeat him.'

'Him?' Faye asked. 'That pumpkin-headed one? Is he ... is he the Devil?'

'Hardly.' Charlotte hefted a leather-bound book from a shelf onto a trunk in the middle of the room. 'He takes the form of a scarecrow to fool farmers.' Kneeling, she flicked through a number of pages with old woodcut illustrations of demons, gods and monsters until she came to one of Pumpkinhead and the falling birds. She spun the book for Faye to see. 'A trickster, from a lower order of demons. Ambitious, cunning, very dangerous, and his like has not been seen in this realm for at least three hundred years.'

'A demon?' Faye asked with a squint.

'One who takes the souls of the dead and resurrects them in effigies of straw. He bends them to his will and draws his power from their devotion.'

'You expect me to believe that?'

'You were ready to believe in the Devil a moment ago.'

'That's different.' Faye thought back to her candle magic and trying to locate Craddock. 'There ain't no such thing as magic.'

'How can you be so sure?'

'Because I tried it and it didn't work.'

There followed a harmonic groan of comprehension from Charlotte and Mrs Teach.

'What?' Faye asked.

'So it *was* you,' Mrs Teach said, pursing her lips in disapproval.

'What was me?'

'Someone has been dabbling in magic,' Charlotte said.

'Someone who hadn't the first clue what they were dabbling in,' added Mrs Teach.

'The power of magic is like a candle in the dark,' Charlotte said. 'As well as showing the way, it can also draw moths to the flame.'

'And this demon is one big bugger of a moth,' Mrs Teach added.

'That weren't me,' Faye said. 'I didn't summon no demon. He turned up before I—'

'Before you what?' Mrs Teach asked.

'Before I *dabbled*. You can't blame him on me,' Faye said, splaying fingers across her chest. 'Someone else must be doing magic and I'm wondering which one of you it is.'

'Neither of us are fools who summon demons.' Charlotte arched an eyebrow. 'Tell us everything, and we shall tell you where you went wrong.'

'I tried to talk to you the other day, y'know,' Faye said, all defensive. 'I came here and told you I found a book, but you were all asleep in the nuddy with a frog on your belly and your goat scared me off.'

'It was a toad, and he's not my goat.'

'You miss your mother, don't you, petal?' Mrs Teach pouted in sympathy. 'Were you trying to make contact?'

'No, I was trying to find Craddock, if you must know. Candle magic, and I didn't summon any demons.'

'Not intentionally, perhaps,' Charlotte said.

'Yes, it's easy to make a mistake when you're dabbling, poppet,' Mrs Teach said, then held out her hand. 'May I see the book?'

'Not until I get some answers,' Faye said. 'Pumpkinhead mentioned you by name at the barn fire, Mrs Teach. He gave you a nod when he first came to the village. What was all that about, eh?'

Charlotte turned to Mrs Teach and tilted her head. 'Oh, really?'

Mrs Teach shifted in her armchair, finding herself outflanked by Charlotte and Faye. 'How should I know what he's on about?' she said.

'Maybe we should ask your Ernie?' Faye said, hands on hips. 'After all, he's the one who had a scarecrow on his allotment that looked just like old Pumpkinhead, and your Ernie is the one who mysteriously came back from the dead.'

'That was not my Ernie.'

'Then what was he?'

'I have no idea.' Mrs Teach produced a hanky from her sleeve and dabbed the theatrical tears glistening in her eyes, her voice trembling. 'It was your magic, young lady. A demon would not risk crossing over unless he got a whiff of something special, and that would be your mother's book. As soon as you started reciting its magic, you drew his attention and he took the form of a scarecrow and now he's created his own army and the only thing keeping him out is us.'

'If he gets the book and uses its rituals, then there would be no stopping him,' Charlotte agreed.

'That's why we're forbidden from writing any of this down,' Mrs Teach said.

'*You've* got a book.' Faye jabbed an accusing finger at Charlotte's leather-bound volume on the trunk.

'Prints and woodcuts, darling,' Charlotte said. 'Reference only. No spells, no rituals, no secrets. It's all up here.' She tapped the side of her head with the bit of her pipe.

'We swore an oath to prevent our knowledge from

getting into the wrong hands,' Mrs Teach said. 'Never mind the Nazis, just you wait till a demon starts sharing our secrets with the whole underworld. There'll be no stopping the scaly-backed buggers.'

'Could you imagine if Vera got wind of this?' Charlotte muttered as an aside.

'Gods forbid.' Mrs Teach rested a hand on her chest.

'Who's Vera?'

'Never you mind,' Mrs Teach said. 'Give us the book.'

'Why would my mother do it?' Faye asked. 'If she knew it was forbidden, then why would she put it all in a book?'

'Because she was like you.' Mrs Teach clasped her hands between her belly and her bosom. 'Never did as she was bloody told, was too curious by half and she never knew when to be quiet.'

'She was, however, an excellent witch,' Charlotte added.

'A powerful practitioner,' Mrs Teach agreed. 'With great foresight. I half wonder if she knew she wouldn't live long enough to train you and that's why she put all of her knowledge into a book.'

Faye looked from Charlotte to Mrs Teach and allowed herself to flop down in an armchair. She thought about the mother she barely knew. The woman who had known and practised magic with these two. An excellent witch. A powerful witch. Faye had so many questions. She wished she could have just five minutes with Mum to . . .

Faye's thoughts trailed off. She realised it was the first time she had thought of her mother without that familiar flash of anger. There was something else instead. Something that might be described as a tiny flurry of happiness.

'You're witches?' she asked and they nodded. 'And my mum was a witch?' More nods. 'And I'm a witch?' The nods became *maybe* side-to-side shakes. 'And this Pumpkinhead fella—'

'Kefapepo,' Charlotte interrupted.

Faye's heart nearly stopped. 'W-wot?'

'That's the demon's name,' Mrs Teach said. 'Though I prefer Devious Bugger.'

'Kefa . . . Kefapepo,' Faye said, nodding like it was the most normal thing in the world to discover your mother had named a bell-ringing method after a demon. 'That's . . . that's a funny name.' She was torn between wanting to tell Charlotte and Mrs Teach everything and listening to the alarm bell at the back of her brain warning her this would be a very bad thing indeed. She heaved herself out of the armchair. 'You know, I've come over all peculiar and I've had a really long day and I'm tired. I think I'll go home now.'

'Leave the book,' Charlotte said.

'No.' Faye shook her head. 'I ain't leaving it, and you ain't burning it.'

'If we are to defeat Kefapepo . . .' Mrs Teach trailed off as Faye let out a little sob. 'Oh, petal, don't make this harder than it already is.'

Charlotte was less moved. 'To defeat the demon,

we start by destroying that book before he gets his hands on it.'

'No you bloody don't.' Faye backed away from them, gripping her satchel tight.

'It's what he wants, Faye,' Charlotte said, closing in on her.

'It will give him more power than any demon has had in hundreds of years,' Mrs Teach added.

'If we destroy it, what will he do to my dad? He'll hurt him, maybe kill him.'

'He might be doing that anyway,' Charlotte said.

'What?' Faye wailed. 'No. You don't know that.'

'We know demons,' Mrs Teach said, 'and all they want is power. The power in that book.'

'I won't give it to him, I promise,' Faye said, bumping into an armchair. She looked around for the way out. The door she came in through was behind Charlotte and Mrs Teach. She was going the wrong way. Trapped.

'I doubt he'll ask for it politely,' Charlotte said. 'He'll take it by whatever means necessary.'

Faye spotted another door to the kitchen. She turned to make a dash for it.

And promptly tripped over the trunk with Charlotte's book and Mrs Teach's teapot and cups. They clattered to the floor and Faye landed flat on top of Charlotte's old leather-bound book.

'Faye.' Mrs Teach came towards her, arms outstretched. Faye couldn't be sure if she was going to help her up or make a grab for her. She didn't wait to find out. Faye kicked her legs like a toddler having a tantrum to scare the woman off. She scrabbled to her feet, dashed through to the kitchen, out the back door and into the wood.

30

A Most Annoying Hostage

'You can think, even though your brains are all stuffed with straw?'

The old man was getting on Suky's nerves.

'Only, what happens when you get field mice crawling up your skirts? You don't have to answer that, of course. A bit too personal, I understand, but it makes you wonder, don't it? I mean, what with you being living, breathing scarecrows and all.'

Suky had not heard from the birds for hours, and she wanted to know if the girl with the glasses was safe, but they no longer flew to the abbey. Scared, Suky reckoned. They had fled the moment Suky and her siblings arrived at the burning barn. No. Sooner than that. They scattered when they caught sight of Pumpkinhead. He was the one who scared them.

'It's marvellous, simply marvellous. Of course, I say living and breathing . . . You're clearly living, but does you have lungs for breathing, eh? Take a breath, go on. What does it feel like? No? Fair enough, you ain't a performing monkey, are ya? I know I shouldn't go on, but I can't help myself.'

Whenever Suky looked at Pumpkinhead now, she felt a tightness where her heart used to be. His smile was fixed in place, though he was quick to anger now. He would rage, then catch himself and stop.

'Do you sneeze? And what do you eat? Ooh, and – bit personal this – but do you need to go the khazi? No, fair enough, I've crossed a line in the sand there. Don't answer. Unless you want to?'

This old man simply had not stopped talking all night and all morning, and Suky was trying to think.

'What happens when it rains? Do you have to wring yourselves out?'

Suky didn't even want him here. She was cross Pumpkinhead had given the order to take him, and now the old man was driving her potty. Oh, she wished the birds were here, she missed their song.

'Do you have to keep yourselves stuffed on a regular basis?'

'Silence!' Pumpkinhead snapped at him.

Terrence – they all knew his name as he insisted on introducing himself to everyone: 'Hello, I'm Terrence. How d'you do? Luvverly to meet ya' – was tied to a stake in the middle of the ruins of Therfield Abbey. He sat on his backside, wrists bound, legs splayed out, cheerily chatting away to no one in particular. Suky was sure he was only doing it to antagonise Pumpkinhead.

'Fair enough, guv,' Terrence said. 'I am goin' on a bit,

there's no denying that. I used to get like this when I was first stepping out with the young lady who would eventually deign to become my missus. She used to say, "Terrence, my love, what on earth are you wittering about now?" She reckoned it was – now what did she call it? – a nervous reaction. Yeah, that was it. When I get nervous I start to waffle on about precisely bugger all till the cows come home. Which is peculiar cos I'm more of a listener by nature. Comes from being a landlord. You have to be a good listener, too. Punters come in after a hard day's toil and they need to let off a bit of steam, so you listen to whatever it is they have to say. And it's not a question of just nodding while you clean a pint glass. Oh no. You have to pay attention, cos sooner or later they'll say, "What do you think of that then, Terrence?" and you'll have to give 'em your twopenn'orth, though of course you don't want to get too involved, so generally you tell 'em what they want to hear . . .'

Pumpkinhead paced around the jabbering man, stopping every now and then to look up into the dimming daylight as if waiting for some kind of signal. The other crow folk languished around the abbey, mindless, floppy, waiting for someone to tell them what to do.

'That's the secret to being a landlord, you're everyone's best friend. Agree with every word they say so long as they keep a civil tongue and buy a round occasionally. I love my job, I really do.'

Suky, for her part, was trying to piece together the flashes of memory that kept coming to her. *Susannah*

Gabriel. That had been her name. That had been her life before. No, it couldn't be possible. She was Suky, here and now. There was no before. Susannah was a lie. The villagers were afraid of them and told lies to spread their fear, Pumpkinhead had warned her. Yes, that must be it.

'How long we gonna be here, eh?' Terrence asked. 'I don't mind telling you my backside is a bit moist, and I don't much fancy another case of the old Chalfont Saint Giles. Anyone got a cushion?'

'Speak not in riddles, man.' Pumpkinhead threw his hands in the air.

'Piles,' Suky said without thinking. 'It's rhyming slang. Chalfont Saint Giles. Piles.' How did she know? One of Susannah's memories? She shook the thought from her head, took the crook of Pumpkinhead's arm and led him away to the abbey's stone steps. 'Why did we take him, my Pumpkinhead?' she asked. 'Why don't we just scarper from this place? We've made the villagers angry and they'll come after us with flames and blades and worse.'

'On the contrary, sister Suky,' Pumpkinhead said, his voice calming after the strain of yelling at Terrence. 'They're scared now. They fear us and they will bring us the book and then we will use it and we will have our home.'

'We won't do him no harm, will we?'

'A cushion. A cushion. My kingdom for a cushion.' Terrence cackled, causing Pumpkinhead to glance back at him.

'I will if he doesn't shut up,' the scarecrow muttered.

'Please don't.'

'I jest, my sister. I promise. No harm will come to him. This will all be over soon.'

'Good, good,' Suky said, then hesitated. 'I must ask, though, and forgive my impertinence . . . Was she . . . ? Was she right about me?'

'The girl at the fire?'

'She said my name was Susannah. And she's stirred up all sorts of strange thoughts in my head, and I'm wondering who I rightly am, and—'

'Hush, sister Suky.' Pumpkinhead took her hand in his. 'She spoke lies designed to befuddle and divide us. Here, let me show you.' He turned to the other crow folk and raised his arms. He didn't even need to speak. They leapt to their feet, ready for action, eager to please. 'Brothers and sisters, come closer, heed me, yes.' He stood behind Suky, hands resting on her shoulders. 'Tell me, brothers and sisters. Who stands before you here?'

'Our sister Suky,' one cried.

'The bravest and wisest of us all,' said another.

'And fair and graceful.'

'His lips are moving,' said Terrence.

Suky felt Pumpkinhead's fingers tense on her shoulders.

'That's very clever, though,' Terrence said. 'What is that? Ventriloquism? Or did you all rehearse this earlier? Either way, marvellous. Well done, everyone. Y'know, a few of us thought you was some sort of travelling circus when you first turned up, and you can see why, can't you, eh? Triffic, really triffic.'

As the old man continued to waffle, Suky felt a stirring inside her. A muddle of shame and hurt. Pumpkinhead relaxed his grip on her shoulders. 'Look at me, sister Suky.'

She turned, finding herself staring up into his hollow triangle eyes.

'You know I only want the best for all of you, don't you? I would not hurt you, or put you in any kind of danger. You understand, don't you, sister?'

'Yes, my Pumpkinhead,' Suky said, though the words came without thought or passion. She just said them because she knew that was what he wanted to hear. Another thought came to her, one that had been niggling her for some time. 'I have a question, though.'

'Ask it and I shall answer,' Pumpkinhead replied.

'You are very powerful, my Pumpkinhead, we've all seen that. You stopped that fire with a clap of your hands.'

'I did.'

'And then you made it start again.'

'Yes, yes.'

He snapped this last and Suky could tell he was getting impatient. 'So, my question is this, and bear in mind this has been swirling around in my head for some time—'

'Suky. Ask your question.'

'If you are so powerful that you can start and stop a fire with just a clap of your hands,' Suky said, her words tumbling out, 'why did you let our jolly brother burn?'

The world fell silent. The wind dropped to nothing, the crow folk leaned forward to hear the answer and even Terrence shut up.

'Craddock set him alight,' Suky continued, hearing the shiver in her own voice, 'and you could've stopped him burning. So why didn't you?'

Pumpkinhead lowered his gaze. 'Oh, Suky, my sister. You break my heart. You think me all-powerful, like the gods of old. I speak plainly when I say that I am nothing without my brothers and sisters.' He stretched his arms out to the crow folk. A few reached back. 'I am nothing without you, Suky.' He took her hand, turning it over, squeezing it, patting it. 'Not a day goes by when I do not weep for our fallen brother. Would that I had the power to save him, to resurrect him, even. Oh, Suky, I was so weak then, but with all of you here I am strong. *We* are strong.' He raised a fist skywards, and all the crow folk – save Suky – joined him with a cheer.

'That's all well and good,' Suky said, 'but you haven't really answered my—'

'Do you trust me, Suky?'

Suky looked from Pumpkinhead to Terrence and to her straw siblings. 'I suppose I must,' she said.

'Good, good, my sister, because without trust we have—' He tensed again and his head snapped around as if he had heard something.

'What is it?' Suky asked.

'Someone is calling to me,' he said. 'Someone is using magic. Brothers and sisters. Our time has come.'

31

A Thin Black Line

Faye struck a match and lit a candle. She stood behind Charlotte's line of black salt at the crossroads by the old Roman bridge. As the burning tang of phosphorous reached her nose, Faye shook the match out, tossed it away and glanced back down the winding road to the village. The only route from the abbey to Woodville.

Faye had cycled here at speed to get a head start in case Charlotte and Mrs Teach chased after her. She had quickly stopped off at the pub to grab the candle and matches. She was tired, hot and whiffy with mayflies in her hair and greenflies on her dungarees, and she spat midgies from her lips.

The Woodville she had pedalled through was a ghost town. It was after midnight. The pubs were closed, shops and houses and cottages locked and bolted. Windows and doors were blacked out, though there was no ARP patrol tonight. Bertie was right. After the barn fire and her father's abduction, everyone had gone home and put on their kettles and wirelesses in the hope it would all blow over by tomorrow.

Faye was on a mission to make those hopes come true.

The moon was high, shrouded in cloud. There was a hint of salty sea air on the breeze. A storm was approaching from the coast. She had to be quick. Faye turned, the book at her feet, as she offered the candle to the north. '*Protect with light that is pure and true, protect my home the whole day through.*'

The east. '*Protect with light that is pure and true, protect my home the whole day through.*'

The south. '*Protect with light that is pure and true, protect my home the whole day through.*'

The west. '*Protect with light that is pure and true, protect my home the whole day through.*'

If using magic was like a flame to a moth, then she would bring the crow folk to her now with this basic protection chant she had found in the book. She wanted something she could do quickly and without any fuss. Simple candle magic.

She turned to the north again. '*Protect with light that is pure and true . . .*'

Shadows moved in the wood. Voices chuckled and hooted as crow folk dashed between the trees, their clumsy feet swishing through the ferns, shaking them like waving arms.

'*Protect my home the whole day through.*' Faye finished and blew out her candle. '*So mote it be.*'

'What's this?' The voice came from the edge of Faye's sight and made her shoulder blades twitch.

As she placed the candle on the ground, Pumpkinhead stalked in from the shadows of the wood. He stayed on the other side of the protective line of black salt. Faye kept her hands on her satchel, watching as his empty triangle eyes narrowed and his zigzag mouth formed a grin. Every move brought with it a creak from his shiny orange skin. Faye had never been this close to him before and her fear stirred up a simmering rage. She wanted to strike out from behind the protective line and smash his squashy head in. Faye wondered if this was how Bertie and the other villagers felt about her now. If they believed the rumours of her putting curses on the likes of Milly Baxter and consorting with witches. She took a calming breath, wondering what Charlotte or Mrs Teach might do. Faye tried to be aloof. She found herself distracted, wondering if she should take up smoking a pipe. When he spoke again, the chills returned.

'Black salt, if I'm not mistaken.' He nudged a boot close to the line and Faye's heart began to race. The tip of his boot crossed over the line of ash and began to smoulder as Charlotte's protective magic did its work. White smoke swirled up from his toes as he began to burn. He drew his foot back.

'You think that will protect you from me?'

'I reckon it might,' Faye said, keeping her voice steady though her mouth was dry and the breeze was picking up. The storm would be here soon. 'Your name is Kefapepo, right?'

Pumpkinhead inclined his head, almost impressed.

'And where did you hear my name, young lady? I'm sure they don't teach that in your churches or schools.'

'I read it in a book,' she said.

'The book you will now give to me.'

'My dad. Where is he?'

More crow folk began to emerge from the wood behind Pumpkinhead, treading lightly on tiptoes as if this was a playground game.

'Give me that.' Pumpkinhead gestured to the book at Faye's feet. 'And you shall have him.'

'Show him to me.'

'The book first.'

'My dad first.'

'The book.'

'My dad.'

'The book.'

'My dad.'

'The book.'

'My dad.'

'*The book!*'

'*My dad!* I can do this all night, chum.'

'I'm sure you can.' Pumpkinhead's face broke into a wide grin. 'You think your bravado hides your fear. That's what my kind feed on, girl. Your dread, your rage, your violence. It's like nectar to us, and you humans provide a never-ending supply. And once again you wage war and I am thrilled. This will be a feast. Your vile, petty disputes will nourish us and allow us to return to our rightful place up here, to rule in pandemonium.'

'Sorry, what was that?' Faye said, inspecting her nails. 'I weren't listening.'

'So childish.'

'Says the man with the pumpkin for a noggin. *Show me my blinkin' dad.*'

Pumpkinhead nodded and beckoned to the wood behind him. Two figures came through the maze of trees. Suky, holding Terrence's hand and swinging it like a child going for a walk, led him out onto the crossroads.

'Hello, Faye,' Terrence chirped. 'Fancy seeing you here.'

He looked chipper, if a little tired, but Faye's dad was always chipper. Faye was sure her dad could be in a room with that Mr Hitler and convince him to give up on this whole war kerfuffle and go back to painting watercolours.

'Are you all right, Dad?'

'Mustn't grumble,' he said with a shrug. 'Bum's a bit damp and I could murder a cuppa, but can't complain otherwise.'

'The book.' Pumpkinhead extended his hand.

'Let my dad go, promise to bugger off, never to be seen again, and I'll leave the book here. How about that?' Faye raised her chin.

'I don't think so.' Pumpkinhead slowly paced up and down. It reminded Faye of the time she had gone with her dad to London Zoo and watched the lions do the same. Looking at her like a snack that was just out of reach.

'You can't touch me. You cannot cross this here line.' Faye remained still, keeping one eye on the book at her feet.

'Indeed,' Pumpkinhead said. There came a distant crackle of thunder and the breeze picked up. 'But I am very, very patient.'

Faye's nose was cold, her lips chapped, and the air was chill. Somewhere in the brambles a mouse scuttled away to take cover.

'Is that your mother's book?' Terrence asked, craning his neck for a better look at the leather-bound tome at Faye's feet.

'Sorry, Dad. I put it away like I promised, honest I did. I was never going to look at it again, but . . . needs must when the Devil drives.'

'You're giving it to him?' Terrence shook his head. 'No, you can't.'

'I have to, Dad. It's the only way.'

Terrence narrowed his eyes, focusing on the book at Faye's feet. There was a glimmer of something, if not recognition. 'Oh no, wait, that's not—'

'Please, for once in your life, Dad, be quiet and leave this to me.'

'Yes. Be quiet.' Pumpkinhead reached out with a gloved hand, grabbed Terrence and yanked him close, whispering in his ear. Old words. Forbidden words. Words of power. Words of pain.

Faye watched helplessly as her father convulsed and cried in agony, his eyes rolled back and his knees buckled. He fell to the floor, his arms and legs twitching.

'Leave him alone!' Faye yelled, fighting every instinct to cross the line.

'Give me the book.'

'No, my Pumpkinhead, no. We said no hurting—' Suky rushed forwards, but Pumpkinhead swung his arm around and slapped her face with the back of his hand. Suky staggered away in shock.

'Do not interfere.' Pumpkinhead gripped Terrence's skull and once more spat words into his ear. Faye closed her eyes tight and clapped her hands over her ears to block out her father's screams.

'Give me the book,' Pumpkinhead said, 'or your father becomes one of us.'

'Stop. Yes. You can have it. I'll give you the book.'

Pumpkinhead released his hold on Terrence, who fell forward, muttering, 'Faye, no, that's not—'

'Dad, will you be quiet.'

'But, Faye—'

'Dad, shut up.'

'No tricks,' Pumpkinhead said, reaching out for it.

'Back off,' Faye ordered, picking up the book and clutching it to her chest. 'Go on, back off and you shall have it.'

Pumpkinhead whispered words into Terrence's ears once more and the old man's eyes widened with the shock of the pain.

Faye felt a cold drop of rain on her cheek, followed by another and another. She glanced down to see fat spots of the stuff pitter-pattering on the road. On the black salt.

'Oh no.'

The storm arrived, the downpour hissing through the leaves and splashing around them. The black salt began to blur. Faye looked up to find Pumpkinhead grinning. The rain was lashing down and the protective line of black salt would be washed away in moments.

Faye looked up into Pumpkinhead's triangle eyes. 'You want this book, you big orange-faced wazzock? You can have it.' Faye spun like a shot-putter and tossed the book into the darkness of the wood.

Pumpkinhead dashed after it. 'Find it, brothers and sisters. Find it and bring it to me now!'

Faye rushed to her father who was curled into a ball on the ground. 'Dad. Up on the bicycle now.' She hefted him to his feet and the two of them stumbled over to where her bicycle lay on the ground. She hauled it upright as he struggled to get a leg over the saddle. 'Come on, Dad. Budge up and hold on,' she said, squeezing herself between him and the handlebars and pushing away before starting to pedal down the road to the village. Her dad might look rake-thin, but the extra weight meant it took her twice as long to get moving. 'Help me, Dad. Push.'

Terrence looked back at the wood where the crow folk were rummaging in the long grass for the book. 'Faye, I was trying to tell you – that's not your mother's book.'

'I know, Dad, I know. And we have about ten seconds before old pumpkin-bonce figures that out. Let's go!'

32

THE GOD OF SCARECROWS

'Master. I have found it, I have it.' Lightning pulsed silently in the clouds above as the scarecrow with the smiling clown face scurried over to Pumpkinhead. Clown-face was holding the thick, leather-bound book aloft like a raggedy Moses descending from Mount Sinai.

'Well done, brother, give it to me.' Pumpkinhead snatched the book and began fumbling through the pages with his gloved hands.

Suky stood apart from the others, watching from the crossroads as rain pelted down and thunder rolled overhead. She knew she should be feeling the cold and the wet, but her only sensation was the shame in her belly.

Her beloved Pumpkinhead had struck her across the face and turned away. Even his name was false. What had the girl with the specs called him? Kefapepo? All of his words were lies. She knew that now. And she knew she did not belong here.

'No. No.' Pumpkinhead raged as the wind began

to whip over page after page of the book. The other scarecrows crowded around him. Suky shuffled forwards and craned her head for a better look. It was a book of old wood carvings. Pictures. Few words. 'This is not it. This is not the book. You fool, this is not the book. This is not the book!' He slapped the book shut, gripped it with both hands and began to beat the smiling clown over the head with it. 'She lied. She lied to us.' Some of the crow folk laughed and clapped and pointed, others backed away in fear as lightning flashed and thunder rumbled.

Suky winced at the memory of beatings from her father when she had been naughty. She had learned to curl up, cover her head and tell herself it would be over soon. Later, they would all sit for supper and smile as if nothing had happened. Suky always joined in with the lie, but she wanted nothing more than to escape, walk out and get lost and never come back. That was another life. The life that kept insisting it was real. The life of Susannah Gabriel.

Suky looked down the dark road to the village. Recollections stirred in her of walks on spring mornings, of daffodils lining the road and pink blossom in the trees, of laughter and a life before the darkness.

All she had to do was take one step, then another, and keep going and she could leave all this madness behind.

'Please, please stop.' The clown-faced scarecrow's cries broke through Suky's thoughts.

Suky turned on her heels, rushed towards the

struggle and shoved Pumpkinhead with all her might, almost stumbling over with him. Pumpkinhead's top hat fell to the dirt, the rain playing it like a drum.

Around her, Suky could sense the other crow folk shuffling back. She took the clown-faced scarecrow's hand and helped him to his feet. His head was misshapen, there was straw all over the ground and he whimpered whenever he moved. Suky wrapped her arms around him, propping him up.

'You are a beast and a bully,' Suky told Pumpkinhead. 'You made us promises about freedom, you made us promises about happiness, but you're just another man telling us all what to do to get what *you* wants. You're greedy and selfish and your head's too big for your body. There, I said it.'

'Oh, sister Suky,' Pumpkinhead said, picking up his top hat and brushing the dirt from it before returning it to his head. 'Greedy? Selfish? Have I not given you life? Have I not given you purpose? Hmm? Brothers? Sisters?' He turned to the others and there were murmurs of agreement, though not as many as usual. 'Have I not given you hope? Have I not promised to fulfil your dreams? Have I not sacrificed every waking moment of my time to making them a reality?'

'No,' Suky said, her shame boiling into anger. 'You have a greater curiosity for that book, if you ask me. That book ain't for us, is it? It's for you and you only. You wants its magic for yourself, don't you, you big greedy guts. Well, I for one am not helping you any more.'

'You defy me, sister Suky?'

'I do.'

'I see.' Pumpkinhead beckoned the clown-faced scarecrow to him. 'Brother, come to me. I must make amends.'

'Don't,' Suky warned, but the clown-faced scarecrow slipped from her arms and staggered to his master.

Pumpkinhead cradled the clown-faced scarecrow's head in his hands, squeezing harder and harder. Suky's mind felt light and floaty as Pumpkinhead drew on her strength and that of her siblings. Suky resisted, pushing away with thoughts and memories of old. They were ghostly and distant, but it was enough to keep her mind her own. The others were not as strong and Suky watched, helpless, as life left Clown-face like air from a balloon. He fell to the ground, his stuffing straw whirling off in the breeze, the rain pummelling his shirt and trousers.

Suky crouched down and took the clown-faced scarecrow's empty sackcloth head in her hands. His red felt smile frozen for ever. She clutched it to her chest as she got to her feet and backed away. 'What are you?'

'I am your saviour,' Pumpkinhead said. 'I am your god.'

'No,' Suky shook her head. 'God is kindness and forgiveness and love for ever in Heaven above. He ain't like you.'

'Then where is he? This kind and forgiving God?' Pumpkinhead looked up to where lightning flickered in the clouds. 'Is that him? No. I think not. I am here.

I am real. The god of scarecrows – yes, I like the sound of that – the god of scarecrows stands before you, Suky. And without me, you are nothing.'

'T'ain't true,' Suky said, gripping the smiling clown's sackcloth head tighter.

'No? Where will you go, sister? Who will give shelter to a wretch like you? A damp bundle of straw in a tatty gingham dress will find no suitor among the boys in the village. No landlady will let you cross her threshold when you look like that. There's no room at the inn on a night like tonight. The stables, perhaps? Yes. You can enjoy my love and protection, or you can fester with the pigs and cows in a barn somewhere. The choice is yours.'

Suky looked to the other crow folk, all standing mute behind Pumpkinhead. 'Why does none of you speak out?' she cried.

'They cannot,' Pumpkinhead said, and she saw the other crow folk were trying to talk, lurching forwards as if retching, their hands moving to their mouths and throats, but no noise was coming out. 'Worship me, Suky, thank me for all I have given you and you shall continue to live.'

He offered his gloved hand for the taking. Suky looked from the hand, to the others clutching their heads and moaning, then back to Pumpkinhead. 'I think I would rather turn to dust,' she told him.

'A shame. Make peace with your god, child.' Pumpkinhead lunged forwards and gripped her head. He drew her closer and Suky felt him try to claw into her mind, prickles of pain stabbing at her brain followed by clouds that threatened to sweep her mind away.

Suky thought of daffodils. Of blossoms. Of her mother's loving smile, of toasted crumpets with salty butter and gooseberry jam, of summer fairs and autumn leaves and crisp snow in winter. These memories of her old self, the ones she had denied before, came much more clearly now. Suky let them wash through her. She recalled how the smell of her father's tobacco lingered long after he left for work, how her baby brother's cries and coughs kept her up. She remembered that final night, when the boy she loved more than sunshine broke her heart, and how she had laced her tea with poison, and death had come for her as she slept.

Suky's love and pain flooded through her and pushed Pumpkinhead out of her mind.

He stumbled back, grinning in admiration. 'Not so feeble-minded as your kin, sister Suky, hmm?'

'I am not your sister, I am not your Suky, I am Susannah Gabriel,' Suky said, her voice raw and breathless.

'No,' Pumpkinhead said, looming over her. 'You are nothing and you will go back to nothing.' He raised his hand as if to strike her, but Suky was faster. She knocked his top hat off and tugged the sack in her hand over Pumpkinhead's noggin. He lashed out, but she ducked under his blow, then shoved him again and ran down the road a few steps. She turned around to see him tumble back again as he struggled with his new face. 'Get it off me, you fools!' he yelled at the other crow folk. One or two tried to help, but the others were too scared.

'I may have nowhere to go,' Suky cried as the rain hammered down, 'but I would rather spend my days with happy pigs and heifer cows in a barn than with you.' She turned and ran towards the village.

The other crow folk simply stared at her, their minds lost on the breeze.

'Kill her,' Pumpkinhead's muffled voice came from inside the sack on his head. 'Kill her, kill them all, just bring me that book, you fools.'

33

Mrs Teach's Confession

'You gave him the book.' Mrs Teach and Charlotte were waiting for Faye by the lychgate of Saint Irene's Church, arms folded, united in their rage. 'You did, didn't you, you little minx? You've doomed us all.' Mrs Teach's lips were like the knot in a child's balloon. Charlotte remained aloof, nose raised in disdain.

As Faye and her father rattled to a halt on the bicycle, she felt a cold droplet on her hand, followed by another and another. The rain had followed her back to the village.

'Answer me,' Mrs Teach demanded, but Faye twisted around to check on her father.

'How are you, Dad?'

'I'm fine, Faye, I'm fine. You shouldn't have come after me, girl. That was too dangerous.'

'What did you do with the book?' Mrs Teach persisted. 'You gave it to him, didn't you?'

Faye leaned her bicycle against a lamp post. 'I gave him *a* book,' she said. 'Not *the* book.'

Mrs Teach squinted one eye. 'Wot?'

'When I fell over your trunk, I landed on your book,' Faye told Charlotte. 'I knew what to do right away. I read it in a detective novel once. They call it a *switch-eroo*.' Faye reached into her satchel and revealed her mother's book, safe and sound, and blew a raspberry. 'Fooled ya.'

'You gave him my book of woodcuts?' Charlotte said, a tiny smirk of admiration on her face.

'I did, though I don't think you'll be seeing it again. I heard the distinct sound of pages being ripped up when old Pumpkin-noggin realised he'd been diddled. Sorry.'

'That book was over two hundred years old.'

'Time you got a new one, then,' Terrence said.

'Well, you are the clever one, aren't you,' Mrs Teach said. 'But the demon will be angry, and he will be coming for us.'

'Demon?' Terrence looked from Faye to Mrs Teach and back again. 'No one said nothing about no demon.'

'Well, Dad, y'know when I insisted he was a scarecrow?'

'Yeah?'

'Turns out I was well off the mark. He's a nasty piece of work, who—' Faye started, then turned to Charlotte and Mrs Teach. 'That Pumpkinhead, you said his name was Kefapepo, right?'

Charlotte nodded.

'Did he know my mum?'

'I'm sorry?' Charlotte narrowed her eyes.

'This Kefapepo fella, did he ever know my mum?

Was she ever . . .' Faye glanced over at her dad, who looked back at her from the sides of his eyes. 'Was she ever consorting with demons and such?'

'What the blazes are you on about, Faye?' Terrence asked.

'Mum was a witch, Dad,' Faye said, waving her hands in the air. 'Though how you could be married to her for so long and not know that, I'll—'

'I knew what she was.' Terrence silenced Faye as the rain fell harder. It flattened his hair and ran in rivulets down his face.

Faye's spectacles began to mist over. 'You said it was a hobby. A silly fancy.'

'I'm not daft, Faye,' Terrence said. 'She told me enough when we was engaged. Though she never called herself a witch as such. But I knew she had some sorta . . . gift? Yeah, I suppose you would call it that. She kept it a secret. All the women in her family did. But she ain't a witch like in the fairy stories. She used to help people. Cure them, make them happy when they was sad. She would sit with the dying, she would make tea for them that was grieving. And yeah, she made potions and did little rituals and all that malarkey, but most of the time she was just a good person, Faye, and she certainly weren't consorting with any bloody demons.'

'When all this is done,' Faye told her father as she got her voice back, 'you and me need a long old chat about Mum.'

'All you need to know is in her book,' Terrence said.

'She done that for you, Faye. She reckoned you might have the same gifts she had, and she wanted to make sure you knew what you were doing.'

'Then why didn't you tell me about it?'

'I hadn't got round to it yet.' Terrence pressed his hands on his chest. 'I'm a busy man, girl. I got a bloody pub to run. I would've told ya sooner or later.'

'Why don't I believe you?' Faye shook her head as thunder rumbled above.

'You believe what you want.'

'I believe you're a great big fibber. Lying to your own daughter.'

'I would not lie to my—'

'Then you was so absent-minded that you somehow forgot to mention in the seventeen years that you've known me that Mum was a witch. I know you're busy with the pub, Dad, but you're not *that* busy.'

'All right, I was scared,' Terrence snapped. 'That good enough for ya? I'd seen what it did to your mother and I didn't want the same thing happening to you. People being frightened of yer. Treating you different. Whispering rumours. I was trying to protect you, girl.'

'Scared? You?'

'Yes. I especially didn't want you turning out like these two,' he said, gesturing at Charlotte and Mrs Teach. 'No offence.'

'Some taken,' Charlotte said.

'Don't be too hard on him,' Mrs Teach told Faye. 'Most folk don't understand what we do, even those who are close to us. The wise ones – like my Ernie and your pa – let us get on with it. And he's right about your mother. She could be trouble, like you. Full of *opinions*, but she was a good lass in her own way.'

'Then why is Kefapepo's name in her book?' Faye opened the book and flicked to the page with the columns of numbers and zigzags. 'She created a bell-ringing method and named it after him.'

'Bells? Really?' Charlotte reached out. 'May I?'

Faye snapped the book shut and tucked it back in her satchel to protect it from the rain. 'Not until you tell me how my mum knew about this demon.'

Charlotte looked to Mrs Teach. 'Do you want to tell her, or should I?'

'Tell her what?' Mrs Teach blinked innocently.

'You *know* what.'

'I'm sure I don't.'

'Then I'll tell her.'

'Don't you dare.'

'Then you *do* know what.'

'Maybe I do, but that doesn't mean we should—'

'Oh, Gordon Bennett on a bicycle,' Faye broke in with a voice that startled an owl out of its nest in the bell tower. 'What did I say about telling the truth? Tell me what and tell it now.'

Charlotte glared at Mrs Teach, who tightened her lips before throwing her hands into the air. 'All right then, but this has nothing to do with our current predicament, I'm sure.'

'I'll be the judge of that,' Charlotte said.

Mrs Teach chewed on her lip like a toddler caught

with her hand in a sweetie jar. 'Before I tell you this,' she said to Faye, 'I want you to know it was a long time ago and I was young and—'

'Get on with it,' Faye said, wiping the rain from her hair.

'When I first met my Ernie, he had the best allotment in the village. He was always winning prizes at the harvest festival and his squashes were the talk of the county, weren't they, Terrence?'

'If you say so.' Terrence shrugged.

'We hadn't been stepping out for long when he lost the biggest pumpkin prize to that crafty bugger Jack Neame. Well, my Ernie was bereft, poor love, and I was a bit of a show-off back then, so I . . . I did a teensy-weensy bit of spell-work to help ensure it wouldn't happen again.'

Terrence was aghast. 'You cheated to win the harvest festival?'

'Like I said, it was a long time ago. We were courting and I wanted to impress Ernie. So anyway, in doing so I may have . . . *accidentally* summoned Kefapepo.'

'What?' Faye snapped, lightning flashing above her.

'Not a manifestation,' Mrs Teach said, raising her hands in defence. 'Just a voice. He said he could help, but I sent him packing as soon as I knew what he was. But I've paid the price. Someone snitched and I've been on probation ever since, forbidden from practising my magic.' She glanced pointedly at Charlotte.

'Don't make me out to be the wicked witch.' Charlotte puffed with indignation. 'We have rules and you know what happens when we break them.'

Mrs Teach curled her hand into a little mouth and made *nyah-nyah-nyah* noises.

Charlotte folded her arms. 'You're the one who risked a demonic incursion to win best pumpkin at the village fair.'

'Ladies, please,' Faye snapped. 'You accidentally summoned a demon, Mrs Teach. What happened next?'

'I told your mother, Faye,' Mrs Teach continued, 'and she did a little reading in a few grimoires and, based on what I told her about him, and what she knew about bells, she started working on a method to drive him off should he ever come back.'

'Why bells?' Faye asked.

'Consecrated bells have long been used to drive away evil spirits,' Charlotte said. 'Though the method she created was never rung, and now he's back and walking among us.'

'*I break the thunder*, *I torment evil, I banish darkness*,' Faye muttered to herself, recalling the words her mother had written underneath the method. 'But why is he back now?' Faye asked. The penny dropped. She opened her mouth in shock and pointed an accusing finger at Mrs Teach. 'Oh, your Ernie. You got him to bring your Ernie back, didn't you? That's why he visited you as a scarecrow and tried to get up your skirts.'

Mrs Teach's cheeks turned red as Charlotte scowled at her. 'You lied to me. You bloody lied to me.'

Mrs Teach looked everywhere but at Charlotte.

'You silly old boot.' Charlotte threw her hands up in the rain. 'What were you thinking?'

'He promised me a chat. That's all I wanted. A few words with my Ernie to say a proper goodbye. He went so sudden and all—'

'And to do this you summoned a demon?' Charlotte raged.

'No. I was having a seance and he came to me. Barged in like an uninvited guest, he did. I sent him on his way. I didn't want any of this, and I didn't want my Ernie coming back as a straw man, but he sent him anyway.'

'None of this matters now,' Faye said.

'It bloody does,' Terrence said. 'She and Ernie cheated on the harvest festival. That's bang out of order.'

'Dad. Please. We all do peculiar things when we miss someone.'

Charlotte glared daggers at Mrs Teach. 'If Vera Fivetrees finds out about this—'

'She won't,' Mrs Teach said.

'Who?' asked Faye.

'Doesn't matter,' Charlotte said.

'I just wanted to hear his voice again.' Tears glistened in Mrs Teach's eyes. This wasn't her usual theatrics. 'He had such a sweet voice. It was all I lived for. Please forgive me.' Mrs Teach held out her hands.

'I understand, I really do,' Faye said, taking one of Mrs Teach's hands and giving it a squeeze. She reached out for Charlotte. 'Miss Charlotte?'

Charlotte's arms remained folded and she looked away.

'If I may offer my twopenn'orth?' Terrence said,

clearing his throat. 'I reckon if there was some way I could hear my Kathy's laugh once more, I would wrestle the Devil himself. No one can know what they'll do till the time comes, so I ain't one to judge. Miss Charlotte, you must have someone special you would want to hear again, surely?'

Charlotte stiffened, tightening her folded arms before shrugging. 'Yes, I suppose I do. But she's been gone too long. The past is dead and that's how it should stay.'

'The important thing is we send this demon on his way,' Faye told them. 'If we ring this method, we'll scare the big orange-headed bugger off?'

'It may be the only chance we have,' Charlotte said. 'And I would very much like to settle this before Vera Fivetrees finds out and has all our guts for garters.'

'Who is this Vera Fivetrees?' Faye asked.

'Never mind, I'll tell you later. We've got bigger problems,' Mrs Teach said, spotting something over Faye's shoulder.

Silent lightning danced behind the church, revealing a row of silhouettes moving fast down the Wode Road towards the village. It flashed again on their sackcloth faces, stitched-on smiles and button eyes.

'Dad.' Faye took her bicycle from where she'd leaned it against the lamp post and wheeled it to her father. 'Find all the Local Defence Volunteers you can and bring 'em to this spot. I reckon you'll need pitchforks and flaming torches, and if they bring their rifles, tell 'em to fix bayonets.'

'What about you?'

'Never mind me, just get a bloomin' move on.' Faye turned to Charlotte and Mrs Teach. 'You ladies, wake the ringers. Start with Bertie, he's closest. I'll meet you at the bell tower. Give Mr Aitch this.' She handed Charlotte the slip of paper with the ringing method.

'Aitch?'

'Mr Hodgson. Hurry. I'll be keeping this lot busy till you get back. Now go!' Faye sent the witches on their way, then turned to face the scarecrows rushing down the street towards her. 'Oi! You after this?' She held her mother's book above her head. 'Then come and get it.'

34

Exit, Pursued by a Bunch of Scarecrows

'What on earth are you doing knocking on my door in the middle of the night?' It didn't take much to rile Mr Hodgson. Typographic errors in *The Times*, verbose children, overfamiliar shopkeepers and women who whistled were all on his long list of irritants. But having two witches appear on his doorstep on a dark and stormy night had just made it to the very top.

'You will come with us,' Charlotte Southill told him. Standing in the pouring rain, her lank white hair rather diminished her usual air of mystery. That didn't stop her from getting straight to the point. 'We must gather your bell ringers and hurry to Saint Irene's where you will ring Kathryn Bright's method to repel a demon.'

'I shall do no such thing. Now be on your way, or I shall call the constable.' Mr Hodgson moved to close the door, but young Bertie Butterworth hurried up the garden path. It was blackout dark, but Mr Hodgson could just see the other ringers standing in the rain by his front garden gate. The Roberts twins, who were also lifeboat volunteers, wore matching bright yellow oilskin raincoats. Miss Burgess stood hands on hips in three-quarter-length hiking shorts and green gumboots, Miss Gordon was in her riding jacket and boots, and the ancient Mrs Pritchett wore her fur-lined coat. They had also drafted in Reverend Jacobs, who had helped them out in the past when they were short. He gave Mr Hodgson a jolly wave.

Bertie, who was still in his striped pyjamas and clogs, broke through the two witches. He stood on the doorstep and looked at Mr Hodgson with pleading eyes.

'How many peals have you rung, Mr Aitch?' Bertie asked. 'Forty? Fifty?'

'Many hundreds, I'll have you know.'

'Crikey.' Bertie grinned, impressed and distracted. 'Hundreds? Really?'

'Young man.' Charlotte nudged him in the ribs. 'Get to your point.'

'Yes, yes.' Bertie turned back to Mr Hodgson with a serious frown. 'And how many of them actually mattered?'

'I beg your pardon?'

'How many of them have saved the lives of everyone you know in this village?' Bertie wiped rivulets of rain from his face. 'I'm thinking the answer would be none.'

'What the blazes are you wittering on about, boy?' Mr Hodgson said.

'You fought in the Great War, didn't you, Mr Hodgson?' Bertie continued. 'A valiant and brave man.

Medals and ribbons and such. I know you would be fighting with our boys now if you could, and I'm the same. You're too old and I'm too crippled, but wouldn't you like to do your bit in your own way?'

'All you need to do is ring some bells,' Mrs Teach said.

'Who sent you?' Mr Hodgson asked, his voice trembling. 'This is Faye Bright's doing, isn't it? This is some sort of witchcraft.'

'Of course it is,' Charlotte said. 'We're witches.'

'Yes, Faye sent us,' Mrs Teach added, 'because she reckoned you wouldn't listen to her, being a young slip of a girl and all, but you might listen to us. I can tell you now, Mr Hodgson, you and your ringers may be the only thing that stands between the survival of everyone in this village and a malevolent demon. And I don't say that lightly.'

'Please, Mr Aitch,' Bertie said, clasping his hands together. 'We can't do this without you.'

'Who is it, dear?' came the voice of Mrs Hodgson from the bedroom.

'It's the ringers and a couple of witches. They want me to ring a quarter peal to repel a demon, or something.'

'Well, get on with it,' Mrs Hodgson cried. 'You're letting a draught in.'

Mr Hodgson looked from the living room to the flickering lightning in the night sky, to the ringers in the rain and to the witches on his doorstep. 'I'll get my coat,' he said.

Suky found herself among gravestones. She had run blind from the crossroads confrontation with Pumpkinhead and lost herself in the streets of the darkened village. She found some bends in the road familiar, and others new and strange with terraces where fields used to be. But the one landmark that hadn't budged an inch was Saint Irene's, visible from wherever one stood in the village. Like some doomed heroine from one of her favourite penny dreadfuls, Suky ran through the rain and lightning towards the church bell tower.

Here, birds warned her off. Jackdaws, black with flashes of grey, had settled on the crenellations of the tower, wings tensed and ready to flee as they *kaw-kawed* at her to leave them be.

'I won't harm you, I promise,' Suky called to them. 'I flew with you, if you remember? In my mind, at least. We soared above the abbey with the sparrows and starlings and robins and more. Do you remember?'

The birds fell silent and lowered their wings.

'I felt another mind in there with us. One like mine. A spirit that had passed over and been brung back, if that makes sense? Someone with unfinished business, I think. Is she there now?'

As one, the jackdaws took flight and circled above the bell tower, wings shivering as they flew, their chattering song now a *chak-chak-chak*.

'I don't know if we can stop him, I know I can't do it on my lonesome, but if we could become one again . . . ? You, me and her. We might stand a chance.'

The jackdaws now sang a warning of *kaw-kaws* as they flew lower, swirling above Suky's head.

'I know,' Suky said. 'I know the price I has to pay, and I is willing. Will you help me?'

ꝭ

Faye pegged it through the rain with nearly twenty scarecrows on her tail as she ran a circuit of the village, starting by Saint Irene's lychgate, then up and around the graveyard. She knew this village like the back of her hand, even in the blackout, and she soon put some distance between herself and the crow folk. She vaulted the church wall and whizzed past one of the scarecrows wandering the gravestones.

Suky.

Faye didn't have time to wonder why she wasn't chasing her like the others, but she gave her a little wave as she raced by. Suky waved back, and it was then Faye noticed the flock of jackdaws circling above the scarecrow girl. Faye wanted to know more, but she had to shake off her pursuers first.

She zigzagged through the church grounds, daring to glance back now and then. The crow folk followed like sheep, bumping into one another and tripping over molehills in the grass. They were clumsy but relentless, and Faye shuddered at the thought of what they might do if they caught her. Visions of Craddock the scarecrow stuck on a cross gave her the boost she needed to hurdle back over the stone wall and leave the church grounds.

Faye took the path past the allotments, peeling off along Perry Lane. The crow folk herded Faye down the narrow alley, tumbling and stumbling about like the Keystone Cops. Half a dozen or so created a blockage which the rest clambered over, their arms reaching out for the book in Faye's satchel.

Faye kept running, turning out of the lane onto the bottom of the Wode Road by the war memorial. Moonlight glistened on the slick cobbles. Faye lost her footing, her shoes slapping as she ran. She leaned forwards like a tap dancer, tumbled and fell hard, scraping her elbow and banging the side of her head. She rolled over, shook her head clear and got to her feet as the scarecrows came haring out of the lane towards her.

Faye had never run so much in one day and this last stretch along the Wode Road to the church was uphill and slippy. Her lungs were aching, along with her legs, arms, back and – strangely – her fingers, but she had to keep going. The lychgate was in sight, but her dad and the Local Defence Volunteers were nowhere to be seen and the bells weren't ringing. The villagers slumbered in the dark, unaware of the strange hunt happening on its streets.

A familiar fear took residence in the pit of Faye's belly. Not just what would happen if she was caught, but what if no one had actually listened to her? It was easy for Faye to bark orders, but who's to say they didn't all head home, make a cup of Ovaltine and go straight to bed? Dad and the Local Defence Volunteers might be having a jolly old laugh over a cheeky pint in an after-hours lock-in. Mrs Teach and Miss Charlotte most likely went their separate ways after agreeing they knew better than a girl who dabbled with magic because she missed her mother.

And what were Faye's choices if that was the case? Keep running? Do another round of the village with this lot chasing after her – which she didn't much fancy – or leg it to the bell tower and lock herself inside until the other ringers arrived, which they might never do?

The scurrying footsteps of the scarecrows were closing in on her. They never got tired, and they would not stop until they had Faye and the book. Faye's legs were feeling heavy, her breathing ragged, and the rain was hammering down on her head. One of the scarecrows moaned as they closed in. The sound was right in her ear.

'Oh, blinkin' flip,' Faye said in fright, gritting her teeth through the exhaustion, doing whatever she could to keep her arms and legs moving. Another moan, and another. Closer and closer, faster and faster.

'CHARGE!' came a yell from the Green Man pub. Its doors burst open and the street was flooded with men wearing armbands and tin hats. They carried flaming torches that sizzled in the rain and rushed to form a line between Faye and the scarecrows.

Mr Paine led the way in his ARP uniform and steel helmet, a fiery torch held aloft in his hand.

'Mr Paine,' Faye managed between breaths, her voice somewhere between hysterical and delirious. 'Put that light out.'

'In this instance, young lady, I shall make an exception.'

'Run, Faye,' Terrence cried, 'we've got them outflanked.'

Faye glanced behind her to see the scarecrows recoiling and running back down the Wode Road as a line of Local Defence Volunteers blockaded the street with their torches. Mr Marshall raised a rifle and took a shot at one of the scarecrows. The bullet went straight through it, ricocheting off the war memorial. The scarecrow looked down at the new hole in its chest, yelped and scarpered. Grinning, Faye found new energy and veered off from the Wode Road, vaulted over the church wall and ran through the graveyard towards Saint Irene's bell tower.

Straight into the arms of Pumpkinhead.

35

The Bells of Saint Irene's

'So kind of you to bring it to me.' Pumpkinhead held Faye with one arm while reaching for the buckle of her satchel with the other. Faye wriggled in his grip, but his arms were impossibly strong and they coiled tight around her.

'Dad. Dad, help!' she cried, and to her relief the ranks of the Woodville Village Local Defence Volunteers came scrambling over the church wall, torches flaming and weapons drawn.

Pumpkinhead threw Faye and her satchel to the ground. He reached into his dinner jacket, drew his cowbell and rattled it at his attackers. The air trembled, the flaming torches were all snuffed out and even the rain softened a little.

The terrible rattling continued as Terrence readied his Lee–Enfield. He pulled the bolt back to load a round into the chamber, but the rifle simply broke apart. Others tried the same, but their weapons fell in useless pieces onto the wet ground, and the sharp points of pitchforks bent back on themselves like ram horns. Pumpkinhead grinned as he returned the cowbell to his dinner jacket.

Faye scrabbled away as he approached her, but with his long legs Pumpkinhead was on her in moments, trying to pin her down. Faye resisted, wriggling, rolling onto her front, holding tight to the satchel beneath her. Pumpkinhead rested a foot on her back and leaned all his weight on her. He took off his top hat, placed it on Faye's head. She felt a sudden numbness in her mind and couldn't move. He pressed down on the hat, pushing her face into the soaked ground.

ẞ

Bertie liked things to be in order. The way the tiles tessellated on the kitchen floor at home, the rows of carrots and cabbages on his dad's allotment, and his alphabetised football cigarette card collection all made him happy in their own little way. But none of these things could match the glory of a well-designed ringing method. That he and his fellow band of ringers could take six, eight, ten bells or more and ring them in such an order they could bring to mind the unfathomable beauty of Heaven itself was nothing short of miraculous to Bertie. And to create this wondrous sound, ringers followed methods. Tried and tested methods, handed down through generations and as carefully notarised as any symphony in clear and concise diagrams. With columns of numbers to signify the bells and red and blue lines to guide the ringers.

Bertie had been ringing since he was twelve and was only just getting the hang of it. Mr Hodgson, on the other hand, was such an expert that he merely had to glance at a blue line to know the method and hear the bells pealing in his head. When he looked at Kathryn Wynter's method, he puckered up like he was sucking on a sherbet lemon.

'This will not work,' Mr Hodgson said as he studied the diagram, pacing in circles in the ringing chamber of Saint Irene's bell tower. 'It's non-symmetrical, it's not a true method. It has no grace, no piety in the presence of God, it is rushed and frenzied and it cannot be done.'

'It'll work, Mr Aitch,' Bertie insisted, then gestured at his fellow ringers, each one of them drenched from head to toe after their dash through the storm. 'We're ready for the challenge. You're always telling us we're the best band in Kent, if not the whole of Great Britain. We've all looked at it and we know it looks half barmy, but you have to admit there's something to it.'

'I reckon it's a work of genius,' Mrs Pritchett added.

'We've seen nothing like it,' the Roberts twins said in unison.

'Truly magnificent,' added the Reverend Jacobs.

'It is rather splendid,' Miss Gordon said, clapping her hands together in excitement.

'Come on, chaps, let's at it.' Miss Burgess marched to take a rope.

Bertie dared to move closer to Mr Hodgson and spoke softly. 'We saw some strange stuff happening in the graveyard on the way here. Faye needs our help and we don't have much time. What do you say, Mr Hodgson?' Bertie's question hung in the air as the tower captain continued to frown in bafflement at Kathryn Wynter's method.

ꝕ

Faye could not move, paralysed by whatever magic emanated from Pumpkinhead's top hat. He pressed down harder, pushing her face further into the ground. Faye's specs fell off her nose. Everything was a blur. All she could make out were raindrops pattering on blades of grass, weeds, dandelions and tiny mushrooms. Rainwater rushed in around her, a puddle filling Faye's mouth and nose. She was going to die, drowned like a rat in a graveyard.

And that's when the bells of Saint Irene's began to ring.

Faye allowed herself a flutter of hope. This was it. Mr Hodgson and the rest would ring her mother's method and the demon would flee in terror. But it only took a moment for Faye to realise they were just ringing up to raise the bells. Nothing magical at all. Mr Hodgson was not ringing her mother's method, and now Faye was going to drown in a puddle.

Pumpkinhead whispered in Faye's ear unfathomable words that crawled across her skin, spreading the numbness. Her eyes felt heavy, her thoughts scattered like leaves on the wind. She was losing her mind.

ꝕ

Bertie rang the tenor, wondering when Mr Hodgson was going to stop ringing rounds and start Kathryn Wynter's method. Ringing rounds was important, of course, they had to raise the bells, but they had been going on far longer than usual and Bertie could see fear in Mr Hodgson's eyes. The tower captain didn't want to ring it, and they were wasting time. Bertie wondered if he should call stand when he caught sight of a familiar figure emerging through the oak door into the ringing chamber.

'Stop this at once.' Constable Muldoon stood with his hand raised, hollering over the clamour of the bells. 'I order you to cease your ringing immediately.'

'Stand!' Mr Hodgson called and the other ringers came to a hurried halt.

'Well, this is a pretty disgrace and no mistaking,' Constable Muldoon said as he strode into the centre of the chamber. 'Merely days after the decree that all ringing be stopped, I find you lot having a right old ding-dong in the middle of the night.'

'Constable, please let me explain—' Mr Hodgson started.

'You can do your explaining back at the station. This is an offence under Article—'

'Oh, give your gob a rest, Noel,' said Mrs Pritchett, hopping off the box she used to boost her height to reach her sally. She marched over and poked him in the belly with her finger. 'Turn around and mind your own business, you lanky streak of—'

'You cannot speak to me like that. I am an officer of the law.'

'I'm still your aunt, Noel, and you're not too big for a clip round the ear'ole. Wait there while I get me box.'

'Constable, could you not make an exception?' Reverend Jacobs asked.

'Officer, my sincere apologies,' Mr Hodgson began, brushing aside a tuft of hair. 'We are, of course, somewhat breaking the decree given to us by the War Office regarding the banning of bells, but I have been assured by *certain* members of the community that it is of the utmost importance we now ring this new method by the late Mrs Bright of this parish and—'

'I don't care,' the constable said. 'The law is the law. Step outside or I'll have you all arrested.'

'No!' Bertie blurted. All eyes turned on him. The glare from Constable Muldoon was like a life sentence, and normally Bertie would have backed down, apologised and vowed never to speak again. But he thought of Faye out there in the rain with the crow folk. He thought of how she took no nonsense from anyone no matter what their standing. And so he limped over and stood before the police officer. 'We know this is breaking the law and we're sorry, but we have to do this. Ringing this method will save lives.'

'What nonsense. Be quiet, silly boy.'

'Please, listen—'

'Silence. There are important matters to discuss.'

'If we don't do this—'

'Lad, I'm warning you—'

'Oh, blimey, Constable, I'm really sorry about this, but if you won't listen, then it has to be done.'

Bertie knew he shouldn't be reaching for the constable's helmet, but he did. Bertie knew he shouldn't take the constable's helmet off the constable's head, but he did. Bertie most certainly knew he should not toss the constable's helmet through the door and down the spiral staircase, but he did. And Bertie knew with every ounce of certainty in his body that he should not have shoved the constable through the door, closed it and locked it with the iron key.

But he did.

'Oh, Lordy, what have I done?' Bertie rasped, his mouth dry.

'What you had to do, Bertie,' Mrs Pritchett said as she hurried to the treble. She clambered back onto her box, took her sally and cried, 'The Kefapepo method, everyone. Look to.'

The other ringers scrambled into position as Constable Muldoon thumped on the locked door, bellowing threats of jail time and firing squads. Bertie joined them, grabbing the sally for the tenor. 'Treble's going,' Mrs Pritchett said, pulling on the sally. 'And she's gone.'

⁂

Pumpkinhead's top hat pressed Faye's face further into the wet soil of the graveyard as she thrashed about trying to break free. Her mind was a fog and, as he spoke his magic, the darkness closed in around her. Sound became muffled, her sight dimmed.

Water flowed into Faye's mouth and she tried to

cough it up, but it had nowhere to go and she could feel it trickle down her gullet. That's when she noticed the bells had stopped ringing, though she couldn't be sure how long for. Time becomes less of a consideration when you're struggling with basic stuff like getting air into your lungs and not losing your mind.

Every now and then she heard a cry and the pressure would be released as Pumpkinhead was attacked, Faye presumed, by her father and the Local Defence Volunteers. The demon would break off, swipe them away and continue trying to kill her.

The bells began to ring again.

Even though Faye had never heard it rung out loud, she recognised the method immediately. It wasn't how bells were supposed to be rung. It was non-symmetrical and the bells were rung too close together, creating a discordant hum that made the air sing.

It was her mother's method. The Kefapepo method.

ꝏ

Bertie's eyes darted from Miss Burgess to Miss Gordon to Mr Hodgson to the Roberts twins to Mrs Pritchett and back to Miss Burgess again as he counted the bells in his head. Constantly listening, constantly counting, though never out loud as the bells moved too fast and they had never, ever moved as fast as this method.

At every hand-stroke he followed one of the Bob twins on the fifth bell, and at every backstroke he followed Mr Hodgson on the seventh, but the constant motion and speed began to make him feel nauseous.

Bertie closed his eyes and listened instead. It would have been a mistake to blindly follow the bell in front of him; he had to stop trying to force this method to be something he wanted it to be, he had to let it take over, he had to relinquish control.

The bells became one sound. A hypnotic hum rising from the clanging chaos, a noise familiar to all ringers from ringing down, but extending long beyond the point when they would normally stop. The hum, a lost chord from some other place, resonated off the tower's stone walls, off every person in the room and settled into Bertie's mind, relieving him of duty. He felt weightless, serene, and loved everyone and everything in existence as the sound escaped the confines of the tower, rippling through the air, rattling every atom it came into contact with.

Bertie and the ringers moved with it in ecstasy through the spectrum of noise, its voice bypassing their ears and moving straight to their brains. *I break the thunder*, it said, *I torment evil, I banish darkness.* It repeated over and over as it used people, birds, animals and scarecrows as sounding boards, like a bat seeking its prey.

It wasn't long before it found what it was looking for.

36

The Kefapepo Method

The demon released his grip on Faye, recoiling at the sound from the consecrated bells. Faye, her face covered in mud, came up coughing water then gasping for air. As the fog clouding her thoughts lifted, she shook the numbness from her arms and legs. She sat up to find Pumpkinhead gripping his temples as the chimes of the bells resonated around him.

I break the thunder, said a voice in Faye's mind, *I torment evil, I banish darkness.*

As Pumpkinhead railed against the wall of sound, there came a wet crunch that made Faye think of the spoon breaking into the runny soft-boiled eggs she had for tea some nights. Faye found her specs on the grass, gave them a quick wipe on her shirt and wriggled them onto her nose.

She watched as Pumpkinhead staggered, clutching a crack running from eye to ear that was beginning to leak. Faye half expected pumpkin seeds and orange liquid to appear, but what came seeping out from the wound glistened black in the moonlight and oozed like thick jam.

I break the thunder, I torment evil, I banish darkness.

Faye felt a pair of hands grab under her armpits. 'All right, young lady,' Mrs Teach said, hefting Faye to safety. 'I've got you.' The older woman moved to stand before the demon and pulled a birchwood cross from her handbag. Pumpkinhead recoiled for a moment then smacked it away, knocking her to one side. He was about to pounce on her when Charlotte rushed over, taking a handful of black ash from a pocket in her dress and throwing it in Pumpkinhead's face.

I break the thunder, I torment evil, I banish darkness.

He roared in agony as his orange skin began to sizzle and his head began to come apart in great greasy globs that dripped between his fingers. Black oily goo pumped from the cracks and he staggered forwards like a drunk.

The crow folk huddled behind a tomb, looking on as Pumpkinhead's body convulsed, his arms spasmed and his dinner jacket ripped at the seams and fell to the ground. His legs snapped like twigs, bending back on themselves like a grasshopper's. The remains of the pumpkin splatted to the ground, revealing a shiny black shell and clicking mouthparts that coughed a clear bile. His spine cracked and lashed out, becoming a forked tail.

'Kefapepo,' Faye whispered.

'Well, it's not the milkman, love, I can tell you that,' Mrs Teach said, dabbing a bruised cheek as she got to her feet.

I break the thunder, I torment evil, I banish darkness.

'Faye, get back,' Terrence cried, rushing forwards with a garden shovel, ready to split the creature in two. He swung the flat blade of the shovel around just as the demon raised a limb to defend itself. The shovel cut through the limb, sending it spinning away. Yellow globs of pus spat from the stump and Terrence recoiled in disgust. The yellow matter became thick as custard, then hardened like tyre rubber, and within moments the limb was as new. Terrence raised his shovel to strike another blow.

'Dad, no.' Faye rushed to put herself between her father and the wretched thing, but he was too fast and brought his shovel down on the demon's head.

'We have to kill it, Faye.' Terrence raised his shovel again, but Faye grabbed his arms.

The demon's shell had cracked, but once again the yellow ooze seeped from the wound and set it like glue.

'Only the bells can do that,' she said. 'Let them finish their work.'

I break the thunder, I torment evil, I banish darkness.

The demon huddled on the ground, coughing up black viscous liquid.

'Everyone, come and see,' Faye called. 'Look what the bells are doing.'

I break the thunder, I torment evil, I banish darkness.

The demon shuddered as the bells continued to sound, their almighty hum vibrating the air. The demon's outer shell began to crack. Its scythe-like claws trembled, reaching out for Faye.

'It's dying,' Faye said.

The demon lurched forwards and everyone scurried back. Everyone except Faye.

'Help me,' the creature begged. Its breath reeked of brimstone as it opened its maw. 'Help me end this.'

'Oh, God, this is horrible,' Faye winced. 'What do we do?'

'Put the kettle on and sell tickets,' Terrence said.

'Dad, we are not monsters. We have to be better than that.'

I break the thunder, I torment evil, I banish darkness.

'It was a scarecrow,' Mrs Teach said. 'Do we burn it?'

'No,' the creature cried. 'No more fire.'

'I know what I has to do,' said a new voice.

Faye turned to find Suky moving through the gravestones towards them. The scarecrow stood before the cowering creature.

'Suky,' it rasped. 'My Suky, you were so very clever, but you didn't think this through. Without me, how will you live? Hmm? Without me to sustain you, you will turn to dust. Listen to me, brothers and sisters,' it cried to the crow folk cowering behind a tomb. 'Suky has betrayed me. Suky has condemned all of us to death. By the next sunrise you will all be gone. I hope you are happy, foolish girl. For it is you who—'

'Oh, stick a sock in it,' Faye snapped, then turned to Suky. 'Is it right? If it dies, you die?'

'It has told many fibs before,' Suky said, 'but it brung us into the world, and I reckon it'll take us with it when it leaves.'

'Then what do we—'

'It cannot be allowed to stay here. It must be destroyed for good and for ever, and I know how.'

'But you'll die.'

'I've been dead before,' Suky said. 'It's not as bad as folks make it out to be.'

'No, no, no, there has to be another way.' Faye turned to Mrs Teach and Charlotte. 'Come on, you two. Think. How do we fix this?'

Mrs Teach said nothing, clutching her handbag tighter.

'None of them are meant to be here, Faye,' Charlotte said. 'I'm sorry.'

'Brothers, sisters,' Suky called, and the crow folk peeked around from behind the safety of their tomb. 'Come to me, quick,' she said, extending her hand.

They shuffled out, uncertain to begin with. A scarecrow with a face like a sunflower was the first to take her hand. The others followed. They formed a circle around the wretched demon.

'You know what to do?' Faye asked.

'Yes,' Suky said. 'Or, rather, they do.' She raised her head to the night sky.

Faye followed her button-eye gaze up as the clouds parted and the moonlight broke through. Jackdaws, black wings shining, flocked around them, whirling and flapping and *kaw-kawing*. The Local Defence Volunteers backed away, but the three witches huddled together as the birds swooped into the circle of scarecrows and formed a vortex around the demon.

Suky began to speak, though it didn't sound like her usual voice. '*I break the thunder, I torment evil, I banish darkness.*'

The other crow folk joined in. '*I break the thunder, I torment evil, I banish darkness.*'

They spoke faster and faster, in time with the bells, and the birds gathered speed to keep up, a tornado of beaks and wings with the demon at the eye of the storm. At first, only the outer shell of its body came apart, tossed up into the wind. Then the rest of it followed, antennae, mouthparts and claws all became flakes on the breeze as the jackdaws spun around it in a frenzy. Faye blinked, then had to close her eyes, shielding them from the debris, spitting bits of demon from her lips. The storm of jackdaws dispersed into the air, banking over the trees and out of sight.

The demon was gone, leaving a graveyard full of scarecrows with nowhere to go, and the bells still rang their hypnotic rounds.

ꞵ

'Miss and catch in rounds after three.' Mr Hodgson's voice broke into Bertie's consciousness like a brick through a window. Gravity pulled at his muscles, air filled his lungs and his ears popped.

'One, two, three,' Mr Hodgson cried. 'Miss and catch.'

With a downward spiral of chimes, the bells fell silent as each ringer tugged on their sally. Bertie wiped his brow and caught his breath. His mouth was dry and his heart beating as if he had sprinted across town.

The ringers all looked at one another, quite unsure of what had just happened. Somehow, they all knew it was time to stop. What needed to be done was done. Everyone's hair was standing on end and for a moment all they could do was blink.

Mrs Pritchett was the first to speak. 'I don't know about you,' she said, 'but I could do with a pint.' She hopped off her box, crossed the chamber and opened the wooden door to the stairwell.

'You are all under arrest!' It was Constable Muldoon, eyes wide, hair a right mess.

Mrs Pritchett brushed him aside. 'Not now, Noel.'

37

The Names of the Crow Folk

They searched the graveyard until it grew dark. They looked for names and dates that might be familiar. The rain had stopped, leaving a sweet smell in the air. House martins, swallows and swifts circled above as the moon brightened.

'Suky,' Faye called as she walked through the stones. All heads turned to her and she gestured to the headstone she had found the other day with Mrs Teach. 'Suky, sweetheart. Yours is here.'

Suky hesitated. Faye couldn't tell from the girl's sackcloth face if she was frightened or angry. Suky began to wring her hands together. Faye reached out, taking the scarecrow's glove in hers. It was cold and wet, but it gripped tightly.

'There, my lovely,' Faye said, and they read the stone in silence together.

Susannah Gabriel
Born 1868, died 1890 in God's Grace
Our 'Suky'

'I have some of her memories, some of her pains,' Suky said. 'I have become something she could never have imagined in her most fantastical dream, and I don't rightly know what that is.'

'I reckon you can be whatever you say you are,' Faye said. 'You want to be Suky, then you be Suky.'

'That's the trouble,' Suky said, turning her head to Faye with a creak. 'I don't think I do.'

A wail came from the far side of the graveyard. 'I want my mummy.'

Faye and Suky hurried to find a scarecrow in a mud-streaked nightgown on her knees before a stone. She was pounding the ground and kicking her feet. Faye read the stone. 'Agnes Shoesmith, born in 1593, died 1600.'

'I want my mummy,' Agnes cried again, wrapping her arms around herself. Other crow folk rushed to comfort her.

'Here's mine,' came another voice, and Faye spun to find the blackbird-faced scarecrow pointing at a marble tomb. 'Benjamin Wexford, that's me. Born 1829, died . . . died 1871.' Benjamin slumped to the ground, cross-legged, and rested a hand on the marble. 'I . . . I had a family.'

More wails came from around them as more and

more of the scarecrows recognised their names and remembered their lives.

'What will become of us?' Suky asked Faye. 'We . . . we don't rightly belong here, do we?'

'No, my poppet, I don't think you do,' Faye said. 'You're welcome to stay, but . . .'

'He said we have till sunrise.' Suky looked to the faint glow on the horizon.

Very few folk passed through the village of Woodville, particularly at night. If any had, they would have stumbled across a peculiar sight. A line of villagers walking hand-in-hand with scarecrows up the Wode Road. Leading them back to the fields where Kefapepo had found them.

Suky's cross in Harry Newton's field was already taken by Craddock's scarecrow, so Terrence, Bertie and Faye made her a new one. Suky chose a spot on a rise where she could see Therfield Abbey and the sea.

Faye took a flask of tea and stayed with her for the rest of the night, holding her hand.

'I might not recall much about who I was,' Suky said, 'but I know I lived and was loved and that is enough. The heart remembers.'

They were joined by a dawn chorus of sparrows, blackbirds, wrens and jackdaws.

'I don't think I've heard anything so beautiful. It

fills me up to hear it,' Suky said, her stitches forming a smile. 'I wants this moment to last for—'

The sun peeked over the sea, infusing it with golden light. Faye felt Suky's hand go limp. Her cross-stitch smile frozen for ever.

38

Vera Fivetrees

Faye trudged back to the village across the fields. Each step weighed more than the last and she was looking forward to a long kip, putting all this strangeness behind her and never dabbling in magic again. Others joined her, including her father, Bertie and Charlotte. No words were said, though she took her dad's hand as they walked and he gave hers a little squeeze.

'I never thanked you,' she told Bertie as they walked.

'For what?'

'You waited for me,' Faye said. 'When I was lost in the wood. Everyone else went home, but you waited for me. I shan't forget that, Bertie Butterworth.'

A jumble of vowels and consonants came tumbling from Bertie's mouth before forming a clumsy, 'You're welcome.' He wiped beads of sweat from his top lip and kept smacking his lips together.

'You all right, Bertie?' Faye asked. He looked pale now, like he might pass out at any moment.

'Hmm? Oh, dry mouth, that's all. Apart from that,

fine and dandy, Faye, thank you,' he said, clenching and unclenching his fists. 'That is . . . there's something . . . What with today's adventure, it made me realise that there may never be a better time to, well, ask. I've been putting it off for months. Years, in fact. So.' Bertie's chest inflated as he took a breath. 'F-Faye, would you consider—'

The roar of a Merlin engine split the air as a black Spitfire swooped low over the fields.

Bertie's courage evaporated and the moment was gone.

'It doesn't have any markings,' Faye said, following the Spitfire as it banked over the village and curved out of sight somewhere near the cricket green.

'Nazi spies?' Terrence wondered. 'Maybe they stole one of our planes and—'

'No, no, no, it's much worse,' Charlotte said, lighting her pipe with all the enthusiasm of someone about to walk to the gallows. 'It's Vera Fivetrees.' She clenched the pipe between her teeth and gave Faye a wicked grin as she puffed white smoke. 'I think we're in trouble.'

Faye wrinkled her nose. 'Who is this Vera woman again?'

ɞ

The black Spitfire had landed on the Woodville village green, churning up quite a bit of turf, much to the consternation of Constable Muldoon. Still befuddled after the night's events – and after a dressing-down from his aunt – he was doing his best to hold back the gathering crowd of villagers with little more than his truncheon and whistle.

The Spitfire was unmarked and painted black from propeller to tail. Its curious cowl – which had a pair of bubbles instead of one – slid back, revealing two occupants. The first, a lithe young woman in an Air Transport Auxiliary flight suit and goggles, hopped out of the pilot's seat and onto the wing. She offered a hand to her passenger. This second woman was brown-skinned and wore a yellow dress with a pattern of black birds and a black headscarf. She descended from the fighter plane with the poise of a queen and marched across the village green with her yellow leather handbag like she had stopped off to pick up her groceries. Head held high, she ignored the curious stares of the villagers who had only ever seen folk with brown skin in newsreel films or illustrations in books and magazines.

Faye let go of her father's hand and hurried after Charlotte to where Mrs Teach waited for them by the duck pond on the green. She wore a beaming smile that belied the panic in her eyes.

'Brace yourselves,' Mrs Teach told them through clenched teeth.

'Why?' Faye asked in a whisper loud enough for everyone to hear. 'Who is she?'

Mrs Teach gave Faye a *Be quiet!* look, then bowed low. Charlotte did the same.

'I am Vera Fivetrees, young lady,' the woman announced as she came to a stop before the three witches. Behind her, the entire village gathered, ready to enjoy the showdown. 'High Witch of the British Empire.'

Faye, unsure how to react, bent her knees in a clumsy curtsey. 'How d'you do?'

'Very badly, I'm thinking.' Vera Fivetrees turned her attention to Charlotte puffing on her pipe, and Mrs Teach gripping her handbag. 'Ladies,' she said, and the pair of them stiffened. 'The most magical activity on one day in this land since 1692, and what felt to me like an incursion by a demon. We've not had one of those since the Middle Ages. Care to explain yourselves?'

'I think a lot of that might be to do with me,' Faye said, raising a finger like a guilty child. 'Y'see, I found my mother's book ...' she started, aware that both Charlotte and Mrs Teach were shaking their heads. 'It's the only thing I have of hers – she passed away when I was little, see – and I started flicking through it and found all these drawings and spells and rituals and such, and I thought to myself, blimey, what's this then? Was Mum a witch? Well, well, there's a thing. And so I sneaked it out. I didn't mention it to my old man, did I? I mean, he's got enough on his plate with the pub and everything. And so I started, y'know, dabbling with little rituals and spells, a bit of candle magic, which I didn't think would cause so much bother, but anyways I reckon that might be what's caused all this kerfuffle with demons and magic and such and I am ever so sorry and I can assure you it won't be happening again, on my honour, so I hope that's cleared everything up.' Faye took a breath and then stopped talking. She caught glimpses of silent gratitude from Charlotte and Mrs Teach.

Vera Fivetrees looked at Faye out of the sides of her eyes. 'You must be Kathryn Winter's girl.'

'That I am.'

'She was trouble, too,' Vera said. 'She left you a book?'

'Not as such. I found it.'

'And it contains spells and rituals?'

'And a recipe for jam roly-poly, but I reckon that was by the by.'

'You realise this is forbidden for precisely this reason?'

'The jam roly-poly?'

'The spells, girl,' Vera snapped. 'Enough of your cheek.'

'It has been explained to me, yes,' Faye said, gesturing to Charlotte and Mrs Teach. 'But I promise it will not happen again and—'

'Destroy the book,' Vera Fivetrees said.

'But—'

'We cannot afford any of our secrets getting into the wrong hands, young lady. Our rituals are handed down from one generation to the next in confidence, from mentor to apprentice. This is how we have kept the peace with the underworld for nearly two hundred and fifty years. They fear us because they do not have our knowledge. We have the upper hand, and we won't be losing it on my watch. And, as you might have noticed, there is a war on and the other side have their own spells and rituals we must combat, so I could do without the additional work.'

'I could hide it.'

'Destroy it.' Vera was speaking to Charlotte and Mrs Teach now. 'Philomena, your probation is ended. Both of you see to it and make sure this girl gets all the help she needs. If she's Kathryn Winter's daughter, she could be very useful. This war won't be ending soon and we need all the help we can get. Teach her everything you know.'

'Yes, ma'am,' Charlotte and Mrs Teach said and curtseyed in unison.

'And you,' Vera said to Faye. 'No unsupervised magic. No more secrets. Understood?'

'Yes, er, ma'am.'

'Good.' Vera turned to the woman on the Spitfire's wing and gave her a wave. 'Ginny, we're going.' The pilot saluted and hopped back in the cockpit, and the Spitfire's propellers whined and turned. There was a *phut-phut* from the exhausts which briefly flamed before the engine growled into life, coughing smoke over the village green.

All the onlookers turned from the witches to this magnificent machine with a collective, 'Ooh!' and a smattering of applause.

Vera Fivetrees raised her arms and closed her eyes, muttering words Faye did not understand.

'What's she doing?' asked Faye.

'Obeah,' Charlotte whispered. 'Old magic. Very powerful.'

'Shush,' snapped Mrs Teach, watching as Vera Fivetrees opened her eyes again and strolled to the duck pond. She took from her handbag a small blue glass bottle and very carefully tapped two drops of a red liquid into the water. Immediately it began to smoke and drift across the village green, mingling with the villagers.

Satisfied, Vera Fivetrees walked back to the three witches.

'They will forget?' Charlotte asked.

'They will remember something different,' Vera said. 'Strangers coming to town. A travelling circus, perhaps.'

Faye's heart sank at the thought of more of Dad's circus anecdotes.

'They will create their own stories that will become memory. Don't' – Vera pointed a finger at all of them – 'make me come here again.'

'No, ma'am,' all three said in unison, with a curtsey.

'Good, I have to be in Stonehenge by lunchtime. Bloody druids are on the sauce again. Good luck and stay out of trouble.' Vera walked through the crowd, stepped up into the Spitfire and squeezed into the rear seat. The pilot increased the throttle and the plane bounced across the green, lifting into the air and turning into the bright morning sky.

point. The week [illegible] small [illegible] [illegible] and very [illegible] two drops of [illegible] [illegible] the water. That [illegible] began to smoke [illegible] the village green, [illegible] with the [illegible].

"[illegible]," Enriqueta remarked [illegible] [illegible].

"They [illegible]," Charlotte asked.

[illegible]

[illegible]

[illegible]

39

A Book Burning

Faye agreed to meet at Charlotte's cottage later that morning. She took a different path through the wood, one that meandered by the stream and carried the scent of honeysuckle. She cycled past two swans on patrol and startled a fallow deer as it drank. She watched as the doe bounced away, the white spots on its coat blending with the dappled light. Bees pestered the fox-gloves at the foot of a larch, and chiffchaffs, willow warblers and blackbirds competed for her attention. She slapped away a horsefly as she got off her bicycle and leaned it against a tree sticky with summer sap. Faye gripped the satchel slung over her shoulder and waded through the ferns.

The world felt as normal as ever, but Faye knew by the time she returned home she would be changed.

When she reached the clearing, a bonfire was already burning and Charlotte and Mrs Teach were waiting for her.

Pine needles scrunched under Faye's shoes as she

walked like a condemned prisoner towards the cottage, watched by the two witches, a toad and a goat with no owner.

'Good morning, Faye,' Charlotte said. 'I'm sorry it has come to this, but I hope you understand why this needs to be done.'

Faye tightened her lips and shrugged.

'You have our word,' Mrs Teach said, 'we will pass on to you everything we know. If you possess half your mother's skill, you have the potential to be a great witch.'

'And we thank you for taking the blame with the High Witch earlier,' Charlotte said. 'You didn't have to do that.'

'Truthfully, the blame lies, in a way, with all of us,' said Mrs Teach.

'But mostly with you, Mrs Teach,' Charlotte said.

'Yes, yes, mostly me.' Mrs Teach bunched her lips.

'I'm sorry, Faye, but this is the price you pay for your kindness.' Charlotte extended her hand for the book.

'*I'll* do it,' Faye said, taking the book from her satchel.

'No offence, petal,' Mrs Teach said with an insincere smile, 'but we would like to check it's the real thing.'

'In case you try to pull another *switcheroo*,' Charlotte added, raising an eyebrow.

Faye ground her teeth together before handing over the book for inspection. Charlotte flicked through its pages.

'We must learn to trust one another,' Mrs Teach said. 'Where would we be without trust, eh? Especially now there's a war on. Is it real?' she asked this last of Charlotte, who nodded and closed the book.

'You still want to do this yourself?' Charlotte asked Faye.

Faye tried to answer, but the words got caught in her throat and she nodded instead.

Charlotte gave her the book and stood aside, revealing the crackling bonfire.

Faye gripped the book.

Her mother's book.

Aside from a few knick-knacks at home, this was all Faye had of her mother. Every word, every sketch, every smudge on a page was a moment in her mother's life. Faye had hoped to study the book for ever. To treasure it and try to be as wise and curious as her mother had been.

The wood fell silent. In the trees were birds of every kind. Witnesses to an execution.

'If I'm to do this,' Faye said, 'I want you to promise me something first.'

Charlotte and Mrs Teach shared doubtful glances.

'No more secrets,' Faye said. 'Not between us, at least. No more being snooty about the villagers, no more looking down on the likes of Craddock.'

Mrs Teach harrumphed. 'Really, young lady. He was the most beastly—'

'He was one of us,' Faye snapped. 'One of our neighbours, a regular in our pub, a man who would get you a bit o' rabbit if you fancied it. And yes, he was a grumpy old git, and he hated women, and I reckon he was probably a racialist, but he was a villager. And I think if we had spoken to him, or just listened to him a little more, then he might have listened to us and we might be better people and he might even still be alive. If we're going to start this coven, or whatever it is, then we need to be trusted by the folks in the village. We can't pretend we're better than them, or they'll just ignore us. We've got a war on our doorstep with the Nazis in France, and we've got trouble beneath us with demons and goblins or whatever.'

'There aren't any goblins,' Charlotte corrected.

'We start from scratch.' Faye puffed out her cheeks. 'Today. We put aside our differences and we work together. Clean sweep, new broom and all that, yes?'

Mrs Teach and Charlotte shared a look. 'Yes,' they replied in unison.

'Good,' Faye said and tossed the book on the flames.

A simple act. A slight movement of her arm and the book spun through the air and landed with a *whumph* on the fire. She couldn't bring herself to look at it, knowing it would break her heart to do so.

'Righto, good. That's that, then,' she said, her voice a whisper. 'I'll see you both tomorrow.'

40

The Hollow Tree

Faye did not go straight home. Instead, she returned to where she had left her bicycle leaning against the tree sticky with sap. She cycled to the hollow oak in the depths of the wood and sat alone among its roots for a while, allowing herself a few tears. She sniffed them away before taking a folded slip of paper from her pocket.

It was a page torn from her mother's book.

On one side was a recipe for jam roly-poly.

On the other side was something quite different.

Faye read aloud from the scrap of paper. '*A ritual for contacting loved ones who have passed to the other side.*'

It was magic.

She wasn't allowed to do any unsupervised magic. She had just made a promise to the High Witch of the British Empire. Faye put the torn page down.

Then picked it up again. And continued reading. There was nothing wrong with *reading*. She was just looking at words on a page and she was definitely not doing magic. '*Gather personal items of the loved one you wish to contact and lay them out before you.*'

Faye took a breath and flipped open her satchel. She took out a hairbrush with an ivory handle, a few cheap necklaces and earrings and a cracked gramophone record of 'Graveyard Dream Blues' by Bessie Smith. She fanned them out on the leafy ground before her. This wasn't magic. She was just looking. And reading.

'*Next, you will require a green candle and olive oil.*' Faye reached into the satchel, taking out an ordinary wax candle and a small bottle of cooking oil. 'Close enough,' she reassured herself, adjusting her spectacles as she squinted back at the book. '*Find a place of solitude where you can be alone with your thoughts*. Yes, done that. *Carve this rune into the candle.*'

The rune sketched on the page was simple enough, looking like an upside-down seven with a couple of lines bisecting it.

Faye couldn't do it. She had promised. She would not do magic. She might accidentally summon another demon or who knows what.

Faye read the rest of the instructions in her head. She did not carve any runes, she did not show the candle to the north, south, east or west. But she lit the candle and placed it in the tree's hollow. What harm could it do? It was gloomy here, anyway. She needed the light.

Faye came to the last instruction. '*Take your mirror and hold it in such a way as to reflect the candle's light.*' It took Faye a few moments to find the small hand mirror in her satchel. It had scratched glass and an ivory handle to match her mother's hairbrush. She angled it to catch the flame of the candle in the hollow, then tilted her head to read from the book. '*And, finally, allow yourself to fall into a relaxed state, breathing deeply. Your arms may feel heavy, your head may feel light, the glass in the mirror may become clouded, but you will soon see your lost loved one in the reflection and you will be able to speak with them.*'

Faye took a few deep breaths and looked into the mirror, her eyes desperate to catch any sign of movement, but there was none. Of course there wasn't. She wasn't doing magic.

There was no sound other than the breeze gently whispering through the leaves.

The days caught up with Faye. Her heart felt heavy, her shoulders drooped and her eyes welled with tears. It was time to go home.

It began to rain and Faye packed her mother's things away.

All she wanted was to tell her mother that she wasn't angry any more. That whenever she thought of her now, she felt a warm glow of love. She wanted to tell her mum that she was going to be all right. She had a purpose now. She could be useful.

Faye reached for the mirror, her eye caught by the twitching head of a sparrow reflected in its glass.

It was joined by a blue tit. Then a robin.

Faye felt a tingle between her shoulder blades. She lowered the mirror and turned slowly to find the old oak dripping with birds. From the lowest branches to the highest twigs, a crowded line-up of swifts, willow warblers, finches, nuthatches, goldcrests, jackdaws and treecreepers, all staring at her.

In a burst of flapping feathers and chirping beaks, they began to sing and swirl around Faye. She danced with them, laughing, breathless, red-cheeked and spinning with her arms unfurled like wings. She could barely speak, her heart filled with a joy she hadn't known since she was a child. Between breaths, she managed two words.

'Hello, Mum,' she said.

THE WITCHES OF WOODVILLE WILL RETURN . . .

MRS TEACH'S SÉANCE

June, 1940

Before and during the events in *The Crow Folk*

1

Her Ernie was gone and nothing would bring him back. Philomena Teach knew that. She understood it in the same way she knew the sun would set at the end of every day. She accepted it as she would showers in April and bitter frosts in the winter, but it did not make the pain inside her go away. Try as she might, she could not rid herself of the weight of grief that wrapped around her. Getting up in the morning involved a lot more huffing and puffing, the butter and jam on her toast had lost its flavour, her breakfast tea was milky and weak. The grief would not go. It was part of her now.

Not that anyone else in Woodville noticed. Mrs Teach was taller than most men, and still kept her chin up when standing in line at the baker's. She was rounder than most, yet still moved on dainty slingbacks when negotiating the cobbled streets of the village. When she stepped out of the front door of her terraced house, she was all smiles.

Behind closed doors, she could be herself.

'I told you to take it easy. Didn't I say you should rest at weekends? You, with your dicky ticker.'

She would have conversations with him as she moved around the house. Telling him about her day as if he were still there, sitting at the kitchen table with some bit of car engine spread across it in bits as he worked to fix it with his blackened fingers. That was his gift. Ernie could fix anything.

'Except your heart, you great lummox. Couldn't fix that, could you?'

It was so quick. He complained about a pain in his chest that afternoon, went to bed and never woke up.

Her last words to him had been, 'I bet it's that steak and kidney pie. You wolfed it down like a little piggy. Chew your food, Ernie Teach.'

He had chuckled and kissed her goodnight. At some point she was aware that his hand had slipped from hers. When she woke, he was cold.

Mrs Teach was no stranger to death. She had nursed many through their final hours, but for Ernie to slip away in their marriage bed had hurt her the most.

His smile had been the first thing she saw in the morning and last thing at night. She missed his warmth, the touch of his hands and lovemaking that was so enthusiastic it would wake Mrs Nesbitt next door.

Death was not unusual in Woodville, and it had become a more regular visitor since the start of the war. Three of the village's sons had perished at Dunkirk, and only last week poor Mrs Rogers got a telegram to say her Danny was lost at sea somewhere off Norway.

Ernie was too old to fight on the front line, thank goodness, but had enrolled at the village police station to join the Local Defence Volunteers. He had been ready to do his bit.

His armband arrived the day of his funeral.

Mrs Teach's only comfort was she knew that death was not necessarily the end.

When you had the gift, the dead could speak.

Of course, this was absolutely forbidden by the council of witchcraft. For a start, no one actually knew if they were *really* talking to the dead. There was a theory – one favoured by Vera Fivetrees, High Witch of the British Empire – that the voices heard at séances were put on by demons intent on winding up those poor souls mourning in this realm. That voice wasn't your dear, departed grandmother you were hearing from the other side. It was some wretched incubus doing a bad impression and getting a giggle from it. Vera's theory was based on her own childhood experience after catching out such a demon in a supposed séance with her mother, who was not only *not* dead, but in the room with her at the time knitting a scarf.

Séances were also forbidden for the very simple reason that you were opening a door to the underworld and that was a door best left shut, locked, bolted, then buried at the bottom of the deepest well you could find, and finally covered in several layers of cement.

Nothing had come through in centuries and everyone wanted to keep it that way.

Especially after what happened last time.

In her youth, Mrs Teach had *accidentally* summoned a demon during a completely unrelated magical act that was innocent and without malice, but had somehow got her on probation from practising magic for nearly two decades.

Thankfully, Kathryn Wynter had helped her sort that out and it was all in the past and best forgotten.

Philomena Teach knew she shouldn't risk incurring the wrath of Charlotte and Vera Fivetrees again, but this séance would be a one-off and no one need ever know. She closed the curtains and arranged four silver hand mirrors around the room. One on the mantel, one on the window sill, one by the door and another in Ernie's old armchair. All faced the small card table in the middle of the room. Philomena fiddled with wingnuts under the table to extend it, pulling it open to unfold a centre section with a pentagram carved into the wood. If her bridge club knew they had been playing on a table used to evoke spirits, they would have had a fit, but it had been in the family for three generations and, even though Mrs Teach had been forbidden from practising magic, she kept the table. Why chuck out a perfectly good card table, even if it it was carved with enough runes to power a demonic uprising?

She placed a copper dish in the centre of the pentagram and poured into it a small, precise amount of ash made from alder and laurel wood. She said a few words known only to witches, and the ash shivered into glowing embers and soon the room was misty with white smoke.

Mrs Teach took what looked like a letter opener – the one with the obsidian handle and a blade that could slice between worlds – from the mantel and placed it on the table, pointing it to the mirror in Ernie's armchair. She then took a salt cellar from her gown pocket and shook a circle around the table on the carpet.

Mrs Teach wafted the smoke towards her face, then sat in Ernie's armchair, resting the mirror in her lap.

The ritual began. A monotonous repetition of old words to budge open the door to the other side. In her day, Philomena could do such a simple ceremony in minutes, but she was out of practice and it took all of her concentration to remain focused.

As her lips moved and the words came without thinking, she quite lost track of time. She heard young Faye Bright and Freddie Paine stroll by on their Air Raid Precaution rounds. The steady beat of two pairs of boots on cobbles occasionally punctuated with cries of 'Put that light out!' was a welcome diversion, but then the church clock stopped chiming at eleven and Mrs Teach knew it wouldn't sound again till six. Silence cloaked the village and Mrs Teach's eyes felt much more comfortable when they were closed. A nap wouldn't hurt. It would help to clear the mind. She could try again in a...

2

Philomena Teach woke to the steady exhalation of the wireless. A white noise of nothingness, peppered with blips and whines from distant crackles of lightning. In her awakening grogginess, Mrs Teach half wondered if she had left the radio on before nodding off, but a séance needed complete silence and she was not the type to have made such an error.

'Phee-Phee?' the voice came whispering through the wireless. 'Phee-Phee, are you there, my love?'

Phee-Phee.

Ernie's name for her.

He had many. Phee-Phee, Pumpkin, Love-Lump. Used only behind closed doors and known only to them.

'Phee-Phee, speak to me, darling. Please.' His voice was filtered through hiss and crackle, words rising and falling with the swell of the airwaves.

The first light of dawn filtered through the curtains, the smoke had cleared and the embers in the dish still shimmered. The door was open and someone had stepped through.

'Phee-Phee? Speak to me, my love.'

How could she be sure it was really her Ernie?

'Pumpkin? Love-Lump? Did you call me? Please speak to me.'

A movement caught Philomena's attention. A face in the reflected glass. An eye in the mirror on the mantel, lips moving in another. A manifestation of Ernie.

Mrs Teach tried to say his name, but her mouth was dry and all that came was a croak. She cleared her throat and started again. 'Ernie, is that you?'

'It is, my love, it is. I'm so happy to hear you again.'

A warmth rushed through Mrs Teach, starting in her toes and flooding her heart. 'Ernie, oh, Ernie, I've missed you.' She knew this had to be too good to be true, but any rational thought was shoved aside as tears came and her lips trembled. 'I've missed you so much.'

'So have I, Phee-Phee.' The voice was still nothing but distant fragments, but it really sounded like Ernie. 'I long to see you again.'

'Where … where are you?' It was the question that everyone wanted to know the answer to. Back when she was a girl and gave her first séances, her nana had told her that folk would ask such questions. Nana warned against giving answers because no one ever liked what they heard. But Philomena Teach wasn't afraid of death. She just wanted to hear her Ernie's voice again.

'I don't know, Phee-Phee,' came the reply. 'It's dark. Dark and cold. I'm scared. Can you help me?'

'Yes, my darling Ernie, just listen to the sound of my voice,' she said. 'Let my love warm you in the dark.'

'I want you here, Phee-Phee,' Ernie said. 'Join me. Cross over and we can be together for ever.'

'Er.' Mrs Teach became aware of the tiniest of alarm bells ringing at the back of her mind. Something wasn't quite right here.

'There are so many of us in the dark,' the voice said.

'I thought you were alone?' Mrs Teach replied, trying not to sound too suspicious.

'We are. We all are.'

'All?' Mrs Teach asked, and she was sure she could hear someone trying to cover up a snorted laugh through the radio noise. 'You cheeky sod. That's not my Ernie, is it?'

'Ah, you saw through my little ruse,' the voice said, filling the room and dropping to a cadence that was one part oil, two parts brimstone. 'I'm surprised you didn't latch on sooner, Philomena Teach.'

'Who are you?'

'Who…? Mrs Teach, I must say I am more than a little wounded that you don't remember me. After all, we got on so well last time.'

'Last time?' It didn't take long for Mrs Teach to flick through her mental address book of demon acquaintances. There was only one. 'Kefapepo, isn't it?'

'At your service, madam.'

'Don't you madam, me. Begone, foul demon,' Mrs Teach said, leaning forward to turn off the wireless.

'Ernie, I can bring you Ernie,' Kefapepo blurted.

Mrs Teach hesitated, her fingers resting on the off dial of the radio. 'Liar,' she said.

'You know I can.' Kefapepo dropped his voice to a whisper again, and Mrs Teach angled her head to better hear him. 'Not for long, of course, but I can bring him to you and you can finally say your goodbyes. That's what you want, isn't it, Mrs Teach? A proper farewell to the love of your life. That's all we want, isn't it? Just a few more moments. I can give them to you.'

'How?' The word was hoarse and dry, and she cursed herself for saying it. Now he knew she was interested. 'A séance?'

'Mrs Teach, you insult me. You're not dealing with those fools who come to have their palms read. No, no, no. I will choose a form for Ernie and he will come to you.'

'A form?'

'A body. A host. You can expect a visit one evening. You will have until the stroke of midnight to make your farewells and all those things you meant to say when he was alive.'

'No.'

'Mrs Teach, this is a unique and generous offer, never to be repeated. I highly suggest you say yes and be quick about it.'

'Why are you doing this? You lied to me before, why should I believe you now?'

'Mrs Teach, how dare you question my—'

'You are a demon, not to be trusted. Goodbye.'

'He will be the first of many,' Kefapepo said. 'My gift to the world.'

'What do you mean?'

'The dead are all around me. I call to them and can summon their spirits. It's one of my gifts. I have studied the old ways and discovered how to . . . breathe new life into them.'

'You won't be doing that with my Ernie,' Mrs Teach said. 'Now, begone.'

She switched off the radio, and the demon was gone. The room lost its chill, and the embers in the dish faded to ashes. Mrs Teach opened the curtains to a pale yellow sun peeking over the bell tower of Saint Irene's Church.

3

After tea and toast, Mrs Teach picked a bunch of sky-blue hydrangeas from her garden. Clutching them tightly, she made her way to the one place she had been avoiding since Ernie's funeral. His stone in the graveyard of Saint Irene's.

He rested in the shadow of an oak tree, side-by-side with strangers. Mrs Teach had seen enough peculiar phenomena in her time to know that an afterlife was certainly a possibility, but that the idea of Ernie floating on a cloud playing a harp was nonsense. She feared that death was cold, dark and lonely.

'Hello, my love,' she said, crouching to rest the hydrangeas at the foot of his stone. 'I got you these. I don't know why we bring flowers to the dead. To brighten the place up, I suppose. Coming here, chatting, flowers, prayers. Everything we do for the dead, we do for ourselves, don't we?'

Mrs Teach stood and brushed her skirt straight. 'It's been three months, three weeks exactly, my love,' she said. 'I'm sorry it's taken me so long to visit, though I suspect you neither know nor care. I'm going to stop feeling sorry for myself and get things done and I'm starting with your allotment, poppet. I haven't been there since … and I know I don't have your green fingers, but all the posters go on about digging for victory, so I'm going to have a go. It has to be better than wallowing in the past, and I know you had no time for that nonsense. But, I promise you this, I'll come here regularly. Fresh flowers and me jabbering to myself. Yes, I'm sure it'll be good for both of us.'

4

Philomena Teach was renowned in the village for many things, but first and foremost she was known for being observant, which was a polite way of saying she was nosey. She would refute this, of course. She simply took an interest in the welfare of others and always lent a shoulder to cry on. Never mind that she would often know that they had something to cry about long before they themselves did. There was no denying that there was little that went on in the village of Woodville without her knowing it.

Which is why she was shocked that it took her all morning to notice what was missing from her Ernie's allotment. She started with a little light weeding – the plot had gone a bit ragged in his absence – and then some watering, feeding and harvesting the few radishes and lettuces that had endured.

It was only when she stopped for a tea break that she sat in a deck chair, surveyed her work, and blurted out, 'Where the bloody hell's Bernie?' causing Mr Loaf digging nearby to jolt, press a hand to his chest and mop his brow with a red polka dot neckerchief.

Bernie was the name she and Ernie gave to the scarecrow on his allotment. The name came about because he was wearing Ernie's old top hat and tails – a left-over from their courting days – and so they named him 'Ernie Mark 2', which became 'Ernie B', which for a while became 'Ernib' and then finally through various convolutions ended up as 'Bernie'.

All that was left of Bernie was his wooden pole.

'Have you lost something, Mrs Teach?' Mr Loaf asked as he negotiated his way around the bean poles and sunflowers of his own allotment. Ever cheery, and camp as a row of tents, Mr Loaf was possibly the only villager to challenge Philomena for the title of 'nosiest person in the village', though his was a professional interest. As the village's only funeral director, he was always on the lookout for new business.

'Someone's pinched our scarecrow,' Mrs Teach told him. 'Why on earth would anyone purloin a scarecrow? I ask you.'

Mr Loaf, a small wiry chap with limbs that at first sight appeared to have a surplus of knees and elbows, adjusted his round specs and inspected the now-empty pole. 'Ooh, you wouldn't believe what some people get up to these days, Mrs Teach,' he said. 'I know we all bang on about the Dunkirk spirit, and *we're all in it together* and all that, but there are some nefarious types out there, I don't mind telling you. Black marketeers, thieves in the night, muggers and villains in this very village if you can believe such a thing.' He thought for a moment. 'P'raps they wanted the top hat and tails? They were still in fairly good nick, and what with clothes rationing and all, some folk will go to any lengths to get their hands on good cloth.'

'Then why take the whole thing, stuffing and all?' Mrs Teach said, a thought sparking deep inside her mind. She tried to concentrate on it, but Mr Loaf was off on one.

'Who knows how these perverted minds think,' he said, patting her hand. 'And you, still in your period of grief and mourning, Mrs Teach. The bounders should be ashamed of themselves. What would their mothers say? That's what I want to know. Where *are* their mothers, hmm? And their fathers? I blame the parents. Spare the rod, spoil the child. Someone needs to tan their hides and teach them—'

'Mr Loaf, if I may,' Philomena interjected as politely as possible. 'Do you recall if it was here yesterday?'

Mr Loaf pursed his lips and rolled his eyes to the sky in thought. 'Trouble is, Mrs Teach, something like a scarecrow, round here … well, it's part of the furniture, isn't it? Part of the landscape. The sort of thing you don't notice till it's … well, till some vagabond half-inches it. But, yes, yes, I could've sworn it was here yesterday.'

'You're sure?'

'As sure as I can be about something like this, which is to say not very,' he said, then added unhelpfully, 'but yes.'

'You've been here all morning? Before I got here?'

'Up at first light,' he told her. 'My one day off and I try to make the most of it, what with the radishes coming through and all.'

'So, no one took it this morning,' Mrs Teach mused. She thought back to last night's séance. Kefapepo's promise to find a form for Ernie, to bring him back in a host of some kind. Had the door been open long enough for someone like Kefapepo to come through and make good on his threats?

'Mrs Teach?' Mr Loaf's voice broke through her thoughts. 'Are you okay, my dear? You look quite lost.'

It was nonsense. A demon from the lower orders wouldn't have the kind of power to cross over. Nothing had happened like that in over three hundred years. It was unthinkable.

'Mrs Teach?'

'Hmm? My apologies, Mr Loaf. This has quite rattled me and my tea's gone cold.' She poured the tea on the soil and screwed the cup back onto the Thermos flask. 'Back to work, I suppose.' She bent at the knees to scoop up her watering can and headed for the communal water butt at the centre of the plots.

Mr Loaf watched her go, his thinning wisps of hair tousled by the breeze. 'I'll be sure to let you know if I hear anything,' he called after her. 'After all, there can't be that many scarecrows in top hat and tails with a socking great pumpkin for a head!'

5

Mrs Teach quietly sipped her gin while the others in the Green Man tried to make sense of what they had just seen. A gaggle of scarecrows led by a tall man with a pumpkin for a head just strolled into the village like a bunch of troubadours and given everyone the willies. They were already calling him Pumpkinhead, but she knew that wasn't his real name. Mrs Teach recognised the scarecrow immediately. It was the one she had thought stolen from Ernie's allotment.

It hadn't been stolen. It had come to life and walked away of its own volition, and all because of her stupid séance.

Kefapepo was here. A demon walking the Earth to create havoc. She recalled the stories that Charlotte had told her of him. Centuries ago, he would appear every year from Easter to Lammas, going from farm to farm in the form of a scarecrow, burning crops, killing sheep and cattle. He was on his own back then, easily scared off, little more than a pest, but now he had a small army of scarecrows that he had somehow drawn to him.

Worst of all, he was more ambitious this time. This wasn't about scaring farmers or killing livestock. He was making threats.

The gin was working. Slowly washing her worries away, stopping her thinking about what was to come. The consequences. This definitely had some whopping consequences. She couldn't bear the thought of letting Charlotte know what had really happened. She would flip her lid, and Mrs Teach could really do without that now.

Kefapepo wanted Craddock. If he got what he wanted, then maybe he would go away. Yes. That would end it.

Mrs Teach took another sip of her gin. Someone was waffling on about Craddock now. Faye called him, 'Poor Mr Craddock.' Mrs Teach would have to set her straight about that.

6

Last night, Ernie had returned.

Already it was a tilting, swirling memory for Mrs Teach. He had come as a scarecrow, wearing his old jumper and dungarees. His face was a saggy sack cloth. He had buttons for eyes and straw for hair, and she was so terrified at first that she took him for an intruder and walloped him with a poker.

It was only after he fled that she began to realise that Kefapepo had delivered on his twisted promise to bring Ernie back. But this couldn't be Ernie, could it? This sad creature, writhing in the grip of Terrence, Bertie and the other Local Defence Volunteers as it was dragged back down the street.

And then it called Philomena by her name and her heart sank inside her.

She finally had her wish. Ernie had returned, or some sad echo of him that was trapped in a body of straw and dust. He was confused, terrified, and he needed someone to help him. Philomena was the only one here who could ease his pain.

She took command at that point. Faye wanted to call a bobby, but this was Mrs Teach's husband and she had to take care of this herself. She gently cradled the creature, and it took her hand.

Mrs Teach leaned close to where its ear would be, and she whispered three questions.

'Do you forgive me?' She held him tighter, the straw in its body creaking. 'I'm so sorry I hit you. I didn't know it was you. I was scared. Please forgive me.'

It gently squeezed her hand.

'Pumpkinhead. Bernie the scarecrow. Was he the one who brought you back?'

It squeezed tighter.

'I'm sorry, my love. I'm so sorry. This is all my fault,' she told him, then asked one final question. 'Do you want this to end?'

A last squeeze.

'Try and rest, my love,' she said. 'I don't think this will hurt. Just try and rest, don't worry about me. I'll be fine, I'll be fine.'

She gave him a long embrace and laid him on the stone steps of the Great War memorial. She pulled his shirt open, buttons popping on the steps and cobbles, and wedged her hand deep inside his chest.

He's just straw. Nothing but straw.

She took him to pieces, one fistful after another, tossing straw behind her like a child unwrapping a Christmas gift.

It's just straw. Only straw.

He lay there like a ragdoll, his button eyes staring. She yanked off his sack cloth head revealing tightly bound straw, and she pulled that apart, too. Before long, there was nothing left but baggy clothes and corn stalks.

Mrs Teach was aware that Faye and the Local Defence Volunteers were looking on in horror. She would have to take care of that. The men wouldn't be a problem – Mrs Teach could befuddle their minds easily enough – but Faye . . . There was something about Faye. Perhaps she had her mother's gift after all? There was no fooling that girl. This would take some delicate explanation.

Mrs Teach was about to speak, but instead could only give a little sob. More threatened to burst out, so she pushed them back down. There would be time for tears later.

7

Mrs Teach didn't go to church on Sunday. She needed time to think. She had promised to meet with Faye on Monday, and she had this half-barmy idea to tell the girl the truth. Why fanny about with lies? The girl wasn't as clever as she thought she was, but she wasn't as daft as half the village either, and Mrs Teach was convinced the girl had more than a little magic inside her. She would tell Faye the truth about the séance if she could get the girl to promise not to say a word to Charlotte. That one need never know.

Oh, who was she kidding? Charlotte probably already knew – she had already interrogated Mrs Teach once – and was no doubt looking for someone to blame. A wicked part of Mrs Teach's mind wondered if she could pin everything on Faye. For all anyone knew, the girl had already started dabbling with magic and opened the door herself. Perhaps Kefapepo's manifestation at Mrs Teach's séance was a result of the girl's unwitting spell casting?

Why else would she have gone to see Charlotte the other morning?

This wicked urge subsided in Mrs Teach. She had no one to blame but herself. She would make peace with Charlotte – yes, the other woman would be cross, but she's always cross – and then they would face this demon together.

Perhaps. Mrs Teach had to clear her mind. She would pick more flowers and go to visit Ernie's stone and say a few words.

By the time she left the house that morning, Mrs Teach's mind had sorted her worries into manageable solutions. Yes, a demon had broken through, yes, it had the potential to do great harm, and yes, it was most likely the result of forbidden magic by either herself or possibly Faye Bright, though Mrs Teach doubted that, but that's where it stopped. Two witches could see off a demon. It would be hard, but it could be done, surely. They wouldn't involve the girl. Not yet. She's not ready. Get this mess sorted, and then they could train Faye properly. There's nothing worse than an untrained witch for creating havoc. They would show the girl how to do witching properly. Like the old days, handed down from one generation to another.

Thank God she doesn't have her mother's book, Mrs Teach thought as she locked her door. *Then we'd really be in trouble.*

ACKNOWLEDGEMENTS

If you have enjoyed this book, and would like to be kept up-to-date with the latest village gossip, get free and exclusive short stories, and receive Miss Burgess' recipe for jam roly-poly, join the Woodville Village Parish Council newsletter here: witchesofwoodville.com

On behalf of the Woodville Village Parish Council, Mr Mark Stay (secretary) would like to thank the following for their contributions . . .

Anne Perry for helping young Faye find her voice and for assisting Mr Stay with his chronicles. We wish Anne all the best in her new venture and she is welcome to return to the village at any time.

Bethan Jones for shepherding the book through the final stages of the edit and production, and we look forward to working with Bethan on future chronicles.

Lisa Rogers for pointing out some two thousand or

so minor errors in the text without tearing her hair out. We also thank her for her expertise on sherbet lemons.

Matthew Johnson for his design skills and Harry Goldhawk for his splendid artwork.

All the fine folk at Simon & Schuster for their diligence and determination in these trying times.

Hélène Butler and the gang at Johnson & Alcock for spreading the good word, far and wide.

Claire Burgess for her thorough explanation of bell-ringing and its hypnotic effects.

Julian Barr, Rhoda Baxter, Lorna Cook, Sage Gordon-Davis, Ian W Sainsbury and Robyn Sarty for reading early versions of the text and offering copious and most helpful notes for improvement.

Paddy Eason for loaning out Ginny Albion for the day.

Steve Mayhew for identifying the John Wayne movie where he breathes through a hollow reed (*Sagebrush Trail*, film fans).

Matt Dench for suggesting the appropriate historical setting.

Sue Strachan, Christopher Johnson, Anstey Harris and Busters Bits for nuggets of historical wisdom regarding pubs and toilets.

And last, but by no means least, Mr Ed Wilson for his splendid negotiation skills and good taste. Thank you also, Mr Wilson, for the offer of the trousers for the church bring-and-buy sale, but we regret that the colours were considered to be a little outré by Reverend Jacobs. He did, however, suggest offering them to the

Local Defence Volunteers who could perhaps cut them up and use them for semaphore practice.

A note on food rationing

Food rationing in June 1940 only extended to bacon and ham (4oz per week), sugar (12oz) and butter (4oz).

Further meat rationing began in July 1940, and cooking fat, meat, tea, cheese and jam wouldn't be rationed until much later. (Source: *The British Home Front 1939-40* by Martin J Brayley, Osprey Publishing).